THE
Orient
EXPRESS

TIMELESS
Victorian
COLLECTION

THE
Orient
EXPRESS

ELIZABETH JOHNS   ANNETTE LYON
NANCY CAMPBELL ALLEN

Interior Design by Cora Johnson
Edited by Cassidy Skousen, Haley Swan, and Lisa Shepherd

Cover design by Rachael Anderson
Cover Photo Credit: DepositPhotos #83431954

Published by Mirror Press, LLC

ISBN-13: 978-1-947152-97-7

TABLE OF CONTENTS

To Break a Berothal

ELIZABETH JOHNS

One

Terrified was not a sensation Kate was used to—yet here she stood, alone on a train platform in Constantinople, trembling. It was not just from the deep chill in the air on this late spring night. The conductor had whisked her luggage away, and sounds of the engine coming to life, mixed with whistles of steam, indicated leaving was not long in coming.

"All aboard for the eleven o'clock departure!" an official called in English and French, his breath leaving a cloud of steam behind.

"I will write to you," Kate told Diya, who nodded.

"Go, or you miss train," Diya said, tears forming in her eyes.

Kate threw her arms around her old nurse in an unladylike, public display of affection. "I love you, Diya."

"And I love you, my Anjushri," Diya said, using the name she had called her charge from the cradle since she had been nanny, nurse, and surrogate mother. "Come visit and bring me babies," she added with a sly smile before turning to leave.

Goodbye had become the common theme in the past month, and now Kate watched her beloved ayah depart, her purple sari quickly fading from view. She had released Diya from her duties—she was twenty years of age, after all, and she no longer had need of a nurse. Diya had accompanied her this far with some male servants, but she did not wish to go to England and leave her own family . . . though she would never say as much. She would have come if Kate had asked.

Feeling her chin quiver, Kate took a deep breath, reminding herself that she was a grown woman. She had wanted some independence, but not at the cost of everyone she loved.

Taking one final look at the Sirkeci Station behind her, the sand-coloured city around, the desert evening cool, she tried to gather her courage. She had come this far already through a succession of boats, trains, and carriages, and she was within a week of her destination.

"You always wanted to go back to England, Kate," she reminded herself as she heard a whistle blow and the chaos of impending departure sounding all around her. At any other time she would have been delighted for the adventure of riding the Orient Express across Europe.

It was different when she had no choice. Now she was finding it impossible to step onto the train.

"Miss, the doors are about to close." A man in a Wagon-Lits uniform was trying to catch her attention.

She nodded to the man and allowed her feet to move forward, refusing to consider why they should not. One step at a time, she climbed onto the massive train. The doors closed behind her, a loud whistle sounded, and the car lurched forward. Kate held on to the railing to catch her bearings.

"This way, miss. You are in compartment number eight."

The conductor, in a uniform of blue with gold trim, led her down the narrow corridor lined with a wall of windows to one side and luxurious wooden panelling to the other. He opened her door and handed her the key, then opened a small door indicating a mirror and washbasin. He pointed out a small table, a seat that converted into a bed, and other features of her berth while she stood wishing he would leave her to wallow in her misery.

"Will you be needing anything now for the night, miss?"

"No, thank you."

"Breakfast is served in the second car to your right. Ring if you need anything else for the night."

He bowed and closed the door behind him.

Kate sat on the banquet seat and watched the Turkish night whirl by through a haze of tears. She had not allowed herself to cry and knew it was best to let the tears all out now and be done with it. Crying for days was unacceptable, and she was not one to be maudlin. If only her last exchange with her papa had not been an argument. Rationally, she knew their fight had not caused his heart seizure, but it was hard not to believe she was partly to blame for his death.

She could not honour his last request—no, demand. She had no intention of marrying Lord Darlington. All she could conjure up when she heard that name was a pudgy, seventeen-year-old face and sweaty palms. That was the one time she had seen him, on her only visit to England. She shuddered in disgust. Of course, he would be a man now, and her subconscious recalled that he did have a startling pair of blue eyes. But she knew nothing else about him!

How could Papa not have understood what a cruel thing it was to form betrothal contracts when they were but children? She cared nothing for the lure of a title. They had argued over and over as their time to leave for England grew near.

"My darling Kate, his father and I were the closest of friends. It was our fondest wish to join our families," Papa had argued through struggled breaths. "Their title is old and honourable."

"I do not know if I can, Papa. Is there no other way?"

Disappointment was etched on his face. "Only if both parties agree to dissolve the contract." He reached his hand out to squeeze hers and then touched her face lovingly. "Please understand we did this because we love you and want what is best for you."

"Papa, don't leave me." She reached over and hugged him, holding on desperately, kissing his face. "I love you, Papa."

She looked into his eyes, willing him to live, but she could see he was losing the fight. His hands were cold, and his lips were already blue.

"Remember, do not mourn for me. I will be with your mother and the Almighty, at last."

She nodded, though tears streamed down her face.

"You will do well, Kate. Despite my failings, you have become an independent, capable woman. You will find your way."

"But I need you, Papa."

"I will always be with you wherever you go." He pointed to her heart.

Those were the last words he had spoken to her.

If only she was not going to England to undo his fondest wish.

Stephen tried desperately to ignore the itch to scratch his annoying moustache, but it was the easiest way to disguise himself. The War Office had asked him to complete one last reconnaissance mission en route to take up the title . . . A betrothal to an heiress was his fate when he returned to England. The estate needed funds, but could he bear such a marriage? He had a little while longer to find out, while he attempted to catch an elusive informer who was suspected to be travelling on the Orient Express.

Never before had his target been a female, but he held no delusions that the task would be easier. He watched as each of the passengers boarded, but he had yet to decide which lady was the traitor—if she was even travelling as a lady.

The description provided by his superiors had been brief: female, early twenties, dark hair, slim, travels as a lady. Known as Anna Smith. That could have described more than half the females of the London *ton*. However, her résumé included theft of Crown documents and the assassination of a government official.

As he stood on the platform, only two females under the age of forty appeared to be passengers, and both were on the manifest for the first-class cabin. The first suspect had arrived and boarded some half-hour past. The young woman, a Miss Hawthorne, was slight of build, wearing pale yellow muslin and a chip bonnet, and looked fresh from the schoolroom. Appearing shy and demure to his eye, she cowered behind a harridan of a chaperone, who snapped orders and made demands of the staff. A most excellent disguise if that were her aim.

The second lady was a more viable candidate, upon his initial appraisal. She was dressed in a bold navy and cream striped silk skirt with a navy waistcoat in the latest hourglass mode, which omitted the bustle, and a matching sailor hat with a single ribbon. Her bearing was confident and assured, despite the fact she apparently travelled alone. Stephen witnessed her have a touching farewell with an Indian servant, and then she stood still, as though hesitant to board. However, if she was concerned about being caught, she had left herself quite exposed for several minutes on the busy platform before boarding, seeming oblivious to her surroundings. Stephen always knew everything going on around him. It was the difference between life and death in his occupation. If she was his target, she was careless.

He slipped on board behind the second lady and observed her go into number eight.

"Excellent. One in eight, another in ten," he mumbled to himself as he opened number nine and settled himself in for the night, thinking of how obliging the conductor had been to place him near the two misses as requested. He tossed his hat on the banquette and halted halfway to sitting down when he heard heart-wrenching sobs coming through the wall from number eight. A spy with a conscience?

It was possible. Stephen did not think he had ever cried thusly, and certainly with none of the deeper emotions her cry espoused. Then again, he was unfamiliar with the emotions of the genteel sex beyond the superficial. Years in the army did not hone skills in that regard.

Mesmerized by the pain he heard in the woman's cries, he sat there listening until she quieted. Invading privacy was commonplace in his trade, yet he felt guilty about doing so in this instance. He could not fathom why.

Shrugging out of his plain brown coat, he pulled off his boots before lying back on the seat. He surveyed the small compartment he would occupy for the next sixty hours. It was certainly an improvement on most of his quarters with the army. The compartment was fashioned with mahogany and teak marquetry, two plush armchairs in red, with an upholstered seat that made into a bed. A small table sat beneath the window, and a cupboard held a wash basin and mirror for his morning ablutions. His batman was travelling as a passenger in the second class, in case their target had chosen to try a different disguise from her normal *modus operandi*, though he could have shared the spare bunk above.

Riding on a train for three days with a suspect was a rare opportunity. How should he approach this task? Should he observe from afar? Or should he attempt to make the acquaintance of these ladies? The latter was the riskier proposition, but instinct was leading him to take the chance. What were the odds anyone would recognize him as Lord Darlington when he later shaved the moustache, trimmed his hair, and removed the spectacles? People saw what they expected to see. He would be certain they saw Mr. Brown—nothing more and nothing less.

Two

By the next morning, Kate was ready to see outside her cabin. The rocking train had lulled her into a deep sleep after weeping, and now she needed some space from the tiny compartment. Diya normally helped Kate dress and style her hair, but Kate rather enjoyed doing for herself. She dressed in a fetching plum-coloured dress with full sleeves, the slim skirt and narrow waist trimmed with black cord *passementerie*, which flattered her height. Her father had always obtained the *Harper's Bazaar* for her somehow, so she was able to maintain a semblance of current fashion even from India. Unlatching the door and stepping into the corridor, she at least felt she looked presentable.

"Miss White, I will show you to your table," the waiter said when she entered the dining car. Kate did not want anyone to know who she was, since she was alone, so she was travelling under a fictitious name. The Worthington name was conspicuous and recognizable in fashionable circles. Besides, her father had warned her over and over that people would try to take advantage of her for her money, and it was best to know and trust a person if possible. It still surprised her to hear the false name, though.

They were passing somewhere between Bucharest and Budapest, and the terrain was already much changed from that of Turkey. The desert had turned to forest, and they were beginning to climb towards the snow-capped Carpathian Mountains. It was still hard to believe her life was so changed in such a short time. It felt as though everything she held dear had been stripped away from her.

Taking a moment to look around the dining car, Kate suddenly felt alone and self-conscious, but she was unused to being by herself. Once in London, she would be required to have a chaperone. A telegram had been sent to her aunt, informing that lady of her impending arrival, but Kate had not received a reply before she departed Darjeeling.

A dozen or so other passengers were seated at small dining tables, some engrossed in conversation and others sipping their morning tea or coffee while perusing the news sheets.

It did not appear that anyone else travelled alone. Another young miss was with her companion or governess, and Kate felt a deep wrenching in her heart for Diya and her father. Having shed her tears last night, it was time to carry on. There were only a few days until she must face her foe, for that was how she thought of him.

What if he was much changed? How had twelve years changed her, she wondered. A gangly girl, she was now filled out with the curves of a woman, and her hair had grown back from that disastrous time when she had thought she wanted a short cut. She would never forget when her mother had caught her, scissors in hand, standing in a pool of long, dark curls. A small laugh escaped her when Kate remembered the look on her mother's face. It had been a horrid cut.

British men often tended to grow fat and bald, however, and she had no reason to think Lord Darlington did not take after his father. She shuddered and cracked the shell of her boiled egg with a spoon. The Earl of Edgewood was a kind and jovial man, but his son was arrogant and annoying. If he could have been but kind to her a little, she might have been able to consider the marriage. There was a reason for the saying a leopard does not change his spots. She cringed and returned her attention to her food. She must stop thinking of Lord Darlington this way, or she would be at a disadvantage when she wanted to negotiate with him. Her plan was to spend a few days spying on him and learning about his habits, his desires, his weaknesses. Her father, General James Worthington, had been a shrewd businessman and had taught her to know thine opponent, or enemy in this case. She intended to do just that. If all went well, Lord Darlington would have a sweetheart and be more than willing to give up this ridiculous betrothal contract. If all else failed, she was willing to offer him twenty percent of Worthington Trading Co., which was no small amount.

"Pardon me, Miss White." The waiter interrupted her scheming. "Would you be willing to dine with another passenger? Our numbers are uneven," he explained. "The gentleman is willing to take a tray in his room, but I thought I would ask if you would mind the company. It is a most unusual circumstance."

"Not at all." Perhaps Divine Intervention would keep her from being lonely.

A tall, though well-proportioned, gentleman dressed in plain brown tweed was shown to the seat across from her, and suddenly Kate thought she should have eschewed manners after all as she felt the scrutiny of ice-blue eyes.

"Miss White, may I introduce you to Mr. Brown, your dining companion?" The waiter bowed as the gentleman inclined his head.

"Charmed, Mr. Brown. Are we not quite the dull pair?" she asked dryly.

"Indeed." His eyes twinkled for a moment. "Good morning, Miss White. I appreciate you allowing me to join you." He looked at her with what she thought might be suspicion. She must be imagining things.

Kate acknowledged her companion with a nod, thinking the man could be handsome without the dreadful moustache and whiskers. Why men thought they needed such adornment was beyond her. It was unsettling to watch a person eat and food always getting left behind—at least in her experience with her father's friends.

"Will you take coffee or tea?" a waiter asked them.

"Darjeeling tea."

"I will have the same," Mr. Brown indicated to the waiter before turning back to her. "Have you travelled to India?"

"I have lived my entire life there. I am returning to England on a matter of business." It was not a complete stretch of the truth.

"Have you ever been to England?"

"Once, when I was a girl. I remember it was cold and damp."

"It has not changed," he assured her, his eyes twinkling again behind a pair of gold-rimmed spectacles.

"No, I do not suppose it would. And yourself?"

"For over a decade, home has been where the army sees fit to send me."

He was a younger son, then, Kate supposed. Not that she gave any thought to such things, but English Society did.

"And have you been to India?"

He inclined his head. "Most of my time in the army has been spent in the Orient. Mainly Burma and Tibet."

"Tibet is not far from where I lived in Darjeeling."

"It is a beautiful place."

The waiter took their orders, and they sipped their tea in silence while they waited for their food. Kate finally broke the awkwardness. She could hardly ignore the man after he had been polite. He had been quite talkative for a stranger—and an English gentleman at that—but he had been away from home and might be lonely.

"Are you on leave to England?"

He swallowed a sip and placed his cup on its saucer before answering. "I am selling out and returning to England to settle down."

"I am certain your family will be pleased to have you home."

The waiter placed their respective dishes before them.

"Bon appetit."

"Merci," Mr. Brown answered in a perfect French accent, before turning back to her. "Do you often travel alone?"

Kate was certain her mouth was hanging open.

He shifted in his seat, his gaze dropping to his plate. "I beg your pardon. That was impertinent. I am unused to being around ladies and have forgotten how to hold a polite conversation. You seem too young to be on your own."

She had already suspected as much from his discourse so far. Stuffing a bite of roll in her mouth so she would not have to answer immediately, she studied the man as best she could without being obvious. A girl on an estate in the middle of nowhere in India, she had not had many opportunities to be near gentlemen of her own age and class. Sometimes British soldiers had passed through the nearest settlement, or her father had had an apprentice, but Father had made certain everyone knew she was promised to another. She now found her tongue to be unusually silent, as opposed to Mr. Brown's. She softened her rigid spine and tried to offer a reassuring smile.

"No offence taken, sir. This is my first time alone. I suppose I am more distrustful of strangers because of it."

"Since I have already crossed the bounds of propriety, may I ask if there is a reason in particular? Not that a young lady can ever be too careful."

Kate felt her resolve leave her. She gripped the chair beneath the table to force her chin to stop quivering. It should not be so difficult to answer a simple question, should it? Clearing her throat, she forced herself to look him in the eye.

"My father died."

Stephen felt like the cad he was pretending to be. He was typically the reserved Englishman she likely expected. This poor young woman was not acting—he would stake his life upon it. But it did not mean she was not the traitor, and there was no other way to discover what he needed to know unless he pried. Perhaps observing her from a distance would have been the prudent choice. She was beautiful, even with her chin trembling. The emotion caused her eyes to darken to a deep emerald and her cheeks to blush becomingly, making her dark locks an even more striking contrast to her fair skin. Thankfully, that same emotion kept her from noticing how he studied her. He wondered how her laughter would sound.

He attacked his beefsteak with fervour, allowing her time to compose herself and the opportunity for him to further study the other travellers. He hoped to put her at ease and loosen her tongue.

Behind Miss White was a French couple who had travelled with him from Bombay. Monsieur and Madame La Roche argued passionately, but he could not discern what about. Miss Hawthorne and her companion sat chewing their meal in dour silence, while a group of gentleman were having a cordial discussion about politics across their tables. The only unknown was an American financier and his wife, George and Vivian Howard. Stephen would need to discover what he could about them, though Howard was a wealthy business-man, if his wife's mink stole and array of jewelry were anything to go on. His mother would have said jewellery at breakfast was vulgar.

"What part of England are you from?" Miss White was watching him intently, so he deliberately tried to hood his eyes and return his attention back to her.

"My family is from the northeast, just north of Yorkshire." He needed to be careful before he gave the whole away, but he found it wisest to remain as close to the truth as possible.

"I do not believe I have been there," she said with a wrinkle between her brows as she tried to recall. "My family hails from Bath."

"A lovely monument to Georgian England."

"Yes, I confess I found Wood's architecture pleasing. My aunt rarely leaves Bath, and only then for London."

"Some people are drawn to Society. I have never understood the fascination."

Miss White gave a gentle shrug of one shoulder. "Widowed and wealth does not loneliness abate. However, it is amusing to read the scandal sheets from time to time. If my aunt's letters are true, people do behave in such a farcical manner!"

"Indeed they do." And often much worse, he thought. After spending more than a decade as a soldier, he did not find the extravagant scenes of idleness to his taste, though it was always the few outlandish members of Society the papers reported on, not the majority who were well behaved.

Miss White signalled the waiter for some more tea, and

some of the passengers were returning to their compartments. Stephen kept one eye on the others, but became more and more curious about the lady across the table.

"What is it like in the northeast?" she asked, before her gaze drifted to the majestic view outside the window.

"Some call it eerie and desolate. I think it is all perspective. There are rolling mountains covered in low foliage, with steep valleys in between. There are desolate moors, which authors delight in instilling fear of the quicksand and marshes— *Wuthering Heights*, for instance. Though I do not feel so bleak in my home as I do when I read the novel."

"Are there sheep?" she teased. "I remember there being sheep everywhere when I visited."

"It would not be England without sheep," he retorted. "It is home to me. Something one despairs of as a youth becomes one's fondest wish the night before battle."

Something he had said caused her to flinch, but it quickly disappeared.

"Perhaps I shall travel the country one day." She smiled wistfully.

"How long do you plan to stay in England?" he asked, encouraged by her openness.

"I have no idea. Everything hinges on how my business progresses."

"Do you not know how your father's estate is bequeathed?" Some people were superstitious about such things. Stephen thought it was a ridiculous notion.

"Oh, I know precisely how it is settled. He has thought to buy me a husband." She did not seem at all pleased with the fact.

"I beg your pardon?" Something set warning bells sounding in Stephen's head, but he chose to ignore them. It was painfully similar to his own situation. "Do you wish it otherwise?"

"It is not what you think. I am not one of those suffragettes who are so consumed by the vote that they eschew men altogether. I would simply prefer to choose my own mate."

"Arranged marriages are becoming less common," he said non-committally, trying not to think of his own betrothal and lose his focus on the mission at hand.

"Of course they are! The very idea is barbaric!" She slapped her hand down on the table to emphasize her point, causing the silver to rattle on the table. Stephen tried not to start.

"Arranged marriages have been occurring since the dawn of creation. There is some sense to it."

Her eyes blazed with passion, and Stephen wondered if she would look that way if he kissed her. His neck warmed at the thought, and he put it out of his mind.

"You sound like my father." She shook her head. "Marriage should be more than a business deal or a merging of estates."

"Ideally, yes. It is still difficult for a woman on her own. I have never viewed one sex as superior to the other. I have always thought God created man and woman to complement each other—one's weakness is the other's strength. Do you not wish for a husband's protection?"

She sat thinking for a moment. "Not if it means losing myself. Every woman desires security and protection. However, I would wish for a partner with whom to share things, to value my opinion and include me in discussions— not dictate to me."

"And this is how you expect marriage to be? I do not suppose I would look forward to that marriage either. They are not all as you describe. My own parents hold one another in great esteem."

"If I marry, I lose my name, my rights, my money . . . I suppose if it were my choice, I could abide it more easily."

Stephen had never thought about a woman's perspective in marriage. He was himself dreading the very life she described—was, in fact, also heading home to marry a complete stranger. Some marriages were indeed miserable. Is that what he had to look forward to?

Three

Kate had never excelled at idleness. She read for a while, then played patience with herself as long as she could bear it, and was exceedingly happy when it was finally time for luncheon. Mr. Brown had been an interesting breakfast companion; once she had overcome her shock at his boldness, she felt comfortable talking to him. She looked forward to more discussion with him.

Unfortunately, he did not come to luncheon. She was disappointed, though she could not fathom why. Mr. Brown was not someone she could contemplate a future with, so it must be she simply enjoyed his company. Talking to him was extraordinarily easy. If only Lord Darlington turned out to be as congenial as Mr. Brown, she would not fear the arrangement so much.

Mindlessly rearranging her peas, she stared out at the rugged terrain where snow still covered the peaks, reminding her of the mountains at home. Would she ever see India again? Did she want to go back?

It was pointless to contemplate her future until her meeting with Lord Darlington. What did he think of this arrangement? He must know of it, for the contract said she was to wed him on her twenty-first birthday—a short three months from now. Of course, her father was to have accompanied her. Kate normally liked to plan, but everything had happened so quickly, and all she could think about was going to England to undo the disastrous betrothal contract. She did not know what would happen when she actually arrived. What if her aunt was away from home?

"May I join you again?"

Kate turned her head and looked up to see Mr. Brown. "Of course, sir."

"I was visiting with my batman, Jeffers, in the other car, and I lost track of time."

He sat down and frowned at her plate. "Is the food off?"

"Oh." She looked down to see she had rearranged all of the food on her plate, but had not eaten any of it. "I do not know yet."

The waiter hurried to bring Mr. Brown a plate as she set to and tasted her roast duck.

"It is quite good, actually."

"Was something on your mind? I am never too distracted to eat," he said with a twinkle in his eye that warmed Kate's insides.

She concentrated on her fillet of cod.

"I suppose there are many things on my mind, not that any of them would be of interest to you, I am sure," she replied with a smile.

"Do try me. I have been told I am a good listener."

Kate still thought it odd that this stranger was so forthright, so interested in her, and that she felt comfortable confiding in him. There was something to be said for the safety of speaking things to strangers never to be seen again.

"Are you worried about the man your father has sold you to?" he asked pointedly.

Kate winced. "It is not quite that mercenary. He said joining me to this family was his fondest wish. He thought he was doing something good for me. There is a way out, though, if the other party agrees to dissolve the contract."

"And if he does not, you must wed him?"

Kate inclined her head, with a wave of her fork for added emphasis.

"Is he a complete stranger, then? No one can force you to marry without your consent in England, you know."

"I could be sued for breach of promise, and I find giving away my father's company to this man untenable." She stabbed her fish with her fork.

"So you have met him. That is the reason you are so against the marriage?"

Kate tried not to squirm in her seat. Mr. Brown was very perceptive. "I have met him once," she conceded, "on my previous trip to England."

"Was he an ogre with hairy warts and five chins?"

Kate laughed for the first time in weeks. Did she truly sound so petty and ridiculous?

"You should laugh more," Mr. Brown said, eyeing her with a smile and a look she could not discern. It was gone before she could consider it.

"Have you anything awaiting your return?" Kate moved the conversation away from her own plight.

"My father will be pleased to hand over the estate management. He did not expect me to stay away as long as I did."

"Why did you?"

"It was his idea to begin with—I was a spoiled youth who needed to grow up, and he thought the army would help with that. The country was not in any major conflicts, so the threat of actual battle was low."

Kate was astonished a man would openly admit his flaws.

She had always found it difficult to mention her own imperfections. Her admiration for this gentleman grew.

"Then what happened?"

"I found something I was good at. For once I had responsibility that could mean life or death for those involved. There is a certain addictive quality to being needed in such a way. But I am not indispensable to the army, and there will never be another chance to spend time with my father."

"You are wise. I would give anything for one more day with mine."

Miss White's situation weighed heavily on Stephen's mind. He kept dwelling on his own betrothal contract with Miss Worthington and whether he could free her from it if it was her wish. He had no idea how he would keep the estate in funds, unless he had her dowry to sustain it, but the thought of having a wife feel as Miss White did was repugnant to him. He vowed that he would look into the situation upon his return and see if there was a way to dissolve the contract, if both parties were willing. He had spent very little time thinking about his betrothal. He knew of it, of course; it would be one of his duties as the future Earl of Edgewood. But it had always been something he could put to the back of his mind. He had met the young lady once, when he was a youth. She had looked like a boy in a dress and had stuck her tongue out at him, but he was nine years her senior and he knew she would have grown up in the intervening years.

But Miss Worthington was for another day. There was a traitor to keep an eye on, first. Jeffers had little to report from the second-class cabin, as Stephen had suspected. He was beginning to feel as if he was on a wild goose chase, but he would continue to keep an eye on Miss White and Miss

Hawthorne. They were not going anywhere for now, so he settled back to relax on his bunk and allowed himself a brief rest.

He could overhear Miss Hawthorne and the dragon practising German. He mentally scratched the young lady from his list of suspects as he heard her whimper when reprimanded over and over for her mispronunciation of *gesundheit*. His instinct could not allow that she would last one day as a spy.

"Thief! Thief!" he heard a shrill, female voice scream. He hesitated a split second before opening his door to see what was amiss. It was unlikely his target would strike someone on board and put herself at risk with no easy means of escape. A discovered spy was as good as a dead spy.

Most of the passengers had opened their doors to see what was happening.

"My beloved brooch has been stolen!" Mrs. Howard wailed to the director, who was attempting to reassure her.

"We were gone to lunch, and when we returned, it was nowhere to be found," Mr. Howard explained.

"What does the brooch look like?" the steward asked.

Stephen could answer that. It was a replica of the ring Prince Albert had given Victoria for their engagement. Mrs. Howard had been wearing it at breakfast, and he had happened to recognize the symbol. How the woman could know she was missing anything amongst the quantity of frippery, was beyond all imagination.

"Perhaps we may have permission to do a thorough search?" the director asked diplomatically. "There is the possibility it may have fallen off, *non*?"

"Who would conduct the search? We must stop and have the police do it," Mr. Howard demanded.

"We cannot stop the train, monsieur, unless it is life and death."

"But he gave it to me for our wedding." Mrs. Howard continued to wail.

"It must be on the train, sir. No one would have stolen it to throw it out of the window," Miss White observed.

"May I offer my assistance?" Stephen stepped forward to Mr. Howard and the director. "I have been an army officer for twelve years and have experience with matters such as these. I can conduct a thorough search before we stop again. No one will leave the train before then, anyway." Stephen did not add that it would give him the opportunity he needed to discover any evidence against his target, though he felt a pang of regret that he still had to consider Miss White a suspect. Though he did not want to believe her capable because he liked her, she was independent, confident, and capable.

Mr. and Mrs. Howard looked at each other as the steward watched hopefully. "I suppose an army officer is as good as a police officer. Very well. How do we proceed?"

"Everyone must return to their cabins, and may not leave until instructed further," Stephen said, and watched as the passengers reluctantly did as they were told. He turned back to the couple.

"Madam, may I ask when was the last moment you remember seeing the brooch? I saw it myself at breakfast."

"Yes. The last time I saw it was when my maid fastened it onto my scarf this morning. I took it off when we returned from breakfast and placed it on the seat."

"And nothing else is missing?"

"Not that I am aware of, but that is quite enough! It must be worth twenty thousand dollars!" Mrs. Howard answered.

"I will begin with your cabin. If you could wait outside, please?"

"You cannot be serious!" Mr. Howard exclaimed. "You think we would pretend to have stolen our own jewels?"

"Not at all, but it is possible they were misplaced. If you wish me to do the job, then I must be thorough. I can proceed more quickly alone."

He shut the door behind him and began to go over each inch of the cabin in a methodical order. He highly suspected the jewellery had fallen off and the woman had not noticed. Things often went missing in army camps, and this was not the first time he had searched people's belongings.

The brooch was not in the Howards' cabin, so he moved on. The dragon had almost spat fire at him when he had searched, but he had to be consistent. By the time he reached Miss White's cabin, he had a rather efficient system perfected.

What he found in Miss White's cabin could not have shocked him more than if she were the spy herself. There were no treasonous papers or confessions of a spy, but instead, a copy of the betrothal contract bearing the name Kathryn Elizabeth Worthington and his own.

ter

Four

Kate waited outside in the corridor, fidgeting with the braid trimming on her waistcoat, as Mr. Brown searched her cabin. There was not much there to search, as most of her belongings were stored in trunks in the luggage car. However, if he read any of her papers, he would discover her real name was not White, and she would be suspect. Why had she ever thought it was a good idea to hide her name? Would anyone have connected her name with that of the heiress to the Worthington Trading Company?

Pacing up and down the corridor with worry, Kate was about ready to go to him and confess to the false name. What was taking him so long? Not until she saw the door open and Mr. Brown approach her with no hint of suspicion on his features, did she relax.

"No luck?" she asked, trying to muster a smile.

"No brooch," he confirmed.

"Has anyone searched the dining car? If that was the last place it was seen, it stands to reason it might have come unclasped and fallen off there, but the loss only noticed once she took off her scarf."

"Not a bad notion. I was going to make my way there

after completing my search of the cabins. I do not believe there was a theft any more than you do."

She nodded and was reaching for the latch when he spoke. "Would you care to search there with me?"

She turned to him and smiled. "I would be delighted. It is tedious to be confined to such a small space as my cabin."

"Never join the army," he rejoined with a chuckle.

"Have you completed your search of the cabins?"

"I have. I saved yours for last. I felt it the least likely place to find it."

"Thank you," she said quietly.

He turned to her and inclined his head as their eyes met. Then he held out his hand for her to precede him, and she tried not to feel disappointed that he had not offered his arm. It was a ridiculous notion, since it was much too narrow for two bodies to walk abreast. The fact that she wished she could have a reason to hold his arm was dangerous. There was no guarantee she could convince Lord Darlington to free her, and she felt bound to honour the betrothal until it was broken, much though it angered her. For now, she would appreciate the friendship he offered to abate the loneliness she felt and nothing more. There was only one more night and day remaining on the train. It should not be too difficult to keep her feelings in check.

The steward opened the doors for them to pass into the dining car, and they stopped just inside the threshold. The train lurched, and he placed his hand on her back to steady her, sending waves of awareness through her as she reached for a chair to keep from falling.

"Thank you. I was noticing the approaching city," she remarked to mask her embarrassment. What was the matter with her?

"Yes, we are approaching Vienna, so the faster we can

search this car the less inconvenienced the passengers will be. I will search the left side and you the right?"

"The tables have been cleared, so should we begin underneath?" she asked as she noticed two waiters preparing linens and silver for the next meal.

A look of amusement crossed his features, and Kate could sense even more appeal to him as she saw his eyes twinkle. She forced her gaze away, reminding herself of the dangerous direction her thoughts were leading when she was not yet free.

"If you would prefer, I will search under the tables," he said. "It is hardly an amenable task when hampered by skirts."

"Nonsense," she replied, already bending to her knees. She needed a place to hide her discomfiture.

It was a tight squeeze. Remaining graceful and keeping her skirts from becoming dreadfully wrinkled was more difficult then she would admit. However, it was better than sitting alone in her cabin indulging in self-pity, and it was exciting.

"The staff have been very efficient. I cannot find even a trace of crumbs under here," she remarked.

The tables themselves had been nailed down, which made excellent sense. Removing her gloves, she checked every nook and cranny she could find along the edge and under the slight opening between the pedestal in the floor of each place. Mr. and Mrs. Howard had been sitting at the farthest table, and her anticipation grew as she reached their table at last. She could barely hear Mr. Brown on his search, for he was as quiet as a mouse. It was a bit disconcerting, as she was noisy in her skirts.

As she crawled to the last table, he had already finished. She could see his neatly polished boots under the table, waiting for her. It was quite gracious of him to allow her to search under the Howards' table. She first tried under the small opening beneath the pedestal, but there was nothing. She then went to the side where the vents were, and there was no sign of the brooch. She sighed heavily with resignation.

Mr. Brown's face suddenly appeared under the table. "No luck?"

"None," she replied, defeated. "I was certain it would be under the pedestal or in the vent."

He climbed under the table with her, and her heart leapt at his nearness. It was suddenly difficult to breathe as his scent of cloves and spice invaded her senses.

"May I try something?" he asked.

"Of course," she replied and attempted to back out of the way but banged her head on the table.

"I beg your pardon, I should have allowed you to come out before I charged in."

"Nonsense, I should have paid attention. Do you intend to remove the grate?"

"Precisely." He took a small knife from his pocket and withdrew a little in order to pry back the metal panel. "Would you care to look first?" he offered.

With as much excitement as a child reaching into the biscuit jar, she nodded with a smile and put her hand into the panel to feel around. When she clasped her fingers around a small metal object, she squealed with glee. Pulling it out of the hole and opening her hand to reveal her find, she gasped with amazement as she took in the emerald and diamond-covered brooch in the shape of a serpent.

Mr. Brown bent over her hand to study the jewellery, and she suddenly found her pulse was racing. Their faces were mere inches apart. If she leaned forward, they would be close enough to kiss. Blinking away her unladylike thoughts, she reminded herself that she was betrothed. She could sense the train beginning to slow and was disappointed that their small adventure was coming to an end.

"Magnificent," he said, taking the small brooch from her hand and examining it, their fingers brushing as he took it from her palm. Could he feel what she did when he touched her? He seemed completely unaffected.

"I suppose we should return the brooch to the owner and conclude this little investigation."

"I think you have managed to divert an international crisis," she added dryly.

"All in a day's work," he said, eyes twinkling again.

He replaced the grate, deftly made his way to his feet, and held out his hand for her. She clasped it and he helped her to her feet, feeling a shock of awareness at his touch. Again, he put his hand on the small of her back to direct her towards the cabins, and a tingling warmth radiated through her. Kate did not know how much more of his temptation she could bear, and it took all her power not to beg him to touch her again. Why did he affect her so? Never before had she been touched or courted by a young, attractive man, but she did not expect it to scramble her wits!

After the brooch had been returned, and the Howards had praised and thanked Mr. Brown effusively, the train stopped in Vienna. They were more than halfway to Paris, and Stephen was no closer to finding a spy. He could not bring himself to believe either young lady on board capable of such deceit. No incriminating documents had been found, although one could consider Miss Worthington suspicious since she was traveling under a false name. Should he reconsider? Was he biased because he knew her to be his betrothed? The thought rankled that he could not answer objectively.

As he was returning to his cabin, the conductor stopped him.

"Monsieur, we will have a slight delay to make an adjustment to the brakes. It is only a safety precaution, I assure you, but if you wish to enjoy Vienna, we will not depart for six hours. It is a short ride to the centre of the city."

"Thank you," he said absentmindedly as he watched the conductor proceed down the corridor and explain the situation to each passenger.

Stephen groaned to himself. He was rather tired after the day's events, but he had a sneaking suspicion that Miss White would wish to see the sights, despite being without a chaperone. He would have to follow her whether she was a spy or not. His conscience could not allow his betrothed to wander about a foreign city alone. He could offer to escort her, but he still needed to convince himself she was not leading a double life. He certainly wished he had more information on the wanted target. Had she been operating out of India, for instance? He did not have enough intelligence about her to completely dismiss her as a suspect.

Entering his compartment, he left the door ajar to see if she went out. He gathered his coat and hat and placed his knife in his boot and his pistol in his coat, not expecting to need either.

Not five minutes later, Miss White hurried from number eight, wearing another striking ensemble in the peridot green which was the exact shade of her eyes. She made a striking picture, and his gaze would not be the only one following her, he was certain.

He slipped into the corridor just behind her and listened as she asked directions from the conductor.

"If you follow the Ring Strasse, it goes in a circle around the centre of town, and you may see most of the sights there are," he explained. "There is the Hofburg Palace, the Vienna Opera House, St. Stephen's Cathedral, and other sites along the way. The Volksgarten is a particular favourite of mine. Shall I hail you a cab?"

"Yes. This sounds delightful. I am in need of some fresh air. Thank you, sir." She handed him a coin for his service.

She descended from the train and waited as cabs were lined up, eager for the custom from the luxury train. Stephen slid into the hack behind hers and directed the driver to follow.

Departing the vehicle with purpose, she walked much faster than any English lady would. He chuckled to himself. She was a refreshing change from Society. He did wonder how she would get on amongst the *ton*, but with her money and pedigree she probably would not care. Stephen rather hoped she did not wish to be the toast of Town, as he vastly preferred the country. Yet again, he assumed she would agree to be his wife. How would she react when she found out? Would she feel deceived or relieved? He must be careful, he cautioned himself. She had still not been cleared as the spy, and women could be wily.

The more he got to know her, the more hopeful he was for their marriage. She had not seemed completely indifferent to him while they had searched the dining car. He could almost imagine that she had struggled to resist him as they sat beneath the table, their bodies almost touching. It was rather wicked of him to try to woo her under the pretence of being Mr. Brown, but he was doing it as much to reassure himself as he was to change her mind about the betrothal. He should not have kept touching her, but he found he wanted to.

Miss White had already reached the Ring Strasse and smiled as she took in the various shops and vendors along the busy promenade. Stephen remained a discreet distance behind, but she seemed completely unaware of anyone around her. No, she did not have the typical characteristics of suspicious behaviour—she seemed much more like a small child surveying a big, new world with wonder.

First, she walked toward the Stephansplatz and to the beautiful St. Stephen's Cathedral, gazing up at the mosaic tiles and steeple that made it so unique. Inside was similar to the Notre Dame in Paris, though it must be quite different from the temples of worship in India. She made her way reverently through the nave and stopped to light a candle and pray in front of the altar. Stephen was tempted to go close enough to hear her fervent whispers.

From the cathedral, she stopped to ask directions from a street-side vendor and went to view the stunning opera house that was done à la Renaissance. She admired it from the outside but continued towards the Hofburg Palace. He would like to be taking in the sights with her, sharing her thoughts, instead of sneaking along behind.

The Volksgarten outside the palace drew her attention, and she stopped to smell the flowers along the way. Spring was evidenced by the first blooms of daffodils and tulips displaying their yellow, red, and pink brilliance clustered in the numerous beds along the pathway. She strolled along towards the fountain, where she stopped for some time, perhaps lost in thought as she seemed mesmerized by the flowing water.

He sat in one of the chairs along the lane, not concerned if she saw him here. It was a public enough place, he could easily excuse his presence. Manicured gardens with blossoms in their early spring magnificence, the flow of a fountain, and the fragrance of freshly cut grass took him back to Edgewood Manor and the smells of his youth. Miss White, or Kate, as he had heard her family call her as a child, would look at home in his garden. Would she remember she had visited Edgewood or the time their families visited Kew Gardens?

He saw she was watching another couple wistfully as they held hands and laughed together. Before he knew what he was doing, his feet were moving towards where she stood by the trickling water.

"Miss White?"

She did not hear him at first. Had she not remembered her false name? He longed to ask her why she had chosen to travel under a pseudonym. One day. He was right next to her before she started at his presence.

"Mr. Brown!"

"You did not hear me call to you. Am I intruding?"

"Not at all. I was remembering a similar garden I visited when in England with my parents. It is a vague memory. I do not have many memories of my mother, but I remember she loved fountains." She paused.

"Memories are God's way of keeping loved ones with us always."

"Yes. My father said something similar before he died." Her chin trembled, and she looked down. He suddenly wanted to bring a smile to her face.

"Have you enjoyed your time in Vienna?" he asked politely, hoping to distract her from her sorrow.

"It is a beautiful city, though it is quite different from those in India. It is refreshing to go about without being a novelty." She smiled shyly.

He wanted to know her better and spend time with her without the preconceived notions she would feel if she knew his true identity.

"Have you been to a café? You have not experienced Vienna unless you have been to one."

"I am unused to going alone to such places. Are ladies even allowed?" she asked.

"I have seen them from time to time. Vienna is more

progressive than most cities. Join me. We just have time to properly savor a *sachertorte*." He could sense her wavering.

She smiled mischievously. "If it involves chocolate, you could not keep me from refusing."

Five

Kate was delighted to see Mr. Brown at the Volksgarten. She had spent the afternoon attempting to enjoy Vienna, but everywhere she went and everything she saw reminded her of travelling with her papa and even her mama, whom she had known so little. It had been twelve years to the day since her mother had died giving birth to a stillborn son, not long after they had returned from their trip to England. These days, she longed for a mother's guidance and advice, for she was only acting on instinct and did not trust it. Mr. Brown was a welcome distraction from her melancholy.

He offered his arm and Kate took it—she could hardly refuse a gentlemanly gesture—but she had never taken a man's arm other than her papa's. This felt nothing like her papa's arm. Large, well-formed muscles flexed beneath the unassuming brown tweed of his coat, and Kate could feel her palms begin to sweat in her gloves. Suddenly, her insides were doing a dance, and her breathing felt forced. What was happening to her?

The perfume of fresh flowers and grass intertwined with his masculine scent of cloves and spice—a heady combination—as they strolled back through the gardens.

When they reached the street, he protectively guided her through the pedestrians and carriages to reach a beautiful, yellowed stone building, which looked as though it could be in the city of London. Inside, there were tall marble columns and archways, with tables and booths set up around the edge. There were no other ladies present, she noticed, but the other patrons seemed too intent on their own conversations to take notice.

"You must have been here before," she remarked.

"My position with the army required much travel. I was fortunate to see many different places."

"Including this café," she stated. "I am certain you have some interesting stories to tell."

"This is a well-known meeting place for dignitaries, poets, musicians . . . we will not be noticed amongst this crowd." He smiled, and she could detect a small hint of a dimple beneath his moustache. She spent entirely too much time thinking about what Mr. Brown would look like without the facial accoutrement, she realized.

Speaking to the waiter in German, Mr. Brown must have requested a table near the window where they could see outside, as he led her to a quaint booth for two. Through the thickness of her jacket, his hand seemed to sear her back as he guided her into her chair. Once they were seated, the waiter handed her a menu written in German. Calling on long-ago lessons, she was able to recognize a few words.

"Do you have a particular request, or shall I order my favourite for both of us?" he asked.

"As long as there is chocolate as promised," she bantered playfully.

"But, of course."

She felt uncomfortable, sitting at the table in a strange place, in a strange city, with a relative stranger. Yet at the same time, she realized she was comfortable with *him*, and it was nice to have company. His eyes were watching and observing, even though discreetly. She could feel his gaze, and it heated her insides in a way which made her thought processes dull. However, sitting here, feeling self-conscious, would not do. There must be something to talk about.

The waiter set a plate of chocolate tortes on the table and two cups of coffee with foamed milk between them.

"Do you intend to partake in the London Season?" he saved her by asking.

"I am certain my aunt will insist. I cannot say I look forward to it with any pleasure. From what I gather from my aunt and old governess, I will be quite restricted as an unmarried lady in your Society. I will not be permitted do such things as enjoy a café alone with a gentleman, in public."

"I am afraid what you say is true."

She took a disgruntled bite of the delectable chocolate cake to comfort her.

"Will you attend the Season, sir?"

He looked surprised by her question, and she could see he was thinking about his answer.

"I, too, have some business to attend to, the outcome of which will determine my course. If I have cause to remain in London, I will likely attend some events." He chuckled. It was a beautiful sound. "That was a very obscure answer to a simple question," he remarked while shaking his head.

"Sometimes there are no simple answers."

"True."

"Unless my aunt has much changed in twelve years, she will be leading the *haute ton* by their ears. I confess, I do not like to think of her ageing, but my father did."

"You and your father were close." He made it a statement, not a question.

"We only had each other, since my mother died in childbirth."

"My condolences." He seemed genuine in his sympathies, as though he had known loss himself.

"Thank you. We made do as one must. I was allowed many liberties sooner than most young ladies, I am sure. Father did not know what to do with me, so he taught me some of the business, and I took over the running of the house."

"You will make a good wife to your husband, I imagine."

She scoffed, which came out almost like a snort.

"Perhaps your betrothed will not be so disagreeable when you meet him," he mused.

"If you recall, sir, we have met." She felt the need to remind him.

"Ah, yes. How recent was this meeting? Have you formed such a loathsome picture of him from this one time?" Mr. Brown's eyes twinkled at her, and she was certain she was blushing. She could feel heat in her cheeks at his words.

"It was during our trip to England—twelve years ago. I suppose it is unreasonable of me to form my estimations from when we were young."

"I would not wish to be judged on my youthful follies. What did he do to colour your opinions so?" He continued to watch her with intensity.

"When you frame the questions in such a manner, I begin to think I am ridiculous. If I were to ask him his opinion of me, I am certain it would be similar to those of my own. I was a gangling girl, and at the time, my hair was cut like a boy." She shook her head at the memory. "He was not more than a boy himself, but he was arrogant and smelled of the stables. And he laughed at me."

Mr. Brown laughed, a deep and hearty sound which

made her want to say more outlandish things to hear it again. She joined him in his laughter, and it felt good.

Mr. Brown picked up his cup and held it out towards her. "May your betrothed be humble and smell nice."

Kate laughed as she held up her own cup and tried to think of what to say to return his gesture. "I feel as though I have done nothing but talk about myself and my woes. I do not know how I might reciprocate, other than to toast to your health and a happy reunion with your family." They lightly clinked cups, and Kate took a sip of the drink. She had heard it described as the essence of Vienna. It was worthy of the name.

"That is a lovely sentiment. We may toast that my betrothed will be as beautiful and delightful as you," he said with an impish half-smile.

Kate choked on her hot drink. She was thankful for the cough, because she had no idea how to respond to such a bold statement.

"Are you all right?" he asked, looking concerned.

"Yes, thank you." She cleared her throat. "I was unaware you were also betrothed."

He paused, looking thoughtful, before speaking. The blue of his eyes caught the last of the sun's rays as they shone in the window.

"Yes, I am sympathetic to your situation. It was a contract made when I was a youth. It is part of the old generation's customs, and some are still grasping for ways to continue to hold onto their estates."

"So, you do not mind? You see it as your duty to your name and land?" She genuinely needed to know, for she cared what he thought.

"That is how I thought, yes."

He was speaking in the past tense and looking at her

meaningfully, his gaze hooded but direct. She swallowed hard, uncomfortable and unused to the scrutiny. It was no good for either of them to express their feelings, for there was little hope of a future with this man. It was little comfort that he seemed to feel the same connection she did.

"And your feelings have changed?" Why had she said that aloud? She looked away.

"I still see it as my duty, but I cannot say I do not mind. You have made me reconsider how my betrothed may feel about such an arrangement. I believe, when I return, I will offer her a release from the contract if she wishes."

"I cannot imagine she would wish to do so," Kate whispered.

Church bells began to chime, and they both became conscious of the time as they looked at each other with disappointment. Kate did not want this moment to end. She knew they were to board the Orient Express for the last leg of their trip, and she would never see him again. Was that how life would be from now on? Little memories, and treasures of experiences, accumulated over short lapses of time to make up the whole?

Mr. Brown paid the reckoning and went outside to hail a cab for them to return to the train. They sat close beside each other to ward off the cold, and perhaps, Kate thought, both of them were seeking some comfort in their mutual misery. She could only hope that her betrothed had become such a man as Mr. Brown, or that Lord Darlington would have the same compassion and also release her.

When back on the train, they said farewell at their compartment doors, and for a brief moment he hesitated. There was something in the way he looked at her. Was it possible he had thoughts of kissing her? It was so swift, Kate was not sure if she only imagined it. She threw herself on her bench seat, staring out of the window whilst thinking Mrs. Brown would be the loveliest title she could imagine. The train began to move forward, and the gentle rocking lulled her into a trance. She was no closer to a solution on how to confront Lord Darlington. Meeting Mr. Brown had not only confused her feelings, it had firmed her resolve against a loveless marriage. But what if Lord Darlington would not release her?

Stephen said goodbye to Kate at her door—or Miss White, as he should be thinking of her. He had almost forgotten himself and kissed her. But he was not free from his army responsibilities yet, and he had best remember it. When he went to open the door to his own compartment, he felt the hairs on the back of his neck rise. He looked around but could not see anything to cause alarm. Shaking off the eerie sensation, he entered his compartment but left his door ajar.

Had a new passenger joined them in Vienna? He would need to investigate. Staying alive for twelve years in the army had not happened without trusting his instinct. Something was sending off warning bells inside him, and he must do his best to determine the source.

It was still another hour until dinner, and they were scheduled to arrive in Paris the next evening. It left him little time to act.

Dressing quickly, he decided to speak with the director and ask to inspect the manifest for new arrivals. He felt a sense of urgency, and he prayed the director would understand the need for the invasion of privacy when he showed him his real identity and papers.

He checked his appearance in the glass and had to smile at the moustache. He was not particularly fond of it himself, but he had seen Miss White look at it and try to hide her displeasure. *What fun it will be to shave it off and surprise her soon,* he mused.

"And I must not forget the spectacles," he reminded himself before venturing on to speak with the wagon-lit's director.

The conductor stood and smiled as Stephen exited his compartment. "May I help you, Monsieur Brown?"

"If you would be so kind, I would like to speak with the director—in private, if I may. It is a matter of some importance."

"Yes, of course. Please follow me. I believe he is in the dining car."

"Thank you," Stephen said, following behind.

He attempted to listen as he walked by each compartment, but he heard nothing apart from the expected noises of people shuffling about, dressing for dinner. The director, Mr. Janssens, was sitting at a table, in discussion with the head chef. The conductor walked over and whispered to the director, who quickly motioned for Stephen to join him. The chef gave a salutation and left.

The director stood up. "How may I be of service, Monsieur Brown?"

"May I?" he indicated the chair the chef had vacated.

"Please do." Mr. Janssens sat back down.

"I apologize if I am interrupting, but I need to know if you have any new passengers since we left Vienna." He pulled his official identity papers from his breast pocket and handed them to the man. "This is to be kept confidential."

The man read them with raised brows before handing them back. "Is the train in any danger?"

"I am unaware of any threat to the train itself, but I have investigated the other suspects who have been on board since Constantinople. I have all but dismissed them. My instinct tells me someone new has boarded."

The man looked hesitant to speak, but did. "There are two new passengers. A French businessman, Monsieur DuPui, is a very regular customer. I cannot imagine him being involved in anything nefarious."

No one would suspect if they were doing their job properly, Stephen thought wryly. However, it was a woman he was interested in. "And the other?"

"An Arab woman—at least, I assume she was since she was wearing the covering from head to toe. All I could see was her eyes."

"A burka."

"*Oui,* that is it."

"Was she travelling alone?" Stephen asked.

Mr. Janssens shrugged. "She had a servant with her."

"And which cabin does she travel in?"

"The number sixteen, in the same car as you."

"Previously there had been a Mr. Smith in the car? And he departed in Vienna?"

"That is correct."

"One more question. What name does this new female passenger travel under?"

"I believe it was a Mrs. Haddad."

"*Merci,* Monsieur Janssens. And please, keep this knowledge to yourself."

The man inclined his head in response.

Stephen walked back to his compartment, slowing by number sixteen, but nothing was out of the ordinary. Considering the new passengers, an Arab woman was as good a disguise as he could make himself, if that were her object. But why had she only now joined the train, instead of in Constantinople? He was accustomed to seeing women in such dress from his travels across Africa and the Orient, yet it was uncommon for one to be travelling without a male in Western

43

Europe. There had to be more to this story, but he had no source for information or any way to get it on a train with no further stops until Paris. Had she been on board the entire trip in disguise and only changed costumes in Vienna?

He felt woefully ignorant yet knew something was afoot. There must be a piece missing, and he could not completely rule out Miss White or technically Miss Hawthorne since he had not captured Anna Smith. Instinct still repelled at the thought of his betrothed's involvement in espionage, yet it was easiest to hide in plain sight. But did she know she needed to hide here?

Six

Kate dressed for dinner with extra care, knowing this could possibly be her last evening with Mr. Brown. The fairy tale of the Orient Express blossomed in her heart. She chose an evening gown of cream taffeta that fell just off the shoulders, with a fitted bodice down to a point which accentuated her slim waist. The skirt was narrow, and covered in a delicately embroidered pattern of pink roses enhanced by green leaves and vines. Carefully pinning up her curls with emerald combs, she allowed a few to hang down and rest on her shoulders.

Hearing the door next to hers latch, she pulled on her gloves and pinched her cheeks. Her appearance was not what it would be with the help of a maid, but it would have to do. Kate walked down the corridor, anticipation building to see Mr. Brown again.

He was wearing a plain brown suit, but he was still handsome to her, and his moustache and whiskers were not as noticeable as they had once been. The admiration on his face and the crinkles around his eyes, when he looked up and saw her, was answer enough for her appearance. He stood promptly and held her chair for her before the waiter could.

"You are in fine looks this evening, Miss White."

"Thank you. I was most fortunate to live where the finest fabrics in the world are made. Father traded tea with the vendors in exchange for some glorious silks." She whispered the last with a grin.

"Ah, you believe you owe your looks to fine fabrics? I beg to differ." He raised a questioning brow at her.

"They cannot hurt." She could feel her cheeks flush

The waiter came to take their order, and they both decided on the *Française noisette* and the *filet de boeuf au poivre* as their main courses.

As they finished ordering, a woman in Arab dress and her maid came into the car and were seated at the adjacent table. From that point forward, Mr. Brown no longer focused on Kate. It seemed beyond all rational thought—for Kate could think of no reason a woman dressed in black from head to toe, save her eyes, would draw his attention away. But that is precisely what happened. He must have been exposed to the Muslim ways if he had spent time in Africa and the Orient. Kate could detect nothing abnormal herself. The woman ordered her food in French and then ate by a slight lift of her scarf. Why, therefore, was Mr. Brown so distracted by this woman?

Conversation became stilted into monosyllabic answers once their food was delivered. Mr. Brown's eyes were constantly, though discreetly, surveying the table to the side, and he scarcely took another bite of his food.

Kate lost interest in her own food as well. An irrational wave of jealousy washed over her, and she began to feel sick. How could she compete with such an enigma?

When the Arab woman left, Mr. Brown's eyes followed her as she departed from the dining car. The waiter brought the dessert, and he did not seem to notice.

Kate set her fork down across the edge of her plate, and placed her napkin on the table. She no longer felt like eating or conversing.

"You have not touched the chocolate mousse," Mr. Brown exclaimed, now that his attention had returned to her.

"My excursion in Vienna tired me more than I thought. I believe I will retire early."

He opened his mouth as though to argue but did not. "As you wish. I will walk back with you."

When they reached their respective doors, he spoke again. "Perhaps we will meet in London. Hopefully, we will both have good news."

"I will throw some pennies in every fountain I see for both of us. Goodnight, Mr. Brown," she said, more curtly than she intended.

"And I will wish on every shooting star I see. Goodnight, Miss White. Pleasant dreams."

Kate closed the door behind her but stood staring at it, wondering what had just happened. Her wretched chin began to quiver, but she refused to allow herself any tears. Nothing could come of a relationship between the two of them, anyway, and her father would have told her she was being silly and whimsical.

She sat down, folded her arms on the table in front of her, and buried her head in her hands. At least he had not said goodbye. She could not have withstood it.

The next morning, Kate took a tray in her room. Melancholy was once again her companion, and it was time she faced her future instead of pining over what could never be. As a child, she had dared to dream of a husband. She had always imagined a handsome man who could make her feel magical inside—as though she were the only woman on earth. Someone who listened to her, who would cherish her, and who would love her as her father had loved her mother. Instinct was telling her Mr. Brown was such a man, but he was already betrothed—as was Kate. She would not allow herself to sit and brood any longer, for there was nothing to be done about it now.

When they at last reached their final stop at the Gare de l'Est station, she waited until she heard Mr. Brown depart before asking the conductor to hire a conveyance to a hotel. Perhaps a day or two in Paris would ease the ache she felt inside. This might have been a success if she had not witnessed Mr. Brown lying in wait for the mysterious Arab woman, and then following her. It was the final blow needed to encourage Kate to forget him.

After two days in Paris, visiting the sites and shops along the Champs Élysées, she boarded another train to take her closer to England to cross the Channel. Once she set foot in England again, she would force herself to forget Mr. Brown and the childish longings of her heart. The last train of her long journey chugged and climbed its way through rolling, green hills of England, villages charmingly situated amongst large stretches of farmland bordered by hedges and wooden fences. She could see beautiful cathedrals and even a castle— along with several herds of sheep. Kate smiled to herself. As the train slowed near the station, the buildings became more frequent and close together, with warehouses and shops, horse-drawn carriages, vendors, and people.

Kate stepped off the train and inhaled deeply to firm her resolve. The Orient Express was now a bittersweet thought. It signalled the end of the most magical and heartbreaking time of her life.

Stephen had allowed his guard to drop, and now, it

seemed, he had unwittingly hurt his betrothed. He would do his best to make it up to her when the operation was over with and he had sold his commission.

Normally, he would not have been so careless, but he had assumed that there were no threats on board and had not considered that the spy might join them at another stop. As much as he longed to follow Kate and confess the whole, he had a job to finish.

Besides having to report to the British Embassy in Paris, he needed to follow Mrs. Haddad to determine if his instincts were correct.

Disembarking from the train as soon as it stopped, he ordered his batman to carry his luggage on to the British Embassy, along with a note informing them of his plans. Then he purchased a news-sheet and positioned himself, with his top hat pulled down, behind a marble column to wait. Once or twice, he felt as though he was the one being watched, but he dared not look up to see if it was Kate who had noticed him. They had not said a proper goodbye last evening, and that had been intentional on his part. Hopefully, she would understand one day.

When he saw Mrs. Haddad and her servant step down from the train, he folded up the news-sheet, tucked it under his arm, and followed her.

His cab followed hers, setting off toward the Rue Lafayette. If only he knew what her mission was, things would be so much easier to determine where she might go, and for what purpose. He contemplated what it might be, but The Sikkim Expedition had just ended and he was uncertain what her aim was. Of course, everyone was always against British rule these days, and it took very little for one of their colonies to rise up against Her Majesty. This spy had a résumé, however, and he had to keep track of her.

Mrs. Haddad's carriage stopped at the Hotel Continental, two streets away from the British Embassy. Would she take a room? Or was her business to be conducted immediately? He instructed his driver to stay back a moment until she was fully ensconced inside the hotel.

Pulling out a piece of paper from his small satchel, Stephen hastily scribbled a note to inform his superiors of his whereabouts and to request reinforcements. He paid the driver handsomely and asked him to deliver the note immediately.

"*Oui, oui, merci!*" The man doffed his hat at Stephen and quickly directed his horse cart towards the ~~Embassy~~embassy, situated two streets ahead.

Stephen then discreetly entered the hotel, taking one of the plush armchairs situated around the lobby. Mrs. Haddad took a room and was shown upstairs.

Stephen was relieved when a fellow agent joined him in the lobby and casually sat in a nearby chair.

He gave a slight incline of his head to Colonel Buchman, whom he had served under in the 9th Lancer's Calvary Regiment when he had first joined the army.

"What can you tell me, Darlington?"

"The target is travelling as a Mrs. Haddad and joined the train in Vienna, wearing a burka. There is one female servant accompanying her."

"I would assume she is upstairs shedding the burka post-haste," the colonel mused.

"Precisely," Stephen agreed. "It did occur to me that Haddad is the Arab version of Smith. The original passenger was a Mr. Smith, and after Vienna Mrs. Haddad was in the same cabin. She could very well be the one we seek."

"Excellent work, Darlington."

"Is there any more intelligence on what she is after?"

Stephen enquired, hoping for more clues.

"There is to be a ball, held at the ~~Embassy~~ embassy this evening, in which dignitaries from our allied nations will be present, not to mention Her Majesty."

"Anyone to be watched in particular? Or do we assume Her Majesty is the prize?"

"Based on Mrs. Smith's history, we know she is unsympathetic to the Crown and against British rule in general."

Stephen considered this for a minute. "What are my orders, sir?"

"Your post here will be taken over by a few agents who have seen her full face before. You are to go and ready yourself for the ball—not in your regimentals, but civilian dress, mind you—and you will be given the signal when she arrives. You will not let her out of your sight."

"Understood."

"Go on, now. I will keep watch until relief arrives."

Stephen sauntered out from the hotel and made his way to the ~~Embassy~~ embassy, to a room provided for senior officers on duty in Paris.

He still wished he knew what Smith's target was, for a ballroom full of dignitaries could become an international disaster.

Seven

"Katherine? Is it you at long last?" her aunt called, leaning over the balustrade overlooking the marble entry hall.

"Aunt Libby!" Kate exclaimed, running up the stairs and throwing her arms around her beloved aunt, who had been her devoted correspondent since her mother died. "I thought I would never arrive!"

"Has it been two months since you left India?"

"Six weeks. It feels like much longer," Kate said as they walked into the parlour. She almost fell into a chair with relief. "I was worried you would not have received my telegrams."

"I hated to hear of my dear brother's passing and you being in that barbaric place all alone, but you were already on your way by the time I received the message. I had expected both of you to be joining me for the Season." Aunt Libby was still a beautiful woman, even though her hair had turned to silver.

"Yes. It was very unexpected." Kate would not bother arguing that Darjeeling was as civilized as most any other place she had been.

"You should not have travelled here alone," Aunt Libby chastised without any heat behind the remark.

"Diya and some menservants accompanied me as far as Constantinople, but I did not feel it was fair to take her any farther. There was little threat of harm once I was on the Orient Express," she said in an off-hand manner. "I travelled under the name of White."

"When you are rested, I want to hear all about that adventure. I am tempted to take a ride on it myself, one day," Aunt Libby confessed, her eyes twinkling.

"I feel as though I have done nothing but rest, yet I am exhausted," Kate bemoaned.

"I cannot believe how much you have changed since I saw you last. You look exactly like your dearest mother, except you have your father's eyes. Dark hair with light green eyes is rather striking—I predict you will be the latest rage. Have you come prepared for the Season? I see you have decided to forgo mourning?" Her aunt looked her over.

"Father expressly forbade it. He maintained we should be happy for the departed going on to a better place."

Her aunt frowned. "I can see you are already outfitted in the latest stare of fashion. I do not know how my dear brother managed it from the other side of the world."

"Business connections," Kate said with a smile. "Is it still passé to work in England?"

"It is becoming less so, I am afraid. Many of the finest families have had to resort to some business to stay afloat. Even so, many of the estates have been sold off to cits."

"The industrial revolution is changing everything, as father predicted it would. I crossed from Constantinople to Paris in only a few days, this time!"

"Times will change, but I cannot say I like all of it. Many of the effects will not be known until long beyond my time."

"I do think you are right, Aunt. But how have you been? Twelve years is much too long to go between visits. Father always wanted you to come to India."

"I am the same as I ever was. I enjoy a good gossip and causing trouble whenever it strikes my fancy," her elegant aunt said, with a gleam in her eye.

Kate laughed. "I shudder to think what you mean by trouble, but as long as it does not involve me . . ."

"My definition of trouble is at odds with that of many unsuspecting bachelors. You have nothing to worry about, since you are already betrothed to one of the most eligible men in the country."

Kate swallowed hard. She did not have the heart to explain her intentions to her aunt. She would tell her after the deed was done or Aunt Libby would exert herself to interfere.

"I shall send to the *modiste* for an appointment. I suspect you will need evening dress, at the very least."

Kate murmured her agreement. "I did order a few gowns from the House of Worth in Paris, but who knows how long it will be before they arrive. I also brought a trunk full of silks with me. You may have any you like."

"Oh, my dear! It will be such fun to have you here for the Season!"

"I must see my father's man of business before I do anything else," Kate recalled.

"Must you? Is that not all resolved?" Her aunt scowled with distaste.

"Unfortunately not. There is much still to be done before my marriage."

"I cannot like this one bit, Katherine. It cannot be too soon for you to wed Lord Darlington and have him take over your father's affairs."

Kate tried to keep her face impassive. She had no desire to rouse suspicion.

"If he returns in time for the wedding, that is," Aunt Libby added.

Kate turned her face towards her aunt in shock. "What do you mean, 'if he returns in time'?"

"You did not know?"

Kate's face must have registered a blank expression.

"His father bought him a commission in the army, not long after you visited here. He had grown wild and indolent, if you wish to know my opinion, and his father sent him there to mature, even though it pained him to send him away."

"Is it not unusual for the heir to go into the army?"

"Not as unusual as it used to be," she remarked. "It is not the threat it was in my youth, when Napoleon was running amok."

Kate did not know what to say. She had thought Lord Darlington an arrogant sloth, herself. But how would she contact him if he were away? Would there be time to enact her plan? Perhaps her father's man of affairs could still look into her betrothed's records.

Kate's heart plummeted in her chest.

"I am dearest friends with his mother, you know."

Kate started when she realized her thoughts had been wandering.

"Are you?" She tried to appear pleased.

"Apparently, he has been quite an asset to His Majesty."

Any mother would say that. "I am very glad to hear it," Kate replied.

"Yes, it seems his father's plan worked. Dear Margaret says he plans to return in time and take over the estate after the marriage. She believes him to be a most dutiful son."

Kate just barely controlled a groan and a grimace. She hated dutiful—the word, the meaning, the very implication— it was everything wrong in her life at the moment.

Stephen managed to remain unobtrusively in the shadows and watch from one side of the ballroom's double stairway while a fellow agent flanked the other side. It was unknown how Anna Smith intended to arrive at the ball, but all were certain she would. During the intervening time, after he had dressed, Stephen had learned that Anna's father had been a British soldier who had abandoned her mother after a campaign in Mysore, and the mother had died giving birth to her. It had become her life's mission to avenge her mother's dishonour and destroy anything British. Aligning herself with the maharajah, whose mission was to see British rule gone from India forever, Miss Smith had been successful in thwarting several unsuspecting allies.

The Queen had already arrived at the ~~Embassy~~embassy, along with more European royalty than Stephen knew existed. He settled down for a long, tedious wait, his eyes never leaving his post. There was always a chance Miss Smith could use an unexpected entrance, since the security was tighter here tonight than at Buckingham Palace. Officers, agents, and guards were posted at every conceivable entrance, and Stephen tried to think of how he would approach destroying someone of importance were he in Miss Smith's shoes. It would not be by conventional means.

He would probably try scaling the roof and descending through a door or open window from the top. A burka would be much too noticeable this evening, since the new fashions did not allow a woman to hide a veritable army's cache of weapons beneath her skirts, though perhaps a dagger or pistol.

Colonel Buchman gave the signal that all guests had arrived. Stephen could not stop the nagging sensation that the threat would come from above. He entered the balcony of the ballroom, where mostly the orchestra, servants, and second-class guests would be. He walked the perimeter, offering slight inclinations of the head to acknowledge fellow guards, and saw nothing amiss . . . until he saw a young, exotic lady flirting coyly with one of the guards.

Stephen's senses heightened, and he pulled his dagger discreetly into his hand and reassured himself that his pistol was ready for swift action. He hid behind a pillar only a few feet away and watched as the lady manipulated and maneuvered the young guard at her whim. The soldier was completely enamoured as Miss Smith smiled and batted her lashes at him. His arm was above her on a column, and he looked as though he would try to steal a kiss. Anna Smith was an exotic beauty, but Stephen could only compare her to Kate and find her lacking. Had he ever been so daft around a beautiful woman? A brief flash of Kate's face and striking green eyes passed through his mind . . . apparently he had. However, if he had been on high alert, never.

Stephen signalled a fellow officer across the way, and the man nodded acknowledgement. Without any ability to raise more alarm, he hoped proper precautions would be taken to warn Her Majesty, whom he spied sitting below the opposite balcony, in the direct gaze of Anna Smith.

Waltzes and polkas were played, though Queen Victoria did not dance. She was still in mourning for her beloved Albert.

"Miss Smith is merely toying with the guard while waiting for the Queen to move," he whispered to himself.

Stealing a quick glance at the dance floor, he found it difficult to locate anyone amongst the twirl of court attire.

He had only glanced away for a brief second, but when he looked back the young guard was slumped over and Miss Smith was aiming a small arrow, bow drawn, at her target below. She must have hidden it beneath her skirts! With no time for thought, he quickly threw his dagger precisely into her shooting arm. The assassin winced from pain and stumbled forward.

"Look out!" Stephen shouted to the people dancing below as Anna Smith began tumbling over the balcony, unable to maintain her balance. Stephen grabbed for her, but his hands met only air. She thudded on the floor below, amid screams from the guests. He ran down the stairs as fast as his legs could manage. Although a crowd of onlookers had already gathered around the fallen woman, his footsteps echoed across the wooden floor in the eerie silence. He pushed his way through the crowd to reach Miss Smith.

There would be no need to apprehend her. He soon ascertained that her neck had been broken by the fall. He knelt next to her and closed the once exotic eyes that now held no life.

A hand was suddenly patting his shoulders. "Nice work, son. You saved your queen's life."

Stephen turned his head to see Colonel Buchman indicating the arrow which had missed Her Majesty by a mere foot.

The breath caught in his throat. Somehow it was little comfort, knowing he had caused this woman's death, even if it had been for the right reasons. He continued to stand there and stare as guards covered the body and took it away. The guests began to chatter again, and in the blink of an eye, his mission was completed.

Eight

Kate donned her smartest suit of dark green wool. It had a black embroidery trim in the military style, with no frills. She was used to men treating her as though she had nothing to offer but a pretty face, and she was prepared to convince them otherwise. She set out with a maid in tow, since her aunt had insisted, and alighted outside the building housing her father's solicitor.

"Mr. Lemmons will see you now, Miss Worthington," a thin young man in a drab grey suit greeted her. He led her down a narrow hallway lined with gas lamps to an office with a large wooden door.

"Miss Worthington," a rotund, bald gentleman said as he stood behind his large oak desk to greet her.

"Mr. Lemmons. Thank you for seeing me so soon."

"Of course, of course. Please have a seat. Shall I send for tea?"

"Oh, no. I am not here for pleasantries," she said with deceptive cheerfulness.

The man's eyebrows gave a slight lift, but he continued to smile. "Very well. What may I help you with? First, may I extend my condolences?"

"Thank you. It was quite a shock. I am here because I would like to see the entirety of my betrothal contract. You may recall I am engaged to be married in less than three months' time."

"Yes, yes, quite a match your father made for you." He beamed.

"So you are acquainted with Lord Darlington?"

"Mostly by reputation, but we handle the Edgewood Estate business as well, so naturally as the heir to the Earldom, we also deal with Lord Darlington."

Kate's heart sank. She would never receive an impartial assessment from him. "Excellent. What can you tell me of his reputation? The status of their estates? I wish to know precisely what I am dealing with." She narrowed her gaze and waited.

Mr. Lemmons' face took on the condescension she was accustomed to from men if she showed an ounce of intelligence. Mr. Brown had been the exception. He had not made her feel insignificant, she suddenly realized.

"Miss Worthington," he began in that dreadful tone. She held up her hand.

"Sir, if you are about to tell me not to worry my pretty little head, then you are in danger of finding yourself without the Worthington business. Do I make myself clear?"

He began to sputter.

"I wish to know everything about my betrothed, and I will see the contract before I leave this office today."

"Yes, Miss." He indicated his head for the assistant to fetch the contract.

Once the assistant had left, Mr. Lemmons took a deep breath and intertwined his hands across his large girth. "There is very little to say but good about the Edgewood family. Theirs is a very old and respected title. Like most noble families, it is becoming more difficult to keep the grand estates turning a profit. The Edgewood Estate is not encumbered and has managed better than most, but it certainly could use the influx of capital your dowry will provide. Lord Darlington has been serving in Her Majesty's Army for some twelve years, now. From what I understand, he has an impeccable and distinguished service record. There is truly nothing ill I can say of Lord Darlington or his family."

"And if I wish to break the contract?"

The man's eyes widened in disbelief. "I beg your pardon? That would be most unwise. Most unwise," he repeated, shaking his head.

"I understand both parties must agree to sever the contract," she continued while he wiped the perspiration from his brow with a handkerchief.

"Yes, but if you sever it, you relinquish all of your rights to the Worthington Trading Company!"

Kate was speechless.

The man nodded.

"I lose every penny I have?" Anger was beginning to overcome her initial astonishment.

"Well, not every penny." The man looked acutely uncomfortable.

The assistant knocked and brought in a large stack of papers. Mr. Lemmons scanned page after page while Kate waited, impatiently tapping her foot beneath her skirts. This was much, much worse than she had ever thought. It was wrong to think ill of the dead, but how could her father have done this to her? She was struggling to keep her composure, willing her wretched chin not to betray her.

"Ah, here we are," he said, holding up the page he was looking for.

"*If Miss Worthington should chuse to sever the*

heretofore mentioned mutual betrothal agreement between the aforementioned parties, she willingly forfeits her claim to Worthington Trading Company to Lord Darlington, heir to the Earl of Edgewood, and will be left with a settlement of fifty thousand pounds sterling."

"This is preposterous! I am the only Worthington left!"

"I am sorry, miss."

She nodded, though she had to bite down on her lower lip to keep from saying something outrageous. She stood abruptly to take her leave, and he stumbled to rise from behind his desk.

"Thank you for your time, sir. I will let you know of my decision after I speak with Lord Darlington."

The man gasped, likely not expecting her response. So be it. A person could surely live on fifty thousand pounds if they spent it wisely, she hoped. Considering the alternative, at least she had something. She signalled to the maid to join her and hurried outside to the waiting carriage.

English soil at last, Stephen sighed. He had enjoyed most of his time in the army, and had certainly matured, but there truly was no place like home.

His valet had just finished shaving him, and Stephen ran his hand over his clean face with pleasure. He hoped Kate would approve. Over and over since he had last seen her, he had debated how best to approach her in London. His father had mentioned she had arrived and was preparing for the Season with her aunt, Lady Bregen. They had come to tea once, and his mother had declared her a delight, according to his father, who was still awake for a chat when Stephen had arrived late the night before.

Stephen was anxious to see Kate again but was uncertain

how she would react. Anger might be one reaction, but he hoped she would be pleasantly surprised. How he had longed to tell her everything on the train! He would never forget her look of disappointment when he had left her in Paris. Now his work was done, he would concentrate all of his energy on courting Kate properly.

How should he best handle revealing his identity? Should he leave his card? Should he call on her? Or should he be properly introduced to her at a ball? What was the most likely situation had he not met her by chance on the train?

Little did she know her courting had already begun. They had had the good fortune to know one another better than many couples on their wedding days. While he did not wish to lie to her, it was probably best not to inform her he had known her identity since Vienna.

Dressed in tan trousers with a fitted navy coat, he thought perhaps he looked smarter than he had as plain Mr. Brown in brown tweed.

Still pondering his best course of action with Kate, he dashed down the stairs and stopped short when he heard his mother's voice discussing the very person he was thinking about.

"Does Libby have any plans to bring her out properly?" he heard his father's voice ask.

"She had not made firm plans, since we did not know when Stephen would arrive. I believe she intends to take her to the Mallards' ball this evening. It is supposed to be a smaller event before the crush of the Season gets into swing."

"Then I suppose we must go and support Katherine." Stephen heard his father snap his news-sheet shut.

"Yes, I had planned on it, but should Stephen go?" There was concern in his mother's voice. "He has just arrived, and I think it might be best if they had some time together before being thrust in front of Society. They have only met once, and they were children at that."

"They are adults, Margaret. I think you had best pose that question to your son."

Her son, now standing at the door, leaned casually against the frame and smiled.

"Good morning, Mother, Father." He walked over to embrace his mother, who had already been asleep when he had arrived.

"I was told you had arrived, but it is so much better to see you in person," she said, giving him another tight embrace.

"It is good to be home, Mother. Did I hear you discussing my betrothed?"

"Indeed you did, Stephen. She is to attend her first ball this evening. We were uncertain whether you should attend with us or if we should arrange something more private for the two of you to become acquainted."

"I had been planning on leaving my card today."

"That is a good start," his mother pondered out loud as she tapped her index finger on her lips. "They will be making calls today."

"Perhaps a ball would be a good place to take each other's measure," his father suggested with a knowing look at his son. Stephen had confessed the story in its entirety to his father the previous evening. "Then you may invite her for a ride the next day, to talk more about your future."

"Excellent idea, Edgewood," his mother commended. "Do you have proper evening wear, Stephen? It has been so long since you have graced a London ballroom."

"I have not been living an uncivilized life, Mother. Of course I have something appropriate to wear," he rejoined.

"Your betrothed is quite beautiful, Stephen. I took tea with her and Libby just last week. I know you may not remember much more than an awkward girl. I wanted you to be forewarned. I had best send a note to Libby and warn her, as well."

"Forewarned is forearmed, Mother. I shall try not to disappoint you tonight."

She beamed back at him.

"First, I must see to some business."

"Business? You have only just returned!" she protested.

"I must finalize selling my commission, and the Queen has asked me, along with a few others, to attend her drawing room this afternoon."

"Is it true there was a recent assassination attempt on her life, in Paris?" his father asked.

"The Queen? She is bestirring herself to receive you?" His mother's question overrode his father's, and he did not wish to speak of the incident yet.

"Perhaps I am mistaken, but my presence was requested at the palace, nonetheless. I shall see you both this evening," he said, with a kiss to his mother's cheek and a bow to his father.

Stephen returned from the palace a few hours later with barely enough time to dress for the ball. He was to be awarded a Victoria Cross, and there would be a formal presentation later, but the Queen had wished to bestow her personal gratitude for his efforts.

The gesture was humbling, but Stephen had only done his duty, as any officer would have in the same position, and he had told her so. The honours should be given out to the foot soldiers who kept fighting when the provisions ran out; when they had walked twenty miles with frost bitten feet, in boots no longer recognizable as such; when injured; when not

ELIZABETH JOHNS

paid for months; when, when, when . . . he had told her passionately. To his surprise, she had listened with concern and had appointed him as an assistant to the War Secretary, to oversee the future welfare of the army's morale so as to prevent such atrocities in the future. With new purpose, he hurried to his chambers to dress for the evening, hoping Kate would be as receptive to him as Her Majesty had been.

Nine

Kate was so intimidated by the prospect of London Society that by the time she arrived for her first ball, she was feeling queasy. Her aunt had paraded her at drawing rooms and teas during the last few weeks, but the more experienced she became, the less comfortable she was. The matrons seemed to think her a barbaric cit brought up in the wild, and the younger ladies seemed to view her as competition even though she was betrothed!

They drove the few streets to the Mallard residence. Carriages were lined up, with passengers waiting for their opportunity to alight. Kate and her aunt had to wait for their turn to be introduced.

"Lord Darlington will be here. Margaret sent word," Aunt Libby whispered in her ear after the footman had handed them down from the carriage.

If she had felt queasy before, she was surely green now.

Why must they first meet again in public? He had left his card when they were out earlier in the day. If Lord Darlington had done the decent thing, he would have arrived a few weeks ago. She could then have investigated him properly, viewed him from a distance and formed a plan. Instead, she was at her worst, caught off guard in a strange place, drat him.

"Smile, Katherine. You will be the most beautiful girl here and are new, so especial attention will be placed on you. And once word spreads that you are Darlington's betrothed, people will clamour in a ridiculous fashion for an introduction," her aunt said as they neared the door.

"How delightful." Fortunately for her nerves, Kate did consider she looked her best, for her gown had arrived from Paris that very morning. It was daring, being fashioned from white silk, with a bold black, swirling, embroidered pattern all over. There were thin, capped sleeves drawing out from the wide V of the neckline that mirrored the V at the waist. The black accents complimented her dark hair, which stood out from the light browns and blondes more common to the English.

There were murmurs and looks when she was introduced. However, when the crowd began to whisper and turn towards the entrance, somehow Kate knew he was there. She had not bothered to watch the door. Instead, she had spent her time foolishly scanning the crowd, hoping to see Mr. Brown.

"I heard he's to be awarded the Victoria Cross," a nearby matron whispered loudly. "I heard he was there with Cousin Alfred, who is also to receive a Distinguished Service Medal."

"You don't say," the gentleman with her acknowledged appreciatively. "Word in the clubs was he was a fine officer, but only men who have risked something great or behaved with valour are given the Victoria Cross."

Kate did not want to hear anything more. She was happy Lord Darlington had made something of himself, yet she could only imagine how it would puff him up in his own esteem. Across the ballroom, it was difficult to make out the features of the man when they announced Lord Darlington.

He was not decked out in dress regimentals, as she had expected, but the more subtle evening dress of black trousers, black coat and tails with a silver waistcoat and a white bow tie.

"How handsome he is!" her aunt exclaimed. "And how modest to appear in his civilian attire."

He did create a fine figure, Kate had to admit, though she could not see details from across the room.

"At least there does not appear to be a moustache," she muttered, with an ache spreading from her heart to her toes. At the moment she would give anything to be back on the train, being plain Miss White with plain Mr. Brown—facial hair and all.

"What did you say, Katherine?" her aunt murmured distractedly, though she was clearly not listening. She seemed to be scheming how best to manoeuvre them to the *ton's* latest hero.

A crowd soon gathered round the newcomer, and Kate had a reprieve for at least a little while. Seeking to ease her way through the crush towards the terrace, so as to escape the overly hot ballroom, she was pleased to see her aunt distracted by a dowager in a red turban. Kate did not deliberate—she took her chance. She knew she was not supposed to go onto the terrace alone. She'd had so much propriety impressed upon her since she arrived that she could write a book about it. But she had to choose between propriety and disgracing herself, because she feared she was about to swoon. Her face felt flushed, her corset was squeezing the breath from her lungs, and a cold sweat prickled her brow.

Almost pushing her way through the crowd in panic, she embraced the fresh air as a welcome escape. It was a cool, dark night, with neither moon nor lamps on this side of the house to illuminate the garden. She squinted and made her way to the nearest balustrade, where she cast her eyes up to the stars.

"How could you have done this to me, Papa?"

Moments passed, precious seconds when she had to wipe away tears of self-pity. There was no one she could confide in who would understand, and it was unlikely Lord Darlington would give up the fortune she would bring to him.

Running away to America or back to India was tempting. It would be hard to be on her own, but was that not what this situation was? She would lose her name, she had already lost her home, and she would marry a stranger who was at ease in this society.

Choking on a sob, she knew she must control her emotions. For all everyone else assumed about her upbringing, she had been brought up a lady.

Reluctantly, she inhaled a fortifying breath and turned towards the doors, where a man now stood in front of them.

"Miss White?"

Could it be true? She had not anticipated actually finding Mr. Brown again in London. Her aunt would be looking for her after so long an absence, and she was supposed to be meeting her betrothed at any moment. She could not see his features in the darkness and against the light spilling through the glass panes behind him, yet she would never mistake his familiar scent or his voice. Her heart beat erratically as he drew so near she could touch him.

"Mr. Brown? I never thought to find you again. We had not exchanged directions, and I—"

"Darlington! Are you out here?" The door cracked open and a bosky male voice called through the opening.

"Darlington?" Kate whispered in disbelief.

"The devil," Stephen cursed under his breath. He had been thrilled to see Kate go onto the terrace alone so he could speak with her, but it had been slow going to make his way across the ballroom. Various persons wanted to offer congratulations and welcome him home. How had everyone found out about his honour so quickly? He had not even had the chance to tell his parents.

And now, instead of telling Kate who he really was privately, some buffoon had followed him and ruined it.

"Do not answer them, and they will leave," Stephen whispered into Kate's ear as he blocked her from the light. Her entire body stiffened when he touched her.

"Darlington?" the voice enquired again. "I could have sworn I saw him go out there. My eyes must be playing tricks on me," the person said to a companion before being pulled back inside and closing the door, taking most of the light with him.

Stephen breathed a sigh of relief. "You must allow me to explain."

She stood staring at him in disbelief. He could just make out her face in the darkness.

"I had to travel in disguise on the train as part of my duty. I could not tell you my real identity without compromising the mission, or your safety. Can you understand that? I never meant to deceive you."

She nodded, though her chin quivered.

"Katherine? Katherine?" her aunt called. There was a hint of fear in her voice.

"We must return now. I had hoped for a chance to explain this to you in privacy, but my betrothed is here tonight, and I must meet her. May I call on you tomorrow?"

"I do not think that will be necessary," she said quietly.

"There you are, Katherine," her aunt said, opening the door and peering around as she tried to make out the two of them in the darkness. "I see you have already found each other. Do come inside from the cold. My old bones object to it." She ushered them back inside. "Katherine, you must not go outdoors alone. I thought I had explained this to you."

"I beg your pardon, Aunt Libby. I was overheated," Kate explained as they followed her back into the ballroom.

Stephen stood there quietly, considering the best way to handle the situation. Kate did not know that he had discovered her identity on the train—or did she? What was it her aunt had said? He had not been paying sufficient attention, being conscious only that Kate was going to be whisked away. Nevertheless, she had also kept her true name hidden. Was she also wondering how to explain this to him?

She opened her mouth to speak, though he could tell she was acutely uncomfortable. People were beginning to walk towards them, so he quickly took her arm.

"Let us discuss this on the dance floor, or we will not have another opportunity tonight, I fear."

She nodded her acquiescence, though she still looked stricken.

He took her hand, placed it on his shoulder and put his other hand in hers. "Have you waltzed before?"

"With my papa," she said sadly, staring at his bow tie.

"Miss White. Look at me," he quietly commanded as the orchestra began to play the Viennese Waltz. He tried not to notice the irony. "Can you forgive me?"

"I am overwhelmed at the moment, Lord Darlington."

"Stephen. Please call me Stephen." He spun her about, giving her a moment to gather her thoughts. She was light on her feet, and she fit in his arms more perfectly than he could have imagined. And he had imagined holding her this way several times during the past few weeks.

"I also have a confession," she offered at last.

"There is no need. I have known your Aunt Libby since I was in leading-strings."

"That is how you knew my name?" she asked, wide-eyed.

"Yes. I know you are Kate Worthington."

"You are not angry at my deception?"

"How could I be? You no more deceived me than I deceived you. I suspect your motivation was to remain anonymous, an heiress to a vast fortune travelling alone."

She gave a barely detectable nod as they danced around the floor. He suspected this was his one chance to determine their future together.

"What I do feel, however, is extremely grateful. I, too, had reservations about marrying a stranger, and for mercenary reasons."

Her eyes shot up and met his with astonishment.

"I now know myself to be blessed beyond measure, to have the chance to marry someone I would have chosen myself had circumstances been different."

"Do you truly mean that?"

"I do. I would have released you from our contract and still will if it is your desire. I will not force you to marry me, Kate."

She drew in a sharp breath.

"Will you allow me to court you properly before you decide?"

She shook her head. "No, Lord Darlington."

Ten

Lord Darlington stiffened and whirled her to the side of the dance floor and then back out onto the terrace.

"I do not understand. Was I mistaken in thinking you returned my regard?"

"No," she whispered.

"Then please explain."

She covered her mouth with her gloved hand, unable to prevent tears from streaming down her face. As she wrestled her other arm out from his, Kate knew she was behaving irrationally, but she could not escape the sensation that he had known who she was for some time—perhaps even the entire time. Had he been toying with her? Her emotions were struggling between happiness, anger, and confusion, and she needed to be alone. Part of her wanted nothing more than to throw her arms about his neck and kiss him, as she had dreamed of doing since Vienna. However, this was her future husband, and too much had happened to dismiss everything else lightly.

"You seem to have the advantage of me," she snapped.

"I . . ." He hesitated too long. It was still too dark to make out the small nuances of his features to guess at his thoughts.

"Forgive me, but I need time to think."

He inclined his head. "May I call on you tomorrow and perhaps take you for a ride? I would like a chance to explain further."

Knowing it would be beyond the pale to refuse, she resigned herself. "I will expect you."

She turned and walked back into the ballroom, searching for her Aunt Libby. She walked as calmly as she could, trying not to draw undue attention to herself, yet she felt the crowds closing in on her. Panic began to broil beneath the surface of her outwardly calm façade. She hoped there would be no resistance from her aunt when she at last reached that lady's side.

Bending forward, Kate whispered in Aunt Libby's ear. "I am going to leave early. I am not feeling quite the thing. Might I have the carriage sent back for you?"

Her aunt leaned back to study Kate's face. She must not have hidden her anguish as well as she thought.

"Of course not, my dear. If you are unwell, I will accompany you home. It would not do for you to leave alone."

Her aunt turned to the lady with whom she was conversing and announced, "My niece is coming down with the headache, so we will be retiring for the night."

Their carriage was summoned at once, and they made polite farewells to their hosts. Aunt Libby organized their departure with an efficiency for which Kate was grateful, and then remained blissfully silent inside the carriage. Not until they had regained the town house did she finally speak.

"I can only surmise this has something to do with meeting your betrothed. There must be some history between you two of which I am unaware."

Kate nodded, barely keeping her composure.

"I will not quiz you tonight, since you are distressed, but I would like an explanation in the morning."

"Thank you, Aunt Libby. I do need time to compose my thoughts." She gave her aunt a kiss on the cheek and an affectionate hug and escaped to her chamber.

Once inside, she gave full rein to her emotions and temper. She beat her pillow with her fist, unleashing the anger and helplessness she felt, since in England a lady was expected to suppress a passionate nature beneath a calm exterior. With that immediate need satisfied, she kicked off her slippers and began to tear the hairpins from her coiffure.

"Perhaps I am the wild barbarian they all think me," she chuckled to herself when she gazed at her reflection in the mirror. She took her brush and started to tease out the tangles as she pondered her options.

"Did Lord Darlington know it was me the whole time?" She did not know if she could forgive him. "How dare he play with my emotions when he knew how I felt? I poured my heart out to him, thinking he was a stranger!"

"On the other hand, I poured out my heart to a stranger, and he might have been afraid to tell me the truth because of it." Kate groaned in frustration. The afternoon in Vienna had been one of the best days of her life. Was that the man he truly was inside? She paused in her brushing, her hand in mid air. She had fallen in love with that man, she realized then.

It still galled her to think he had been capable of such deception. Would he return to such guises once the first blush of romance faded? Was it truly just that he was doing his job for the Crown? The real question, she knew, was could she trust him?

"But can I bear to walk away?"

Setting her hair brush down on the dressing table, she doubted she would solve her dilemma that night. She should give him a chance to explain—and allow herself to know him better—or she would regret it. There was still time to do so, and much to lose if she did not.

After a restless night's sleep, Kate woke up to the sun peeking through the gold curtains. She stretched and recalled what she must face that day. It was not a feeling of dread inside, but excitement and anticipation to see Lord Darlington again. She hoped it was a good sign and he would not leave her disappointed. It would be difficult to bear.

First, she must face Aunt Libby and explain her rash behaviour at the ball. She rang for the maid and dressed before going to her aunt's apartments. She rapped lightly on the door.

"Enter," she heard.

"Good morning, Aunt," Kate said, closing the door behind her.

"Have you broken your fast?" her aunt asked. She was lounging on a white chaise near the window.

"Not yet."

"Jenny, please fetch another tray for my niece."

"Yes, my lady," the maid said before bobbing a quick curtsy and leaving the room.

"Join me, my dear, so I do not have to strain my neck to look up at you."

Kate smiled affectionately and sat down on a nearby chair. She was very thankful to have her aunt's guidance.

"You look better this morning. Are you prepared to tell me what happened?"

Kate sighed loudly as she accepted the cup of tea her aunt passed to her.

"You know I met Lord Darlington when I visited England as a child. I do not have fond memories of that first meeting," she confessed, taking a sip of tea. Her aunt raised her eyebrows but said nothing.

"While on board the Orient Express, I was, by chance, seated with an English army officer who was also travelling alone. We became friends of sorts, in the less formal atmosphere of the train."

"I gather you were rather fond of this gentleman?" her aunt asked.

Kate could feel herself flush, but she met her aunt's brown gaze. "Yes, I did. In fact, my feelings solidified my intention to come here and dissolve the betrothal contract with Lord Darlington."

Her aunt gasped. "You cannot mean it!"

"It was my intention before I left India," Kate affirmed. "I could not talk Father into dissolving the betrothal for me. He was convinced it was a good decision, while I could not abide the fact that I would be married to a stranger against my will. Remember that he made a distinctly foul impression upon me when we met."

"But you were children!" Aunt Libby objected.

Kate waved her hand. "No matter. The gentleman and I departed in Paris, and I never expected to see him again."

"But then you did meet him again—at the ball?" her aunt asked, guessing at the source of her dilemma.

"Indeed I did. However, that man was Lord Darlington, not the Mr. Brown I had grown fond of on the train."

Her aunt was looking at her unnervingly over her spectacles. Kate stared at the bottom of her tea cup, sure a reprimand was imminent. It did not come.

"What do you plan to do?"

"He said he would call today and perhaps take me riding."

"Do you wish to go? If you need more time I can arrange it."

Kate's heart gave a squeeze at her aunt's consideration. "I suppose I should give him a chance. He asked for the opportunity to court me properly. He said it was necessary to travel in disguise as part of his duty."

"Ah, there is a simple explanation!" her aunt exclaimed with a satisfied clink of her tea cup.

"Perhaps . . . except that he seemed to know who I was already. I feel foolish and deceived." Kate stood up and began to pace the room.

"Then you must decide if you can forgive him. Though you stand to lose a great deal if you dissolve the contract—and is Stephen willing to do so?"

"He is. That is one decent thing that came from our time on the train. As for the other, I cannot yet answer. Hopefully it will become apparent quickly. There is little time left."

Stephen was as nervous as he had ever felt before any operation, for this meant much more to him. He wanted Kate, not the Worthington Company. Stephen had to make her see that she was who he wanted, not a convenient wife for Lord Darlington and the future Earl of Edgewood. It had taken every ounce of willpower he could muster not to run after her and make a scene the previous evening. He had to believe that good sense would prevail. If he had forced her hand then, she would likely have walked away forever, and that was not an answer he would accept without a fight.

After mounting his grey, Animo, he set off at a slow pace to call on Kate, trying to prepare his mind. Hopefully, she would listen to him.

Cook had filled his saddle bags with a picnic, and he prayed Kate liked his favourite spot as much as he did. There was a flower stall selling bouquets of tulips on the corner, and he stopped to purchase some for Kate. Hopefully she would remember them from Vienna, as he would forever associate their beauty with her.

A few moments later, he was handing Animo over to a groom and directing him to make sure Miss Worthington had a mount prepared.

The butler showed him in to the morning room, where Libby was waiting for him. His godmother welcomed him affectionately as always but patted the seat next to her with a concerned sigh.

"Has Kate told you the story?" he asked.

"Indeed she has. You must tread wisely."

"Yes, I am all too aware of that."

"What have you planned? Please tell me you do not intend to take her to Hyde Park!" She looked sideways at him.

"Indeed not. I am not of a mind to share her just yet. I was going to take her to Kew Gardens, where she visited as a child. There is something there I wish to show her."

"That is a considerable ride for an afternoon, but I trust you completely. And I trust that you will not ruin this!"

"I have the most to lose, Libby. Shall we send for Kate now, please?"

"Yes, of course." She rang the bell and sent for her niece while Stephen rose and paced the room. When Kate entered, Stephen could not help but smile. She was wearing a dashing riding habit of brilliant blue, designed to make a man forget himself. He knew this woman was meant to be his forever, but how to convince her?

"Miss Worthington, may I say how lovely you look today?" He handed her the tulips and, by the change in her expression, could see she remembered that day in the Volksgarten.

"They are beautiful, thank you," she said as she held them to her nose.

"I shall have them placed in a vase, Kate. You had best be going so you have enough daylight." Libby ushered them out to their awaiting mounts.

Stephen took the opportunity to touch Kate by criss-crossing his hands and boosting her atop her side-saddle. Her cheeks took on a rosy hue, and he was pleased to see she was still not indifferent. He mounted his grey and began to lead them through the streets of London, a groom following a discreet distance behind. When they had passed through the last toll-gate and the traffic grew sparse, he reined in his horse to her side.

"Where are we going?" she asked.

"A few more miles, to one of my favourite places. I think you will be pleased."

"My curiosity is piqued," she said with a slight smile, and he hoped that was a good omen.

"Do you feel up to a faster pace? I confess myself eager to arrive."

"Lead the way!" she commanded.

Kate was a rather good rider, which surprised him, and she kept pace with him as they rode across the rolling green hills towards Richmond. He paid the one penny fee as they entered the gates, and he led her to a place they could leave the horses for a rest. He helped her dismount, and then unhooked his saddle bags and slung them over his shoulder.

They strolled for some time through the vast wooded park. There was a red brick palace, where the royal family still spent some time, and it was surrounded by beautiful gardens. Kate had stopped and was looking around with some sense of familiarity. He had suspected that once she saw the gardens or the Chinese pagoda it would all come back to her.

She gasped as awareness and recognition struck her.

"This is the garden I remember visiting with my parents!" She turned in a circle as she surveyed her surroundings.

He walked slowly to stand beside her when she stopped before the fountain of Hercules wrestling with the serpent Achelous.

"That day in Vienna, this is what I was remembering," she said softly, just audible above the fountain's trickle.

"I thought it might be."

Finally, she turned her gaze to meet his. "When did you know who I was, Stephen?"

He knew that his suit depended on how he answered, and all he could offer was honesty.

"The day I searched your compartment, before we arrived in Vienna."

She swallowed hard. He wanted to pull her into his arms and reassure her it had only increased his regard for her, but knew it was too soon.

"Come, I will explain further over a picnic." He held out his hand, and she hesitated. "There is chocolate," he said, trying to coax a smile from her.

"That is a very low trick, my lord," she retorted.

But it worked. Her smile nearly stopped his heart, but he forced himself to walk on to his favourite spot overlooking the river, which was well hidden from other visitors. He took his time spreading out a blanket and setting up the picnic, while attempting to discern her mood. Nothing she had said or done this morning indicated she was averse to him, yet nothing made him feel overly confident. However, he might not have another chance.

"Shall I help?" Kate asked. He had been so absorbed in his thoughts, he had not said anything.

"Yes, thank you. I hope you will be pleased." And he trusted Cook would have done the food justice. He smelled the delicious fragrance of cocoa when Kate lifted the lid of the basket.

"Sachertortes!" she exclaimed.

"I assumed I would need every weapon at my disposal," he said wryly, moving to sit next to her.

"Are you waging a war?" she asked with an adorable cock of one brow.

"That depends on how my peace treaty is received today."

She handed him a plate bearing a slice, and took one for herself. She placed a bite of the delicate chocolate cake in her mouth and sighed with obvious pleasure.

"How was step one in my plan?"

"I would say that the initial negotiations were not rejected out of hand. But before you go any further, may I ask some questions?"

"Of course. I would not have anything between us."

"I feel like there is much I do not know about you. I became quite comfortable with Mr. Brown until the Arab woman arrived."

He sighed deeply. He was afraid he had hurt her. "During my time in the army, I was a reconnaissance officer. Sometimes I gathered information and sometimes I spied. I was on my last mission on the train which is why I was traveling as Mr. Brown."

"The Arab woman was your mission?"

"Precisely. I had been told my target was an Anna Smith, so I actually suspected either you or Miss Hawthorne as the only two younger ladies on board."

"I was a suspect?" she asked indignantly.

"You were, and I am so very thankful." He gave her a look full of meaning, and he could see her visibly soften.

"It is why you were so forward," she stated as she thought back to their time on the train.

"I feel very fortunate we had the time together and will always remember it fondly," he said, meeting her gaze.

"As will I," she said. "So what happened after Paris? You were following the woman."

"You noticed quite a bit," he remarked. "I followed her to a hotel near the British Embassy, and there we unraveled her plot to assassinate the Queen."

"And you were successful."

"Only just. I barely stopped her from putting an arrow through Her Majesty."

"And what became of Anna Smith?"

He looked away. He had seen much death in the army, but Anna's eyes would always haunt him. "She did not survive." He swallowed hard. Kate reached over and touched his hand in sympathy

"And this is why you received the honour from the Queen."

He nodded.

"What is the next move?" she asked, changing the subject. He was grateful that Kate seemed willing to capitulate.

"To undermine my worthy opponent's defences," he whispered, reaching up to tuck a lock of her dark, silken hair behind her ear. Her breath hitched, and her eyes darkened. That was enough encouragement to lean his head forward and taste her lips. His touch was gentle at first, before her hands came around his neck, pulling him close. He savoured each sensation of her skin, her silken hair, her scent of orange blossoms, but as desire rose within him, he slowly pulled away until only their foreheads touched. He cradled her face in the palms of his hands, and their eyes met.

"Can you forgive me, Kate?"

"I might want to know what comes next, first," she replied, her eyes twinkling. She looked as though she had been thoroughly kissed. She could not have been more beautiful.

"You little imp," he teased, giving her another swift kiss.

"I must admit, having the time together on the train allowed us to know one another with a freedom we never would have been allowed had I been Miss Worthington and you Lord Darlington. I had rather made up my mind," she said shyly.

"I had noticed." He took a forkful of cake and fed it to her, then moved until he was on bended knee and placed her hands in his.

"Kate, I *want* to marry you. I want to spend my life with you and everything that entails. Do you think you could be happy married to me, in truth?"

She looked taken aback.

"You do not need to answer now." Had he misjudged the moment and moved too quickly? He stood up and turned his back to her. "I just want you to know it was you I fell in love with, not your dowry or the promise of the Worthington Company. I would have been pleased to have married you as Miss White. However, I will respect your decision and release you from the contract."

For a few minutes, the only sounds were those of the river flowing by and the birds chirping their songs. Suddenly, two arms came around him from behind with such force that he had to steady himself to keep from falling.

"You win. I surrender," she murmured into his back. One hand lifted and waved a white napkin in front of him. He turned in her arms and lifted her into an embrace.

"I do not believe I have ever been happier, Kate," he managed to say before closing his mouth over hers. Resistance was futile, after all. His heart had been captured.

Then and there, they sealed their future with a kiss, leaving no doubt in his mind that both opponents were entirely satisfied with their capitulation.

National bestselling author **Elizabeth Johns** was first an avid reader, though she was a reluctant convert. It was Jane Austen's clever wit and unique turn of phrase that hooked Johns when she was "forced" to read *Pride and Prejudice* for a school assignment. She began writing when she ran out of her favorite author's books and decided to try her hand at crafting a Regency romance novel. Her journey into publishing began with the release of Surrender the Past, book one of the Loring-Abbott Series. Johns makes no pretensions to Austen's wit but hopes readers will perhaps laugh and find some enjoyment in her writing.

Johns attributes much of her inspiration to her mother, a retired English teacher. During their last summer together, Johns would sit on the porch swing and read her stories to her mother, who encouraged her to continue writing. Busy with multiple careers, including a professional job in the medical field, author and mother of small children, Johns squeezes in time for reading whenever possible.

Detective Grace
Meets Her Match

ANNETTE LYON

One

Constantinople

Grace stood on the railway platform, looking about casually as if she were any other traveler on any other rail line. As she did everywhere she went, Grace let her gaze skim across the people milling about her, never staying in one place long, and made mental notes about everyone and everything she saw.

She'd always been observant, even as a little girl, and the talent had served her well. Not many people could make a living based primarily on observation and a keen mind. Even fewer women could, or did. Being hired to investigate various situations—some criminal, some not—tended to be an avocation reserved for the men of the world.

At least, that's what most people seemed to think, but her client list tended to tell another tale, full as it was of wealthy women desperate for help—help that Grace, as a private investigator from the Harward and Sons Detective Agency, was more than happy to provide. The *and Sons* part had been a hopeful gesture on the part of Grandpapa, a wish that never did come true, as he had only three children and all daughters.

More than that, he'd failed in mustering any interest regarding detective work in any of his five nephews or three grandsons.

Only Grace, his youngest grandchild, caught the passion. Her surname, however, was not Harward, but Thompson.

At first, she'd taken over the finances of the agency, out of pure necessity, as Grandpapa's secretary fell terribly ill. Grace discovered that she had a knack for numbers and budgets, and she'd never left the position. Through her efforts, she created quite a reputation for Harward and Sons, and she continued building the reputation when Grandpapa himself retired to his deathbed. Now, half a dozen years after Grandpapa's death, the agency flourished under her ownership and management, which consisted of one person and one person only: Grace Thompson as owner, detective, bookkeeper, and secretary.

Not that the public knew that the agency was so small. She'd strategically placed her desk in front of an imposing door, so people would assume that a male descendant of Harward of some stripe kept his office there. She never dispelled the assumption that when she worked at the desk, which seemingly guarded the door, that she was something other than a secretary. The fact that clients never did meet any Mr. Harward or a son—that they presumed the owner was merely unreachable when they inquired—added to the mystique of the agency, a reputation she credited with delivering more clients.

Upon Grandpapa's death, she'd quickly learned that she had no need to place notices in the papers, not with the quick-as-blazes society gossip chains spreading the word of her services.

Grace had once assumed that if anyone knew how she supported herself, she'd be shunned from society, and the business would therefore collapse. Even now, she had a suspicion that if too many men sniffed out the truth, her fate would lie in their shocked and horrified hands. So far, praise be, that hadn't happened. She'd gotten by quite handily thanks to specializing in clients who were both wealthy and female, and who therefore had a special type of loyalty toward the woman who had helped them in their time of need. The only times Grace had found herself the subject of whisperings were when one friend in the upper classes needed the type of aid Grace could provide, and a former client quietly passed along her name. Such women were willing to pay a pretty sum to learn about their husbands' misdoings, whether they included visits to unseemly neighborhoods, skimming money from the family estate or business, or things far more nefarious. Grace didn't divulge the full scope of her position at the agency even to her clients—not that anyone would have believed that a woman could be so successful in business.

With that anonymity, and her income, she found herself remarkably free for a woman living in the late nineteenth century.

Her gaze glided over a group of rail workers carrying trunks, then dwelt briefly on a young, upper-middle-class family: father, mother, governess, and two young children. The mother and governess both looked weary and travel worn but happy enough. The youngest, a babe of perhaps a year, lay cradled in the arm of a governess, who sat on a bench. The father sat with a newspaper in hand and a pipe in his mouth. The older child whined and complained, pulling on her mother's skirts until she was lifted onto her mother's lap.

Grace let her gaze move on. Not for the first time, she wondered if she could ever be in public without her finely honed observational skills demanding to be used. Noticing those around her—determining their life situations, ages, personalities, and more—came second nature, almost like a reflex she could not control. She hadn't always possessed the skill—nor a dozen others, including lock picking and lipreading—but Grandpapa had encouraged her. "If you lack the requisite skill," he'd always said, "learn it." Simple as that. So she'd learned all of those things. And continued to learn.

Being a quick study and a good improviser did wonders when circumstances required.

Yet at times such as this, when she'd finished a job and anticipated a rest from her labors, she wished she could snuff out the instinct to observe and note and file away details. Her mind deserved a vacation too, did it not? How, precisely, to provide one, when she was so used to analyzing everything she saw, heard, and smelled? On the other hand, in a world filled with conniving men who used their stature and influence to wreak havoc on women's lives, keeping oneself attuned acted as a protection for a woman and proved wise.

If Grace had learned one thing over the course of her career, it was that men were not to be trusted. At least, no man since Grandpapa. He remained the one truly good man she'd ever known. Her mother, God rest her soul, had claimed that Father had been a good man, but he died before Grace had any memory of him. Besides, she'd seen man after man—dozens, if not hundreds—prove her beliefs correct. They were scoundrels, all of them. Part of her wished she'd lived in Grandpapa's generation, which clearly had at least *some* good men. Instead, she had to keep a lookout for men whose lives were spent seeking to indulge their carnal desires no matter who paid the price. Usually the women who loved them most: their wives, their mothers, their fiancées.

Not me. Grace sighed happily at the knowledge that no man could manipulate her. She'd learned long ago that hearts and emotions were fickle things, which was precisely why men preyed on those things. No, she'd wisely locked up her heart and weak emotions and had then learned to use men's egos against themselves.

Keeping an eye out for men who might try to take advantage of her tended to be tiring, especially while traveling, but it was far preferable to being swindled. Retaining her defenses did not have to be entirely unpleasant, however; if she batted her eyes and tittered around the right men, they sometimes bought her dinner before she gently let them down. She made sure to never be too cold about her rejections, however. If the man was flattered but told no with an accompanying regretful story she concocted—*Oh, I so wish I could visit your estate. I'm sure it's divine. But my fiancé is expecting me first thing this evening. Surely you understand*—she stayed in his good graces. That, in turn, allowed Grace the opportunity to protect other vulnerable women from him should the need arise.

And it usually did.

Which man would she need to watch out for on this trip? Three days in close quarters meant plenty of opportunity for a man to ply his devious trade, hurting women in the process. If she could prevent other women from falling prey, which required finding the shadiest man in the lot and not giving him the opportunity to swindle anyone or break any hearts. Unfortunately, that usually meant flirting with that same man, making him think she was a good mark as a way of preventing other women from falling victim. Grace considered her ability to protect other women a skill and therefore a duty—part of her work, but not one she ever got paid for, unless the man decided to pay for her dinner.

Not having identified any obvious suspect so far, she rotated to her right to see that side of the platform better. There on a bench, she spied a woman who sat with a prim and proper posture, wearing a gown that looked like it had been made of a dozen yards of pure golden silk and finely tailored in precise lines. An elaborate arrangement of hair sat beneath an exquisite hat bearing feathers that looked to be from an exotic bird. Every inch of this woman was made of an amount of money Grace could only imagine having.

Even though Grace couldn't see more than the toes of the woman's boots peeking from the hem of the grand dress, she had no doubt that the footwear hiding there cost more than Grace earned in a year. Everything about the woman told a familiar tale that Grace could have recited. The straight back and demure way the woman sat with her gloved hands clasped on her lap said that she'd been reared under the watchful eye of a governess. As a young lady she'd likely gone to finishing school. And now she was married with a luxurious life complete with a lady's maid to tend to her every whim. Such a woman wouldn't travel without such a maid, so the servant would surely appear soon, likely with refreshment for her lady. As if on cue, the maid appeared right then, carrying a tall glass of white wine.

A gentleman in an equally fine suit walked up to them. His mustache was oiled and shaped precisely, and he smoothed it with his fingers as he sat beside the woman. A second, slightly older man, clean shaven, with gray at his temples, took his position to the side of the bench—the husband's valet, no doubt. Neither of the men had the certain quality Grace recognized as being a particular danger to women. If anything, the husband in this case might have a mistress at home, and the valet would be preoccupied throughout the journey with serving his master.

He must be elsewhere. Finding the man to guard against didn't usually take so long. She didn't give much credence to the idea that perhaps *this* trip could be free of any such dangers. After all, she'd always found at least one.

She casually looked to the other side of the platform again, where a young couple arrived and stopped by a column. They dropped their bags at their feet, but with eyes solely on each other, someone could have walked away with their bags and they wouldn't have noticed. Newlyweds, most likely. The man wouldn't be a genuine threat for a few years.

The couple's slightly worn bags and clothing—attractive and fashionable, pressed and clean, yet lacking polished cuts and expensive materials—told her that they came from a relatively comfortable life but not one of significant wealth. The lack of any servants told the same tale. Many couples took tours of the continent for a honeymoon, but few did so on a conveyance as extravagant as the Orient Express. This groom must have saved his hard-earned income for quite some time to afford this trip. Something about his spectacles made her think that he likely worked with ledgers or some such. At a bank, perhaps, or at the courts, keeping records. If she were to draw closer to see his hands, she'd have been able to spot telltale signs of what his work entailed. Calluses, stains, and even the state of one's nails and cuticles, all spoke volumes.

How much interaction would she have with each of these passengers over the next few days? Which would strike up conversations with her? Which would keep to themselves? Would any keep to their compartments altogether? *Was* any of these men a threat? She couldn't imagine the train pulling into Paris without her finding one. Perhaps she'd let her skills grow soft.

A whistle blew, marking the time to board. Grace withdrew her ticket from her purse, picked up her bag, her trunk having been loaded before, and walked toward the queue. She stopped at the end, behind the newlyweds.

From behind her, a deep voice spoke. "Ever traveled on the Orient Express?"

Grace turned about, startled that she hadn't been aware of the man before. That kind of thing would not do at all. If she hoped to remain independent rather than having to rely on some man for support, continually sharpening her mind and skills further was paramount. In a single quick glance from his toes to his hat, she took in the appearance of the man who owned the voice. In a trice, she did the standard mental evaluation. Near thirty years old, perhaps aged two years either direction. That crooked smile and flirtatious tone could mean only one thing: a bachelor, or a married man with a string of mistresses. If his handsome looks were any indication, he was long since married, yet he seemed to be traveling alone. No valet.

The Orient Express was typically a destination unto itself; such an expensive trip did not draw single travelers. What was he doing on board, apparently alone? Her suspicions slowly rose, even as she reminded herself that she, too, was alone, and that was hardly suspicious. Then again, she was not a typical woman in many regards.

He waited for her reply, brows raised in anticipation, his mouth curved into a welcoming and—to most women, disarming—smile. Grace's mental inventory had taken longer than usual, and for the tiniest second she forgot what he'd asked. Then she remembered and put on her practiced voice.

"Never been aboard the Orient Express, no." She made a half step toward him, closing the distance between them somewhat, then coyly tilted her head and added, "I'm rather excited for the adventure. You?" She looked up at him, so close she could faintly smell his cologne. She never ceased to be amazed at how easily she could put on the airs of a flirtatious nitwit, nor at how easily dishonest men believed it. She waited to see his reaction to her overtures.

Some men stepped back when she drew so close. Such

men were far more likely to be aware of societal conventions and the appearance of impropriety, which meant that any dangers they faced would be in private. This man withdrew not an inch. The only change she noted was a broadening of his smile. *He's a bold one.*

"This is my first time, too," he said. "I imagine it will be, as you put it, an adventure."

Their eyes caught, and something flipped in Grace's middle, making her catch her breath and nearly step back—as if *she* were the weak one. She needed to regain the upper hand, immediately and securely. She mentally broke the threads that seemed to connect her to this man. All the while, she continued to gaze into his eyes, hoping he hadn't seen her falter even for a flicker of a moment. She waited for him to look away first. He didn't, only kept smiling at her.

I found him, she thought. *I knew this trip would have one.* The threads appeared again, and she felt a tug of not just attraction but of respect. She allowed the respect to stay but deliberately severed all others. She could respect an adversary; in fact, doing so tended to be wise so one didn't underestimate his abilities. But feeling attraction toward the man would, quite simply, be unacceptable. Before she could think too much on any other emotions threatening to crop up, she put out a hand. "I'm Grace."

Tarnation! Why didn't she give a false name? She hadn't made such a ridiculous beginner's mistake in years. As before, however, she refused to reveal the misstep in her expression, voice, or movement. To somewhat rectify the matter, and so he could not find her after the trip, she added a false surname. "Grace Harward."

Yet even that was too close to the truth. If this man knew about Harward and Sons, he might suspect something. And who in London *hadn't* heard of her agency?

Without breaking eye contact, he too reached out a hand and took hers. A pulse of energy zipped up her arm. She flung the sensation behind a mental curtain with the remnants of her other attempts at not feeling anything toward this man but respect and suspicion.

"I'm Marshall," he said.

She shook his hand, purposely leaving hers in his a moment longer than necessary. Small gestures, like a lingering handshake, gave men additional encouragement. Only this time, she genuinely did not *want* to remove her hand; she liked the feel of his strong, warm hand around her thin gloved one. And *that* was disconcerting. "Pleased to meet you, Marshall."

His given name or his surname? She quashed the question and replaced the curtain with something much stronger—a mental brick wall. *Stop wondering about him.*

His name mattered not a whit. Nor did knowledge of his family connections, marital status, or personality. Only two facts mattered: whether he had a quick mind intent on wooing unwary women, and whether she could make herself the recipient of his attentions so she could prevent victims.

"Miss? Your ticket, please?" another voice called.

She whirled around to discover that the queue before her was gone; the passengers ahead of her had already boarded, and others waited behind her and Marshall for their turn. She felt her cheeks go hot as she hurried forward, ticket outstretched. When she boarded, she heard Marshall chuckling behind her, which made her cheeks flame even hotter. She couldn't bear to look back and have him see her blushing.

How am I not seeing my surroundings? Worse, how have I let myself feel the slightest bit of attraction toward a man? For she'd finally admitted the simple fact to herself, if for nothing else than to acknowledge the need to conquer it.

Showing, or rather, feigning attraction toward a man to prevent him from hurting someone else was one thing, but whatever she'd experienced a moment ago was something else altogether. She'd have to spend time in her compartment to shake away the feelings. More importantly, she'd need time to make a plan for how to manage her dealings with Marshall. She'd become so adept at managing the male sex that she hadn't needed to make such a plan in at least two years.

Clearly, she'd been working too much. She was wearied and not at her prime. A vacation was past due, and as soon as she returned to her flat in London, she'd take a well-earned, much-needed break.

If Grandpapa were here, he would insist on one. And with that thought, she held out her ticket to the porter, climbed into the train car, and sought out her berth, where she'd freshen up and make her plan.

Grace Thompson had never been in greater need of a holiday.

Two

Marshall Bailey, known to the reading public as Eldrick Stiles, watched the pretty woman ahead of him board the train. He absently handed his ticket to the porter while keeping half an eye on the train and its windows. He hoped to catch another glimpse of the intriguing young woman he'd just interacted with.

Something about her was different. He could not quite put his finger on what it might be, but the fact remained that this was no typical woman. Perhaps he could tell these things from his experience as a novelist. Readers praised his attention to detail, the vividness of his characters—qualities his stories had thanks to his cultivated skill of noting those around him more than others did. Indeed, Marshall watched people, listened to them, always keeping part of his mind open to future details he could jot into one of his many notebooks for use in a future book.

That said, as he boarded after Grace Harward, he wasn't thinking about modeling a character after her. He wasn't thinking about writing at all, which was a relief. He'd decided to return to London via the Orient Express instead of a more modest conveyance for the specific purpose of a holiday. He'd been away from his flat in London for over a month—nearly a week traveling to the Holy Land by other means, then four weeks serving the poor and sickly there regardless of religion or creed. He was weary and needing a rest. Surely, the Orient Express would allow him just the kind of holiday he needed, away from large groups of people prying into his business. Yet he had yet to board the train and had already found his mind gravitating toward his notebooks anyway.

He'd been under the weight of so many deadlines and pressures, from public appearances to his editor's insistence that he answer every letter received in the post from excited readers, that after his latest publication six months ago, and after the accompanying tour across Scotland and England, he'd refused to extend the tour by months to visit America. He'd told his publisher and everyone in his life that he would simply be unavailable for several weeks—perhaps several months—and headed off to the Holy Land. While helping so many people had been rejuvenating in spirit, his body now needed rest. He wished he'd had the courage to agree to a stop in his hometown of Dublin on his tour, but he feared too many things about such an appearance, including his hard-won proper English accent slipping and relatives from his rough childhood appearing, likely drunk and making a scene. No, best to visit the Emerald Isle quietly, in the countryside, and not as Eldrick Stiles.

Despite his plans to ignore anything and everything to do with writing, he'd been unable to ignore the tendency altogether, and over the course of the journey had filled three notebooks with observations: details of dress, speech, appearance, differences in cultures, and so much more. He'd begun notebook number four that morning and knew he'd be adding more on the rail trip, including a full description of Grace Harward. Apparently, someone who had made a life out of telling stories did not easily stop thinking in terms of story-telling.

So far, he'd managed to travel incognito. The addition of a close-cropped beard, now fully filled in, had done the job of obscuring his appearance for the few people who might have attended one of his appearances or seen a photograph of him in a newspaper or poster. Truth be told, he'd had such an easy time that he had a suspicion that the beard had not been entirely necessary. People seemed to be fully aware of who Eldrick Stiles was, but few knew what he looked like, so he'd walked among strange streets without a single person accosting him, demanding an autograph. Many people simply assumed that Eldrick Stiles was twice his actual age, perhaps gray and wrinkled, spending his nights before a fire in a wingback chair, reading a book, pipe in hand.

Any time a reader at an event saw him and expressed surprise at his appearance, Marshall chuckled. To his credit, he never mentioned that some owners of pen names were even less like their real identities. George Eliot, for example, was a woman. Marshall had come to like the appearance of his beard and even considered keeping it after he returned to his London flat. But he would not feel fully relaxed and at ease until his next visit to Dublin, where he could let his Irish brogue free over a pint.

Unfortunately, he did not board in time to catch up to Miss Harward, so he had no idea which berth was hers. *No worries. You have three full days to interact with her and to discover which it is.* He'd have ample opportunity to uncover more about the unusual woman.

He quickly found his own cabin and went inside. After admiring the polished wood, the built-in sink, the electric lights, and more, he unpacked his travel bag and arranged his items quickly. He'd done so enough times over the last several weeks that he'd become adept at completing the task quickly. That chore done, he left, hoping for some light refreshment in a dining car—and hoping to perhaps cross paths with Grace. With his door shut tight behind him and the key in his vest pocket, he made his way to the nearest dining car.

With every step, he deliberately tamped down the hope that Grace would be there. He would order a coffee and pastry, and with his notebook and favorite fountain pen in hand, he would write down all the things he'd seen since his last entry.

The pastry was divine, but his journal writing quickly became laborious in a way he'd never experienced, though not because it wearied his hand or because he'd tired of such exercises. Quite to the contrary, on both counts. Rather, every time he tried to record his impressions of the past day: leaving his hotel, the streets of Constantinople, the train station, the foods—especially the fruits—and some of the locals he'd encountered along the way, his pen kept returning to the intriguing Grace Harward, even twenty minutes after the train had left the station. Why his mind could not stop thinking about her, he had no idea, but the fact was infuriating.

Very well, I'll write about her first. He quickly wrote a description of her and recorded their brief interaction. Getting his thoughts onto paper removed them and freed his mind. The technique had always worked, and it had been a boon for him as a struggling young man, allowing him to cease dwelling on a situation.

After writing down the entire encounter, he tried to write about something else and settled on the interior of the dining car. When his mind wandered once more to Grace, he wrote about the train station at Constantinople and compared it with the one in Paris. Four sentences in, he was once more thinking of Grace. Every description, every vignette, every subject he tried to distract himself didn't work. Inevitably,

Grace's face and voice returned to his mind like a powerful perfume impossible to ignore.

I'm mad, he thought. It was utter ridiculousness to think that a single person could have such an influence on him after such a brief exchange. He'd likely have to journal for an hour tonight to get her out of his head.

Then again, why did he need to exorcise thoughts of her at all? He'd boarded the train with the intent of enjoying himself, and thoughts of Grace were, indeed, enjoyable, if not explicable. The countryside of Turkey zipped past the window as the train headed west, the station long since left behind. He closed the notebook and laid his pen atop it, then watched the landscape outside and let himself enjoy the sights—as well as any thoughts of a certain pretty Englishwoman.

When little remained in his coffee cup but the dregs and his pastry was but a memory, the door to the dining car slid open. The sound briefly drew his attention as it had the other half a dozen times the door had opened since he'd taken his seat at the small table with a linen tablecloth and a lamp with an intricately designed base. But instead of one of many unknown passengers appearing in the doorway, there stood Grace Harward, her spine straight, shoulders back, and head held high. In her hands she held a beaded clutch purse.

Three

Instead of looking for her waiter, as others typically did upon entering, she scanned the dining car, her gaze moving from one table to the next until it landed on him. Marshall suddenly became aware of two things: first, the knuckles of his right hand had gone white because he'd unconsciously picked up his pen and was gripping it hard. Second, seeing Grace again, in the flesh rather than in his mind, made him hold his breath, which he released only after she spotted him and he felt the weight of her stare on his chest. She'd changed into a pale-yellow dress of a flowing material. Thanks to whatever other magic she had performed to freshen her appearance, she looked nothing short of a Greek goddess.

When their eyes met, her pretty mouth curved into a smile, revealing teeth and dimples. Once more, his breath caught, only this time, he ordered his body to keep inhaling and exhaling, in an orderly, normal manner.

Don't blush, he ordered his face. He felt relatively confident that it obeyed, but when she headed toward him with purpose and then took a seat across from him at the little table, he decided that he should have ordered his heart to beat at an even, slow pace instead of the erratic, faster rhythm it insisted on.

Grace laid her clutch purse beside the lamp, made a show of elegantly crossing her legs in the aisle, then leaned across the table. "Marshall, wasn't it?"

His throat had tightened so much at her entrance that he could *not* find his voice. He merely nodded and tried to smile casually. There was good reason why people of his temperament became writers. He got along far better alone or interacting with people he knew well than he ever did with strangers, especially gorgeous ones like Grace Harward. Over the years, he'd received many comments after lectures and appearances about how he mustn't be shy at all, not as he was rumored to be. Surely, they declared, no shy person could get up in front of a large group composed of dozens, if not hundreds of people while looking at ease and confident. *Being* at ease and confident. What they didn't realize was that speeches and appearances were things one could rehearse and, in large measure, control.

He most certainly could not control social interactions, and in his case, his scant abilities to interact with others tended to abandon him entirely when he found himself before a beautiful woman he admired or wished to become better acquainted with. He was yet a bachelor, as finding a wife, particularly one who could be a partner he could be utterly at ease with, required a level of conversation he had yet to master with anyone who was not a family relation or a schoolmate from his youth. And if this woman's alluring flirtatiousness was any indication, he would turn into a bumbling ninny about three seconds after opening his mouth.

The mysterious intrigue she carried about her seemed at odds with the far more approachable version of her from the platform. That version he could imagine—granted, only in flights of fancy—becoming acquainted with on an intimate level. She seemed quick and smart and funny, someone he might enjoy telling about his latest projects.

Even better, he could imagine telling her about his daily stresses and even silly things, such as of the letter he received two months ago from an offended reader. The writer, a woman, was certain that Marshall had gone to Manchester to spy on her life and had then written it all out in one of his books. He could easily imagine being such good friends with the woman on the platform that he could laugh great belly laughs with her. At least, the woman he'd imagined she was—a woman turned friend . . .

And so much more.

But this version of her had stolen his tongue and all coherent thought. That, unlike their meeting before, was *not* pleasant. The storyteller part of his mind briefly felt tempted to ask if she had a twin she was traveling with, and if so, could he please speak with her. Of course, he knew better. She was traveling alone, as he was.

Which version of Grace Harward was the real one? He suspected the former version, but why did she put on a show now? The whole thing made him uncomfortable and uneasy in his skin, as if ants walked in lines all over his body.

"Is the coffee any good?" she asked, then briefly looked at his used cup before her gaze slid back to his and pinned him in place.

Find your tongue, man.

"Y-yes, it's quite . . . quite good." He could hear himself stammering and forced himself to keep speaking. His voice would even out. He hoped. "And the pastry was excellent. I had a raspberry scone with orange zest. It was ex-extraordinary."

"Mmm," she said, leaning a little closer, but she didn't

look at what remained of the scone, only deeper into his eyes. "Sounds divine."

Was it his imagination, or had her eyebrows lifted ever so slightly, as if in expectation?

Expectation of what?

"I love raspberries," she said.

And then the reality dawned on him: she wanted him to purchase her a scone. He gestured toward his empty dishes. "Would you like some coffee? And a raspberry scone?" His anxious mind churned, sure he'd said something wrong. "That is to say . . . raspberry is not the only type they have. I believe they also have orange marmalade, cranberry, blueberry, and apple. I'm probably forgetting some. And various biscuits and cakes."

You dolt. You find your tongue but lose your mind. No woman wanted a man to recite a menu to her.

Grace, however, gave no indication that he'd said or done anything awkward. "Raspberry would be perfect," she said, then licked her lips, making them shine. He couldn't take his eyes away from them.

A waiter appeared right then, breaking the spell. Grace turned to him expectantly but did not speak, clearly waiting for Marshall to take the lead.

"The lady will have what I had," he said.

"Very well," the waiter said. "Would you like another coffee, sir? Or another pastry, perhaps?"

"Another coffee would be wonderful, thank you," Marshall said. "That will be all, I believe." He looked at Miss Harward for confirmation, which she gave with a nod and a smile. And, he thought—or might have imagined—with a wink. Marshall cleared his throat in an attempt to free it from the constriction the sight created.

The waiter bowed slightly at the waist. "I'll return with your order in a moment."

Marshall looked after him wistfully. Having a fellow member of the male species nearby, someone of the same approximate age, felt easy, natural, and Marshall would be able to speak to Grace more easily if the waiter remained. If only he could apply the same ease to conversing with Grace as he'd felt in that oh-so-brief exchange on the platform.

World events. The theater. Weather. He couldn't decide if any topic he came up with would suffice. Definitely not the weather; he knew that much.

She reached over to the window and played with a tassel on the drape tieback. "So what do you enjoy doing, Marshall?" She paused and considered him. "Rather, I should probably be saying *Mr.* Marshall, shouldn't I?"

"No. That is, Marshall is my given name. My surname is Bailey."

"Marshall Bailey. Fascinating." She dropped the tassel and leaned against her arms as she considered him.

What was "fascinating" about his real name? The longer he sat there with her, the more he wanted to escape to his quarters. How had he spoken to her on the platform at all? Approaching her and speaking with her the way he had was entirely unlike him. That had been unplanned and spontaneous.

The waiter returned but then stopped suddenly, making the coffee cups slosh and spill onto the tray. "My deepest apologies." He tried to dab the minor spillage with a linen napkin, but the tray trembled in his grasp despite the fact that nothing had spilled onto the table, the floor, or the guests.

"It's quite all right," Marshall said. "Here, let me take the cups for you."

"Thank you," the waiter said, holding out the tray. When the drinks and scone plate were safely on the table, he turned to Marshall with wide, amazed eyes.

Marshall's middle dropped at the sight. He knew what was about to happen, and he could think of no way to stop it. *Oh no.*

"I did not mean to eavesdrop, but I couldn't help overhearing . . ." The waiter paused. He glanced at Grace as if she were in on the secret. Marshall gritted his teeth to face what he'd managed to avoid for over a month. "You're Marshall Bailey? *The* Marshall Bailey?"

"Oh, I'm sure there are many Marshall Baileys," he said with a wave of his hand, on the minuscule chance that the waiter *didn't* know.

The waiter nodded toward the half-filled notebook, which was bound in red leather, as Marshall's notebooks always were. "And that's where you keep your notes?"

"Some of them," Marshall said. He instinctively placed a hand protectively over the cover. A relatively minor percentage of readers knew that he published under a pen name, but even fewer knew his real name. The information had been mentioned in a few papers, and if this man happened to be one of the few who knew that information, if he'd attended a tour appearance, if he recognized Marshall's penchant for red leather notebooks . . .

"Eldrick Stiles," the waiter said slowly.

And there it was.

"I can't believe it. You're Eldrick Stiles."

Marshall groaned silently and kept his attention on the waiter. He could not bear to see Grace's expression. If she'd been flirtatious with a socially backward twenty-nine-year-old, she'd turn into a bird of prey after discovering that he was the world-famous Eldrick Stiles, who was worth ten thousand a year.

The waiter took a half step back as if he'd drawn too close to royalty. "I'd recognize you anywhere, even with a beard."

He shook his head as if he thought he was dreaming. "This is amazing. Could you—would you—if it's not too much trouble—"

"I'd be happy to," Marshall said, interrupting the request. The young man probably wanted Marshall to sign a book, but even if he wanted something else, Marshall would do whatever favor the young man wanted to keep him quiet. He leaned toward the waiter, who bent down to hear him whisper, "Could you please not tell anyone? I'm trying to enjoy a peaceful holiday."

The waiter looked at Marshall for several seconds. "Can I *never* tell anyone?" he asked in an almost desperate voice. His voice squeaked, which made him sound ten years younger than he surely was.

"After we reach Paris, and after I'm safely on my way across the Channel, then you may tell someone. Not a moment before." Marshall pierced the young man with a stare that, he hoped, would leave a firm impression. "If you keep the secret, I'll have a handsome reward for you in Paris. But you'll get not one penny if the secret gets out."

"I'll tell no one. You have my word." The waiter seemed to be thinking deeply, as his forehead creased and his eyes focused on the tablecloth. "I'll, um . . . how about . . . well, we can discuss what I was about to say later."

"My thoughts exactly."

The damage was done as far as Grace Harward was concerned, but hopefully Marshall could convince her to not mention his pen name during the journey either.

The waiter straightened and nodded politely toward her. "Enjoy." He turned to leave and nearly stumbled on a table leg, catching himself and nearly taking its linen cloth to the floor in the process. The waiter steadied himself, secured the tray, and quickly left the car.

When Marshall could avoid the moment no longer, he

sighed and looked at Grace, bracing himself for the inevitable treasure-hunter look—one element of interacting with people, men and women alike, that he understood all too well. After they realized he had money, he was suddenly worth knowing. Those kinds of people didn't make him nervous; they made him angry.

But Grace didn't say a word, and he couldn't make out the meaning of her expression, so he ventured into the breach. "Well, now you know."

The simple statement only made her eyebrows draw together in confusion. She looked out the window briefly, then took a sip of her coffee as if she needed it for strength. "Are you saying that you lied about who you are?" she asked in a flat, tight tone. "You *aren't* Marshall Bailey at all?"

If he'd been asked to list a hundred possible reactions, this one wouldn't have made the list. Nor a list of a thousand. "Excuse me?"

"Why would you lie about your name to a woman you don't even know?" she demanded. "What did you have to gain? It's not as if you think I have ties or a titled family or an estate you can benefit from. You had *nothing* to gain by not telling me your real name." She shook her head, looking every inch disgusted. "Men of this generation make no sense, but they're still all the same."

"Wait one moment," Marshall said. "You're accusing me of a lot of things—and I'm not entirely sure of what all—but let's start with the first: What do you mean that I have nothing to gain by not mentioning that I'm Eldrick Stiles?" He looked about surreptitiously, hoping no one heard him. "I have a world full of reasons not to travel under the name." Literally anywhere in the world that had an English speaker, his books could have traveled, and anywhere with a reasonable English-speaking population likely had seen his books.

She rolled her eyes. "How about just *one* really good reason," she said drily.

"Isn't it—obvious?" Marshall said slowly, confused himself now.

She blew out in frustration. "I'm an intelligent woman, Mr. *Stiles*, a good deal more intelligent than many men I know who have graduated from Cambridge or Oxford. Please do not insult me by saying that I should be able to read your mind." Her flushed cheeks, increased rate of speech, and the slight flaring of her nostrils all told him one thing: whatever she'd felt a moment ago had been entirely replaced by anger. He'd never encountered *that* reaction to Eldrick's name before.

Slowly, a possible explanation for the situation offered itself to Marshall. He ventured to settle the matter with a gentler, indirect approach. "Do you read much?"

"Must I recite Shakespeare or write out Newtonian calculations to prove my mettle?"

"Not at all. I—"

She lifted her eyes to the ceiling. "The nerve of some men." Though he did not like having Grace angry with him, he'd disliked the sultry, flirtatious version of her even more. That mask had now fallen. The woman before him now, though filled with rage, was far closer to resembling the one he'd spoken to before. Better yet, he found himself far more able to speak to *this* Grace.

"That's not at all what I meant, I assure you. I merely—" How to put this in a manner that would not make her angrier? The simplest way to say it would make him look arrogant, and that was *not* something he wanted to risk. He'd simply become so accustomed to the public knowing the name and work that he'd assumed she'd know who he was on hearing it, whether or not she'd read a single one of his novels. And whether or not she hated his work. He was still trying to find the best way to explain when she leaned back in her chair and folded her arms.

"You merely *what*?"

"What I was asking was not *whether* you can read, but whether you *enjoy* reading or do so often. Novels, in particular." He waited for her to answer, hoping against hope that her angry flare would soften. Oh, to have her smile at him again. Or not hate the sight of him. He'd settle for that.

"I don't read many novels." Grace narrowed her eyes, seeming more suspicious now than angry. "Why?"

He wanted to give proper explanation, but he didn't dare spend time on even a brief history. The plain truth would be best, and as quickly as he could say it—well, both quickly *and* quietly. He cleared his throat and leaned forward to speak in a whisper. "I'm a writer—a novelist. Eldrick Stiles is my pen name. My real name *is* Marshall Bailey." He could scarcely take a breath until she answered.

"Oh." Her arms relaxed, and the mixture of anger and suspicion lessened. She lowered her gaze to her lap and seemed to be pondering something.

Oh. That was her entire reaction to learning that he went by another name? Ironic, considering what he'd seen on her ticket. He sat back in his seat and crossed his own arms as she had a moment before. "I'm surprised you'd get upset over a silly thing like a name, considering your own circumstances."

Her head come up suddenly. "What do you mean?" Gone were all coyness, flattery, and hint of feminine wiles.

"You know precisely what I mean." He tilted his head to one side, his face a portrait of incredulity. "I find your shock and disgust rather hypocritical, seeing as *you* didn't give me your real name either."

He let the words sink in but didn't see the emotional

reaction he'd expected. Her eyes remained studied pinpoints trained on his. She'd donned a straight face to hide her true feelings; of that he was quite sure. *Time to call out her lie.*

Casually, he stood, tucked his chair under the table, and buttoned his suit coat before sending one final volley. "Have a lovely trip, Miss *Thompson.*"

Her face fell, the color in her cheeks drained, and her eyes became saucers. Ah. Now *there* was the reaction he'd been looking for.

Satisfied with his moment of recompense, Marshall Bailey strode out of the dining car and returned to his room.

Four

Grace remained in her seat, her back ramrod straight, as Marshall—Eldrick?—walked past. She clasped her hands below the table, a nervous habit she made sure to hide whenever she felt a bit off-kilter. She stared at the empty chair across from her. She heard Marshall's step retreat, the dining car door open, two more steps, and it closed again. Only then did she move—her eyelids fluttered closed nervously.

What had just happened? How had she let her guard down so much that someone—a man—had noticed her name on the ticket?

Who, aside from people in her line of work, noticed such things? Who *looked* for them? Was Marshall Bailey a detective, then? A constable? A military man? Could he be a foreign spy? What if he wasn't even British, but American, putting on the accent?

The more her mind spun out possibilities, the more her frame refused to still, and instead, her limbs trembled.

She curled her toes in her boots and pushed the soles to the floor. She pressed her ankles and knees together and pressed her interlaced hands against her knees. So long as she didn't rise from her linen-draped table until the trembling eased, no one would know anything about her was untoward. The waiter reappeared at her side, startling her. After a quick intake of breath, she looked at him, praying that her eyes didn't reveal her fright.

"Could I get you some refreshment, miss?" he asked in a gentle tone. Clearly, he knew that she was shaken.

"Um . . ." She'd entirely forgotten about her cup of coffee, and the scone seemed about as appealing as chalk. Wait, was *he* part of the Marshall/Eldrick ruse?

Don't be foolish. It's thanks to this young man that the false name came to light. I should be grateful to him. And yet. This waiter proved to be one more person with a keen eye for detail. What were the chances of that? The train had built up speed, and the countryside flashed by in a blur of colors. The car felt small and cramped, and she yearned for fresh air.

"Miss?" he said again.

Grace's attention had drifted again. She rearranged her expression, took a calming breath, and smiled at the waiter. "I'd like a sloe gin. Thank you." Her voice came out so quiet that it was a wonder he heard her, but sure enough, a moment later, he slid a crystal goblet before her, bowed, and retreated.

The drink helped her slip back into the persona she'd let fall. She leaned back into her chair. Crossing her ankles, she lifted the glass and pressed the rim to her bottom lip. The berry-flavored gin burned as it went down. The sensation sharpened her senses.

Of course, too much drink would dull them. It was a matter of pride to her that she never let herself drink enough to become tipsy. She knew how to behave with a little drink in her, something that benefited her efforts more often than one would think. She found it downright amazing how frequently men, jovial from partaking of strong drink, divulged secrets from the depths of their hearts to a stranger, especially if that stranger happened to be a woman. If the man happened to be altogether tanked up on alcohol, the revelations flowed to her like a river. She hardly had to do anything but ask the next question.

The door on the far side of the car opened, and the young family she'd seen on the platform entered, first the wife, with the baby on one hip and the toddler holding her other hand. The husband followed behind. The valet and female servant— lady's maid or governess?—didn't appear. They were probably in their own quarters or eating in a different dining car, one where servants would be more likely to congregate.

While the servants' absence wasn't surprising, the children's presence was. Very young children, or children of any age, for that matter, tended to stay with a governess, to be trotted out briefly before special company. Otherwise, they remained unseen and unheard. Yet here, a well-to-do family took one of the larger tables with their two very young children. The wife sat at a chair, placing the babe on her lap, after which she selected a spoon from the place setting and held it out for the child to take in her chubby, little hand. Meanwhile, her husband settled the toddler on the chair by the window, then sat across from his wife.

They began a conversation, and while Grace sat too far away to make out the subject matter, the snippets of their voices and their warm expressions told her volumes.

Grace decided to focus on them to get her mind off Marshall Bailey. She watched them from the corner of her eye for several minutes as they interacted with their children and talked about books and even politics. Of course he found his young wife attractive, but he seemed to enjoy more than her appearance, pretty as it was. They seemed genuinely happy, both of them. Having their children nearby didn't appear to be a burden. More remarkably, the father seemed as interested in them as the mother. Grace had never seen the like from any man, let alone someone of his status.

The husband chuckled at something, reached across the table, and stroked his wife's cheek. She leaned her face into his open palm, then turned her lips to kiss his palm. He mouthed something that any non-detective would have been able to decipher the meaning of, but which Grace understood immediately.

I love you.

Unnerved at the tender display, and unable to reconcile it with her own experience, Grace shifted to look out the window. She took another sip. When the burning of the drink had passed, a different pain got stuck in her chest.

Most of the time, she successfully kept her tender emotions locked behind a padlock. That was the safest way to live as an unmarried, employed woman of a certain age. Potential clients were far more likely to enlist her services if she didn't appear emotional and fragile, as the fair sex was typically assumed to be.

More importantly, she could do her work far more effectively if she didn't allow complicated things like emotions to blind her. Her methods worked well; she'd solved many a complicated riddle that even the police hadn't been unable to unravel, and she lived a comfortable life.

But a solitary life.

At one time, she'd wanted to be a mother, a wife. She'd come to terms with the realities of her situation. She'd never had an opportunity to be courted properly when she was of a marriageable age, and when she reached the upper end of that age group, Grandpapa's declining health meant that she'd a lot of time helping him in his last days. By the time he passed, she was nearing thirty—long since doomed by society to old maidenhood.

The old desires and dreams flared from time to time, but rarely. And today, it happened when she'd least expected it.

She sipped her drink again, looked away from them—again—and determined to avoid the thoughts and emotions they brought up. She wanted to leave, to flee to her quarters, but she didn't dare quite yet; she had to be certain that Marshall would be nowhere in sight. She could not bear to cross paths with him a third time in one day.

A heavy thud sounded, followed by a high-pitched cry. Grace's head came around, back to the family, where the toddler stood on her chair, jumped up and down, and cried, tears streaming down both cheeks. She'd dropped or thrown something to the floor, most likely. The mother looked distraught, reaching across the table while trying to balance the baby.

The father grabbed the child, and in a flash, dual emotions flared inside Grace's chest: dread for the little girl sure to be paddled, and a heavy streak of satisfaction that her beliefs about men remained intact. Men were *not* kind and good. They were harsh and cruel.

All but Grandpapa.

Better to remain unmarried than to be shackled to a cruel taskmaster. Surely this father wasn't as kind a husband as he'd appeared either.

The thoughts and feelings flew through her brain faster than the train sped down the track, faster than the father moved to grab the child. But he didn't spank her. Grace's brow furrowed, her gaze on the father and his every move, even as she tried to keep her attention hidden by half-closed lids and her glass held to her lips. Too bad she'd left her hat in her cabin; it would have provided more cover for her to observe unnoticed.

The father plopped the little girl onto his lap, with her

feet dangling into the aisle. She leaned to her side, into his chest, and he wrapped one arm around the little shoulders. He leaned down and looked into his daughter's eyes. She returned his gaze with love and trust and comfort.

The father tugged a handkerchief from his pocket and wiped his daughter's tears, first one cheek and then the other. Then he held the cloth by one corner and pretended it was a dragon or some other fantastical animal intent on tickling her. Just the kind of thing Grandpapa used to do.

Grace's vision clouded with unshed tears, and when the girl's laughter rang out, she closed her eyes, and tears made twin tracks down her cheeks.

That man may be kind and good like Grandpapa, she thought, desperate to get the padlock back into place to lock up her heart so she could stop hurting and missing him so. *Such men are one in a generation.*

She slipped her own handkerchief from her clutch purse and dabbed at her cheeks and the corners of her eyes. When she trusted in the control she had over herself again, she tucked the kerchief into her purse and left some coins on the table before heading for the door. She left more than enough to cover her own drink—enough to pay for Eldrick's order as well, as he didn't appear to have paid a penny.

Back in her berth, she locked her door from the inside and imagined turning the padlock in her chest, locking away the melancholy of wishing for someone kind and genuine to share her life with.

He doesn't exist, she reminded herself as she closed—and locked—her door behind her.

Most likely, there would be no way to avoid seeing Marshall-Eldrick entirely. That's how she'd come to think of him: the combined name of *Marshall-Eldrick*. Barring the dreadful idea of staying in her small compartment, alone, for three days straight, what could she do to minimize contact with him throughout their rail journey until they reached Paris?

She sat on her bed and played with her necklace as she debated how to spend her time on the luxury train line. She would use her eye for detail to note when and where he was most likely to appear and then avoid those places. Granted, such deductions typically required observation of more than two or three days to achieve. But if she viewed Marshall-Eldrick as a puzzle to solve, if she funneled her detection skills into deciphering who he was and how to avoid being taken advantage of, perhaps she could reach Paris unscathed.

Yes, that was what she would do. Instead of staying in her berth, she'd take the unsettled energy Marshall-Eldrick Bailey-Stiles had awakened in her and use it to unmask the rake and scoundrel he surely was. She'd find evidence that he, too, lived to serve himself and no one else.

Unlike most men, he hadn't proved easily duped by her flirtations. Where a detective could not predict a response or outcome, one learned that the best course of action tended to be the one posing the smallest risk to oneself. In Marshall-Eldrick's case, that meant observing from a distance rather than seeking him out, as she was used to doing. She could already tell, even from their brief interchanges, that while Mr. Bailey was no doubt untrustworthy, he had a wit and intelligence she'd rarely seen. She would have had an ample amount of diversion flirting with him. Truly, it was a shame that she needed to avoid him. She'd have much rather spent her time flying along the rail line across Europe while discussing all manner of topics with someone handsome and intelligent.

For someone who dislikes parties and other large groups of people, I've become strangely tired of being alone.

Grace shifted and lay back on her bed. Staring at the ceiling, she felt the rumble of the train wheels below her and sighed.

Five

Marshall lay on an unfamiliar bed, between unfamiliar sheets, as the track rocked him back and forth. Normally, such movement, combined with the darkness, lulled him to sleep. That was especially true of nights that followed his charitable trips, as he was inevitably fatigued from weeks of physical labor.

Tonight was no different in respect to his overall level of weariness, but it was most definitely different in the fact that despite having been in bed for well over an hour, he could not sleep. No amount of keeping his eyes closed helped him nod off, and staring into the black ceiling above him did no good either.

The cause of this mischief was clear, as again and again his mind returned to Grace. The mischievous glint in her eyes, her laugh . . . and her look of dismay. And the look of something else he could not pinpoint, something he'd seen right after using her correct surname. Her cheeks had colored, but the rest of her face seemed to have lost its color. She'd released her coffee cup and put both hands under the table, where the subtle flexing of her forearms hinted that her hands were clenched in fists or clasped tightly together. The movements were so small that others wouldn't have noticed—no one, probably, save someone whose line of work, as his did, necessitated developing a habit of noticing precisely those types of things.

What emotion had she reacted with? Fear? Doubtful. A woman as confident and devil-may-care as Grace Thompson wouldn't fear a bachelor of nearly thirty who was intimidating in neither stature nor influence; after all, she didn't know or care about Eldrick Stiles. She had no reason to be intimidated or afraid of him.

Yet he could not entirely dismiss the idea. He'd seen a swift change in her, and the details could have reflected fear. If so, he was the cause. And what had he done? He'd sauntered off as if he'd won a cricket match. What kind of ungentle-manly, boorish behavior was that?

Maybe he'd seen anger in her—a far more likely theory, for several reasons. For a significant portion of the time they'd spent interacting, she'd expressed that very emotion. Yes. Anger. That must have been it. The conclusion did not sit well with his conscience either. Anger, he knew, tended to be a manifestation of inner hurt.

I might have hurt her, he thought. *No woman deserves such a thing, and certainly not from a strange man.* That thought was quickly followed up by hating the thought that he was a stranger to her. *Would that we were long acquainted, and I could not only determine her emotions accurately but know her well enough to prevent hurts and frights.* He stopped the spinning thoughts long enough to examine them and realize that he was quickly devolving into a sentimental fool.

Yes, he'd won a match of wits at whatever game they were both playing—he'd called her out of her own deception, though he didn't judge her for using another name. How could he, when he did the same? His curiosity burned to learn why she, too, traveled incognito. She certainly had a story, and he wanted to learn it. In her eyes, however, he had to be a knave or a louse.

He closed his eyes again, intent on sleeping now that he'd solved the puzzle as much as he could for the moment. But not a minute passed before he rolled over, punched his pillow into a different shape, and for the umpteenth time that night, closed his eyes and tried to sleep. Several deep breaths later, he could feel his heart rate gradually speeding up instead of slowing down. The faster it went, the more Grace returned to mind, along with guilt for treating her like a pawn in a game rather than as a gentlewoman. Like an adversary to defeat rather than another person—a woman—with feelings and thoughts and a life of her own.

He groaned, knowing he'd be unable to sleep at all unless he wore himself out another way. He threw the bedclothes off, sat up, and shoved his toes into his slippers. In a heroic effort to expend the uneasy energy brought on by unceasing thoughts of Grace, he paced the narrow room. The path amounted to a few steps in one direction and a few steps in the other.

The exercise did no good, of course. Perhaps if he were in his own flat, he could have worked thoughts of Grace out of his mind, going around and around the block of the London city street on which he lived for as long as it took. Even pacing the length of a train car would have been more likely to work, but he couldn't very well do that in a striped nightshirt, even if he put on a dressing gown on top. Getting fully dressed seemed foolish, when the object of doing so was an activity intended to help him sleep.

On one of his trips back to the outer edge of the car, he stopped by the narrow window looking into the darkness outside. He could make out precious little save a bright swath of stars across the sky and a glorious silver moon with wispy clouds that looked like an expensive scarf adorning a socialite's delicate neck.

Such a scarf would look divine on Grace. No sooner had the thought crossed his mind than he groaned and shoved both hands through his hair. Why could he not get her out of his mind?

Was it her beauty? He crossed his arms and stared out the window, demanding answers of the night sky.

No, it wasn't merely her beauty, and he didn't need the stars to confirm the suspicion. For while he was quite certain that she possessed the quality in ample amounts, he could not think of an individual feature he admired. For that matter, he could not clearly summon her face to mind, and not for lack of trying. Were he to see her again, he'd recognize her on sight, but apart from quick snatches—those teasing eyes, her long fingers, that honey-gold hair—he could not remember specifics. Shouldn't he be able to remember such things about a woman his mind was apparently obsessed with? Yet he couldn't have saved his own life at the moment by correctly recalling the shape of her face or the color of the dress she'd worn.

Marshall turned from the window and resumed pacing. If the draw was not her appearance, then what was it?

I've gone without writing anything significant for too long, he thought. *Yes, that explains it.*

Something about Grace—her temperament, manner of speaking and moving—tugged at the novelist lying dormant inside him, the part of him yearning to escape from its prison cell. The writer in him needed to once again frolic in literary sun by writing a new story. He hadn't done so since leaving for Jerusalem. While he'd filled several notebooks along this journey, the volumes contained no stories, merely observations. Writing such notes did nothing to satisfy the storyteller part of his soul.

Then I'd better do something to scratch the itch.

He felt about in the dark for a few seconds before finding the button that illuminated the cabin's electric lamp. The change in brightness nearly blinded him, and he blinked to clear his vision as his eyes adjusted to the light. He fetched his newest notebook from his satchel, and soon he had it and his favorite fountain pen—made of polished mahogany, with an intricately engraved gold nib—before him. He hastily got to work, writing not only his observations about Grace Thompson, but also imagining her as the heroine in one of his stories. He turned her into a character sprung from his own mind—a character that, granted, highly resembled a sliver of reality, though he tried not to think too hard on that fact.

The more he wrote, the more he had to write. Despite the cramping of his hand and the drooping of his eyes, he went on, his script becoming sloppier and nearly illegible by the time he finished the character sketch and a ten-page treatment of the story he imagined for her.

Satisfied, he drew the nib of his pen, twice, across the bottom of the last sentence, then went back to the start of the night's writing session and labeled the first page *Grace*.

Only then did he cap his pen, lay it on the small table before him, and sit back with a sigh. There. Now that he'd exorcised the ghost of Grace from his mind, he'd be able to sleep. After switching off the light, he removed his slippers and lay down once more, pulling the bedclothes atop himself. With a deep breath, he closed his eyes, then rolled to his side, waiting for blessed sleep to claim him.

But as before, his mind floated directly back to Grace— her voice, the shock when she'd heard him use her true name.

On paper, he'd created a full back story and an entire plot for a novel based upon their chance meeting, and in the fictional version, he wasn't the cause of her pain. Yet in his mind, there in the darkness, he felt as if he knew her so well that he had to comfort her. To hold her, assure her that she had nothing to fret over, that he would make sure of it.

For in the process of creating his sketch and story outline, he'd also created a compelling explanation for her sudden shock—fear caused by a source unrelated to him or his actions. But in the foggy recesses of his mind as he drifted to sleep, he knew that he was indeed the one who had caused her pain. He needed to apologize and beg her forgiveness.

But for the moment, in his dreams, he could let something else play out. In his mind's eye, he could clearly see her being comforted by the hero of the story—a hero who looked like him. No, he *was* the hero.

He held out his arms to Grace, who collapsed in them and cried into his chest. He held her close, kissed the top of her head, and whispered, "Everything will be all right now. The men seeking your father's fortune will never find you or hurt you. I will see to it that you are safe."

Her breath hitched, and she looked up with tear-stained cheeks. "But how can you be sure?"

He stroked her hair and leaned down and kissed her. And though it was all a dream, he could feel the weight of her body in his arms and the warmth of her lips against his, sense their heart rates speeding up in unison.

Marshall Bailey, known by some as Eldrick Stiles, let himself slip into the dream and remain there throughout his slumber.

It was easy to do. After all, it wasn't real. His mind was merely working on a new book, working out the characters and their story as vividly as he could.

Six

Grace enjoyed a lazy morning, sleeping far later than she ever allowed herself to do at home. She dressed just as slowly as she wished, savoring every moment she didn't have to rush to meet a client or hurry to another part of the city to confront an unfaithful husband, or manage the dull bookkeeping side of the Harward and Sons Detective Agency, which, of course, most people assumed was all she did there.

She requested breakfast to be brought to her compartment—two eggs over medium, toast and marmalade, and a side of ham. The simple meal might well have been one of the best she'd ever partaken of.

Eventually, however, she grew tired of staying in her quarters, which seemed to shrink an inch with every hour she spent in them. She needed to leave, to find some diversion. Perhaps the drawing room car she'd heard about would provide just the thing she needed.

She opened her door and turned the handle but didn't pull the door open. So long as she stayed in her cozy-yet-suffocating compartment, she could be sure to avoid seeing Marshall Bailey. The moment she stepped across the threshold, however, nothing would be certain.

Though such thoughts had been a significant part of why she'd stayed in all morning. Even so, she resisted the notion that any man, least of all a stranger who happened to be able to spot her act, could be the reason she withdrew from seeing anyone on the train. Even her brief interactions with the waiter who had brought and taken away her breakfast tray had made her uneasy. She could not have said precisely why; Grace was not a weak, fragile woman by any stretch. But she was usually in control of situations, and yesterday, Marshall Bailey had soundly turned the tables on her. And what had she done in response? Hidden away like some frightened kitten.

Since when have I ever been afraid of a man? She scoffed at the thought, though the truth niggled at her mind. Her work had taught her to be plenty afraid of the male half of the species—or at least that having a man in one's life in any permanent way would inevitably lead to sorrow. She'd seen far too many women destroyed in too many ways—most of their heartbreaks not visible to outsiders—to trust anyone but Grandpapa, who lay under the cold earth in a cemetery outside London. She'd viewed men as potential dangers, but ones she knew how to control.

Marshall Bailey had left her reeling utterly *out* of control. But fearing him . . . No. She could not bear that. She discarded the idea as if it were an old stocking with holes, then opened the door. She straightened her back, lifted her chin proudly, and stepped into the corridor. Grace walked to her right, away from the car in which she'd had the interaction with Bailey, hoping to find the drawing room—and *not* him.

A relatively short search through three cars to find the drawing room ended without crossing paths with Mr. Bailey. She indeed found the car she'd been looking for, one lined with sofas and tables. Several passengers she'd never seen were scattered throughout the long room. Some played cards at a table. A man read a newspaper, legs outstretched on a footrest made of the same rich wood and red velvet as the sofas. And in the corner nearest her, she spied the young family she'd seen on the platform.

The father held a sleeping baby over one shoulder as he read a book, and the mother quietly read aloud from a different book to the slightly older child, who sat on her lap. The girl was leaning back against her mother, thumb planted in her mouth. The girl's hand held her mother's sleeve, and she rubbed the silky fabric between her fingers. She absently glanced up at Grace and grinned around her thumb.

The heartwarming sight, combined with the girl's bright smile, filled Grace with longing. She smiled back and waved. The girl waved, too, which prompted both parents to look up.

Grace stood there, suddenly feeling sheepish. "Hello," she said, now waving at the parents, too. "Your daughter is an angel."

"For the moment," her father said with a laugh, ruffling the girl's hair.

"Do you like fairy tales?" the girl asked. "Mama's reading one. This whole book is fairy tales."

Grace looked from the girl to her mother, to her father, and held out a hand in apology. "I'm sorry. I didn't mean to intrude—"

The father closed his book and set it aside. "Not at all. Would you like something to drink? A waiter should be by again soon."

"I—" Grace's voice cut off. What to say? Was this man offering to buy her a drink? Surely he wouldn't attempt to turn on his charms in front of his wife and children, would he? On the other hand, every time she thought she'd found the depths to which a man could sink, she found one who could sink even farther.

"Oh, do join us," the mother said. "I could so use some female conversation, and my lady's maid has taken ill."

"Well . . ." Before Grace could formulate a decision, let alone a response, the little girl hopped off her mother's lap and tugged Grace's hand.

"Yes, come."

"Betty," her mother chided. "That is not how we speak to our elders."

"I'm sorry, Mama." The girl—Betty, apparently—turned to Grace and curtsied. "Do come spend some time with us," she amended. "Please?" Her eyes pleaded even more than her sweet little voice. No one with half a heart could have resisted.

"I'd be delighted to join you, Miss Betty," Grace said with a proper nod.

Betty giggled at being spoken to as an equal. Grace followed her to the sofa and took a seat. She expected to listen to the tale that Betty's mother had been reading, but the little girl had another plan. She daintily climbed onto Grace's lap.

"Betty . . ." her father warned.

"She's as nice as the man who read to me in the breakfast car this morning," she said, defending herself. "I can tell."

And which man was that? The image of Mr. Bailey's face flashed into Grace's mind, as it had been doing regularly since she'd awoken. There was no reason to assume the "nice" man who'd read to Betty had any connection to Marshall-Eldrick at all.

"I don't mind reading to her," Grace assured the father. She held out a hand and added *less* truthfully, "I'm Grace Harward, by the way. I'm a governess." A story that would assure them that she liked children, which she did. It would also explain why she was unmarried at her age and help avoid any questions poking about such topics.

"James Miller at your service," the father said. He stood

slowly, balancing the sleeping baby over his left shoulder, and reached out to shake Grace's hand, after which he made the rest of the introductions. "This is my wife, Martha. And this little bundle"—he indicated the sleeping child with a tilt of his head—"is Ellie."

"What about me?" Betty said with a clap.

"And this is Betty," James said, holding his hand outstretched. He winked at his daughter and returned to his seat.

"I'm three." Betty held up two fingers easily and propped up the third with her other hand to show the result to Grace.

"I'm pleased to meet you all." Complete truth.

She was intrigued with this family, or rather, with this James Miller. She'd never seen a father actively involved in his child's care, yet here he was holding his sleeping babe, with no apparent intention of passing her back to his wife.

Before returning to his seat, James leaned down and kissed Martha's cheek. The couple exchanged a look that couldn't have lasted more than half a second but for Grace seemed to halt time. Each gazed into the other's eyes with pure joy and love. Both husband *and* wife. James squeezed Martha's hand, then returned to his seat across the aisle. He continued reading where he'd left off, holding the book with one hand and gently patting baby Ellie with the other.

And he hadn't given Grace another glance before returning to his book. She could hardly believe what she'd witnessed. Not only did his attention not stray to another woman, but he'd shared a tender moment with his wife, one that seemed as natural to them both as breathing.

Perhaps that is an everyday thing for them. Grace could not fathom such a thing existed, though she'd hoped for it and wanted it, only to be convinced that kindness and chivalry and romantic love had died with King Arthur's knights.

Her eyes clouded a bit as tears welled up in them. She blinked quickly to clear the moisture; she would *not* cry before this family she'd only just met, and certainly not over the fantasy of love. Holding back the emotion proved harder than she expected, however—she'd witnessed evidence that such love yet existed and perhaps had not died with Grandpapa and Grandmama.

All the more reason to be cautious for myself, she thought, settling her face into a smile. *If there is one good man walking the earth, he sits before me now.* What were the chances that two such men were on the same train at the same time?

"Betty got turned about this morning and wandered away from us," Martha said. "James and I were worried, of course, but we knew she had to be on the train and would turn up."

"I was scared," Betty piped in. "But then a nice man helped me find my way." She returned to playing with her mother's sleeve, now running her fingers along the lace at the cuffs.

"How kind of him," Grace said, picturing the porter or a waiter aiding the child.

"Oh, it was," Martha said. "He needn't have accompanied her the entire way. Most people would have found a member of the staff to handle such a situation. So few people understand children or are willing to interact with them at all, as if they're another species, or they have a catching disease." She chuckled, and Grace joined her, knowing that her words were all too true for many people.

Not for her. She dearly wanted children of her own but had accepted her reality as one that took a different path. Even so, she'd dreamed of teaching lock-picking techniques to both a boy and a girl—she'd once hoped to have at least one of each.

Sometimes she still let herself imagine such moments, though she had to skip over how she would become a mother without losing her freedom to a man.

James looked up from his book to join the conversation. "I don't think I've ever seen a man taking such care of a child."

"You excepted, my dear," Martha added.

Feeling a mixture of piqued interest and uncomfortable suspicion, Grace adjusted Betty's little form on her lap and leaned forward. "Who was this man? A waiter?" She said the last hopefully, though something in her middle told her that fate enjoyed playing games and that the mystery man was not, in fact, a waiter, or the porter, or anyone else employed by the Orient Express. Nor was he some elderly grandfather figure. Somehow, she knew.

Martha looked at James. "What was his name? Bailey?"

"Marshall Bailey, yes."

"Of course it was," Grace murmured under her breath— or thought she did.

"You know him well?" James asked.

Betty clapped again. "He's the nicest man in the world."

"Ahem." James grinned.

"You're not a *man*," Betty said with a laugh. "You're *Daddy*."

"I stand corrected."

"I met Mr. Bailey briefly yesterday, is all," Grace said as quickly as she could. Best to rid the air of that conversation topic at once.

"You seemed well acquainted when you shared a table," Martha said thoughtfully. The Miller family had been in the dining car. Grace wished she could melt away from the room and magically appear in her own cabin.

Martha continued, though Grace wasn't sure to whom she was speaking. "Now why would Mr. Bailey be looking for Miss Harward?"

Alarm shot through Grace. She schooled expression and her voice. "Pardon?"

"He was here not half an hour ago, looking for you," Martha said.

"Perhaps he was looking for someone else," Grace offered.

"No, I'm quite certain he was searching for a Miss Harward."

James nodded and turned a page. "Indeed he was." He looked up from his book and lifted one eyebrow at Grace. "Lest you think I wasn't paying attention, I assure you that I was. I'm skimming this book."

The comment brought humor to the moment, and Grace chuckled. "Why would you skim a book? Is it not to your liking?"

"On the contrary." He closed the cover with a snap. "I've read it a dozen times."

"At least," Martha added.

She did not add what Grace was thinking—that in spite of the luxuries aboard, passengers had precious little to do, so it seemed logical that if one found a book they enjoyed that they'd devote their attentions to it.

"It's true. This is my favorite novel, not only of Stiles's work, but of all time."

"Of . . ." Grace had never been one to be at a loss for words, but hearing the last name of the author, she suddenly could not manage to find the use of her tongue, nor any words for it to speak.

"Eldrick Stiles is a genius," James said. "A treasure. I only hope he lives a bit longer; he's rumored to be ailing, but no one knows for sure, as he's such a private person."

So private that much of the world had no idea he likely had decades of life ahead of him, that he was in prime health, and that he was on this very train. Grace opened her mouth to say as much but suddenly could not get herself to reveal his secret. Inside, she knew at least a kernel of why: she, too, lived a private life, and she instinctively respected another's need to do the same. For her, the dual identity was a matter of survival, financially and otherwise.

If Eldrick Stiles's presence were to be revealed, what would the consequences be for him? She doubted they would be disastrous, but even so, she could not betray the confidence.

He helped a little girl find her parents, a little voice in her head reminded her—her conscience. Yes, he'd done a good deed. But one good deed did not make a person worthy of praise or confidence keeping. Yet she wouldn't tell his secret. Not here, not in this moment.

"Have you read any of Eldrick Stiles's work?" James asked.

"No," Grace said. "Before boarding the train, I'd never heard of him." Absolute truth, that time.

"Here." James held out the green-covered book.

Grace raised a hand and shook her head. "I can't take your favorite book in the world."

"Just to borrow it," James said.

"I'm not a fast reader," Grace warned. "I probably won't finish before we reach Paris."

"Then send it to me by post when you finish it," James said. "Our address is in the front cover there. I'm quite serious. I have all of his work and a library filled with other books to keep me busy until *Of Ash and Flame* is returned." He held the book a little closer.

After a moment of eying it, Grace took it and hefted the weight. She could not have said whether she would read it, but she also could not deny a burning curiosity about its author.

She stayed a bit longer, even reading a fairy tale to Betty, one about a boy who gets kidnapped by an evil queen living in a palace of snow. Had it not been for the green volume at her side, she would have been delighted to stay with the Miller family for hours. Instead, she lingered only long enough to not appear to be rude.

With *Of Ash and Flame*, by Eldrick Stiles/Marshall Bailey, in hand, she could not bear to leave the pages unread a moment longer.

"I'm afraid I'm feeling a bit unwell," Grace said. A truth, but a misleading one. She wasn't ill, but her nerves had sent a swarm of butterflies aloft in her middle, and she wouldn't be able to quiet them until she could be alone, open the green-bound cover, and read at least a few pages. She slipped Betty off her lap and onto the sofa.

"Oh, I'm so sorry to hear that," Martha said. "Hopefully we'll see you again later."

"I hope so, too." Grace rose, thanked the Millers for a delightful conversation, and swept out of the car. She kept her steps as slow as she could manage, which took considerable effort, as she wanted to run. Entering her own car brought a sense of relief and excitement. She withdrew her key from her skirt pocket, eager to get inside her cabin.

The key turned, and when the door was open but a crack, she heard someone enter the car. She glanced over, intending to acknowledge a fellow passenger, but the greeting froze on its way from her lips. "Hhh—"

"Miss T—I mean, Miss Harward."

"Good day, Mr. Bailey." She turned back to her door, the book in her hand suddenly feeling like a hot poker. He seemed intent on speaking to her, as evidenced by the fact that instead of walking, he called after her and broke into a run. "Grace! Please wait. I must speak with you."

In a panic, she reached into her cabin and threw the book. Where it landed and in what condition, she did not know, but she no longer held the damning volume for him to see. She cleared her throat and turned his direction, only to find him within arm's reach. So close. And he smelled good, too. A tiny whimper escaped her, one she prayed he didn't detect.

She straightened her back and lifted her chin, her practiced manner of showing confidence toward anyone who intended to cow her. "What is it, Mr. Bailey?" She placed her hand firmly on the doorknob so he'd understand her intent to retire to her room.

He looked over his shoulder in the direction he'd come, then over hers. "Could we go somewhere else to talk? Please? I've been looking for you all day."

"May I ask why?" Normally, Grace would have tried to maintain a distant tone, but she couldn't, not with him so near, and not when she wanted to know the answer so intently.

He gestured about the corridor. "This isn't the most conducive location for a conversation."

"I meant why do you wish to speak with me?"

"I know." Marshall scratched his beard as if he wasn't quite used to it. "I won't take long. Afterward, if you'd rather not speak to me again, I'll abide by your wishes." He sounded perfectly serious.

Couldn't he have been rude and angry, rather than kind and, it seemed, deeply concerned about something? She thought of James Miller—a good man who deeply admired Eldrick Stiles.

"Very well." She smoothed her skirts to avoid looking into his eyes. "I was going to lie down, as I am not feeling entirely well, but I suppose I could take a moment to speak with you first."

"Thank you." His face softened with relief. "It won't take long."

She looked up, unable to withhold a half smile. "You already said that."

His mouth quirked into the hint of a smile as well. "I suppose I did." He gestured for her to follow him down the corridor.

After pulling her door closed and locking it again, she followed, and some emotion flowed through her, though she couldn't be entirely sure what it was. Regret that she hadn't gotten into her room and closed the door and begun reading his work? In part, yes, but also enjoyment at speaking with Marshall again and even—dare she admit it?—a seedling of attraction for this stranger.

He knows which room is mine, she thought, and wondered at herself for *not* feeling concern over the fact. And her lack of concern was concerning in itself. An idea flashed through her mind of Marshall walking her back to her door after a pleasant evening—of Marshall *kissing* her before she went inside. Of herself enjoying the kiss.

She shook her head and berated herself. *Yank that seedling out of the ground before it takes root.*

Seven

Marshall felt the weight of Grace's gaze as they walked down the corridor, and it was not altogether pleasant. She'd made her opinion of him quite clear and had nearly refused him the opportunity to apologize properly. If she hadn't agreed to talk elsewhere, he would have attempted an apology at her door. He sensed, quite rightly, he was sure, that going to a more comfortable place, such as a quiet corner in one of the dining cars, would be far more likely to elicit forgiveness than a drafty corridor ever would. A place where they could be seen—but not necessarily overheard—would likely serve him well if she cared for things like the appearance of propriety.

Yet her silence didn't bode well. He didn't dare look back, not even to smile. He could hear her step behind him, along with the swishing of her skirts. He'd made a point of noticing what she wore this time. Today, her dress was dark blue. And her eyes were green, another detail he'd missed before. He'd have to look right at her longer to be able to describe her features in greater detail.

They reached a dining car—the very same in which he'd last seen Grace. There was the table they'd argued at. He stepped into the car, mostly so she wouldn't be stuck in the space between them. As soon as they were both inside, he turned about.

"Let's go to the next dining car. I'm sure it will be more to your liking."

"This will be fine," she said before he could move.

Her tone seemed to hold a meaning of its own, but maddeningly, he could not interpret it. She moved past him to the same table they'd sat at before and pulled out a chair for herself. Not the seat she'd had last time, but the one *he'd* sat in.

She clasped her hands atop the linen and looked up at him, noting that he hadn't moved. "Are you joining me, or no?" This time her tone somehow sounded both challenging and playful at once, though he didn't know how that was possible. Perhaps her ability to change her voice and blend multiple emotions meant she was an actress. Regardless, she seemed to be testing him, gauging his reaction to her taking his prior seat, and not allowing him to move this meeting to a more neutral location.

He had no intention of being cowed by her challenge. He'd say what he'd come to say. For goodness' sake, he'd spent most of the day first trying to decide how best to apologize and then trying to find her. After so much effort, he would not surrender his cause so easily. Never taking his eyes from her face, he reached for the back of the chair opposite her, pulled it out, and took a seat.

"You look lovely today," he said, entirely sincerely, though he wondered whether she'd believe him.

Was he properly playing her game of cat and mouse—or whatever she was up to? How, exactly, did one manage to apologize when the other individual was intent on wearing masks and playing games? Once more she held herself, including her face, in the elegant yet superior manner of the mask she'd worn yesterday—before it had fallen away as a result of his unkindness. Would that he could determine how to rid her of the mask for good so he could see the real Grace, and do so without wounding her again.

"I haven't told anyone," she said suddenly. "About you, I mean."

"Thank you. I am most appreciative, truly." He noted that she'd been discreet enough to not refer directly to his pen name, though they were alone in the car. Of course, at any moment, someone could enter. He needed to speak quickly, and if someone did enter, he needed to be prepared to speak vaguely enough for others to not understand while making his meaning clear to her.

He could feel the weight of her gaze on him once more, but this time it lacked any unpleasantness. What did she see when she looked at him? Did she find him wholly loathsome, or did he have even one redeeming quality? He self-consciously scratched his itchy chin. He liked how the beard looked on him, but perhaps she preferred clean-shaven men.

Grace smoothed back her hair as if taming a stray lock, though she seemed to have nothing of the sort. "May I ask what this interview is about?"

How was it that he could speak before hundreds of people crowded into a town hall, but he quaked when speaking directly to one woman? Especially to *this* woman. He knew why, at least in part: crowds consisted of strangers he'd likely never see again and who already had a high opinion of him as Eldrick. He easily slipped into the role; Eldrick Stiles had practically become a character unto himself.

This situation was different in every way. He could not hide behind Eldrick's persona. His audience of one had no reason to look upon him with any shred of good opinion. And he *wanted* her good opinion.

Nothing to it but going through, he thought—the same advice he gave himself when faced with the blank page and insecurities about his ability to write another word that anyone would want to read. He'd simply speak the words he needed to say and do so without thinking long on them.

"I must apologize for my behavior yesterday."

"You . . . really?" Grace pulled back an inch. Or had he imagined the movement? Her eyes widened slightly; he was quite sure of that much.

She didn't expect an apology, he realized, then decided to hurry on and finish the speech before she could reject him soundly.

"The name you use to introduce yourself to the world is a personal matter. I had no right to intrude upon your privacy. Doing so was hypocritical of me, when I am in a similar situation. I regret declaring the surname I saw, regret it more than you can imagine. It was entirely ungentlemanly of me. I was up late into the night stewing over the matter."

And over Grace in general, but she needn't know that.

"You were?" She tilted her head to one side, and the formal, superior mask she seemed intent on maintaining slipped just a bit. "You lost sleep over"—she moved her hand in a circle, indicating their table—"what happened here?"

"Yes," he said, unable to hold back a smile. "My mother would be furious with me if she knew of my abominable behavior. She probably *is* furious from the other side, God rest her soul. If she could, she'd send me to bed without dinner and lecture me over how she raised me to be better than that. And I'd have to agree with her."

"About going to bed without dinner?" Grace asked with a glint of humor in her eye.

He chuckled at her attempt at levity but then fell silent. He'd said his piece. Now he had to wait for her response to it.

For several seconds, Grace regarded him but said nothing more. He felt her studious gaze pass over him and felt not unlike a sheep at market, being weighed and measured to determine its worth. Would he be found wanting?

At long last, her gaze reached his hands, and then she ended her inspection by looking at her own hands. "You look like a bookkeeper."

Since the wee small hours of the night, when he'd decided to apologize, he'd imagined a thousand possible responses Grace might give. *You look like a bookkeeper* was not one of them.

"Pardon?" he said rather lamely.

"Your fingers are covered in ink." She gestured with one hand at some blurry black marks on his hands. "I never imagined a novelist with hands like that."

"Well, I . . ."

"They weren't stained yesterday."

"You noticed that, did you?" Marshall was impressed on the instant, though he instinctively rubbed his thumb over the ink, wishing he'd been more careful refilling his fountain pen last night. The dim lamp hadn't provided the best light, and the rocking of the train, combined with general fatigue, hadn't made his hands as steady as they usually were. At home, he often had ink-stained fingers, especially on days he wrote for several hours at a stretch, but in public, he took better care to keep his hands clean. At least, he did when he traveled as Eldrick.

"What changed?" she asked, as if she genuinely wanted to know.

He wanted to tell her—at least some of what happened. "I couldn't sleep last night, so I wrote for a spell." About her, of course.

"You really are a writer, then."

He sat back and regarded her in much the same manner as she had him a moment before. He folded his arms. "You didn't believe me."

"I hadn't heard of Eldrick Stiles," she said. "I've since learned that he is indeed a novelist of some acclaim. But I had to ask; Eldrick Stiles is assumed by some to be quite old and feeble. I couldn't be sure that you were he."

"Well, I am him. Or is that, 'I am *he*'?" He laughed and shook his head. "I'm better writing words than speaking them, I'm afraid."

"I wouldn't know."

"As you've said." Marshall disliked attention from strangers, and he disliked being known solely for his books when he was so much more than the words bound in his novels. Many people imagined his life to be one of glamorous travels and servants waiting on him. They didn't know how mundane his daily life looked, how dull and boring and painful and frustrating and even depressing his work could be.

Readers rarely considered that he had a life outside of his books. They never imagined that yes, he, too, got blisters from walking too far, suffered head colds in the winter, and misplaced belongings like anyone else. He grew hungry and tired and heartsick like any other person.

Being treated like a regular person instead of a famous one was refreshing. But to have found someone who'd never heard of his books or his pen name at all, and for that person to be someone about his age, and from London, no less, was a slight blow to the ego.

"What do you write about?" Grace asked. "I've heard one of your titles, but it didn't tell me what kind of book it is."

"Which title is that?"

"*Of Flame and Ash*."

"Of course. I should have guessed." That book was his first big success.

"What is it about?"

Goodness, how to answer? He'd observed enough of Grace Thompson to know that she had a quick wit, an extraordinary intelligence, and a keen eye for detail. Did she want to know about his work because she genuinely found the topic interesting, or would the information be ammunition for her next volley?

When he didn't answer right away, she prodded him. "I can always read it to find out." Her tone was half threat, half teasing.

"Maybe I should insist on it. That would mean another sale."

"As if you need more." She shrugged one shoulder. "If you're as successful as all that, I can find someone who owns the book and will to lend it to me." Her words seemed to hint that she disliked him, but everything else contradicted that. She leaned forward on her arms against the table. Her voice had warmed and softened to the point that it no longer resembled the aloof one from before. She seemed to be enjoying herself, as he was.

He leaned in, matching her position and drawing their faces closer together. "Borrow and read as many as you please."

"Tell me what it's about." Her tone implied a dare.

"Very well. I'm sure you have better things to do with your time than read my books."

"Hmm," she said, as if debating the point. "Perhaps." But her closed-mouth smile revealed sparkling eyes and dimples.

He was suddenly willing to divulge every moment of his past if doing so meant gaining her favor. *Except, perhaps, about where I grew up.* She might be sympathetic to a childhood of poverty and a lot more he'd experienced, but centuries of difficult history had created a rift between his homeland of Ireland and England. He'd found success as a writer as many Dubliners had, but he'd also followed many of them in coming to London for an education, learning how to speak properly, and making his name as a Londoner. No one asked about the city he'd been born in, and as the stories of his past fit as easily in England, he didn't correct others when they assumed he was born there.

"I write about things I've experienced and seen."

"That's broad and potentially dull. Please tell me that you write about more than the shapes of smokestacks and the colors of cobblestones."

"I might have mentioned those things in passing, but my books are about people and the common struggles of life—families torn apart, poverty, illness, tragedy."

"So they're happy, delightful reads." Her dimples deepened.

He blushed slightly. "They're not easy subjects, but my stories leave readers with hope. At least, they do for me."

"How so?" Her easy, relaxed manner and genuine question took him off guard but in a very good way. Again he wanted to tell her about his life, share something with her that he hadn't shared with others.

"I hope to show triumph over adversity, particularly over trials that are thrust upon those who do nothing to deserve or cause their misfortunes."

Grace's eyes grew more serious. "Have you experienced those things, then?"

"Which things?"

She seemed to ponder before repeating the list he'd given a moment before. "A family torn apart, poverty, illness, tragedy . . ." She counted them out on her fingers, and as her voice trailed off, he found his chest tightening with emotion he hadn't felt in ages. Emotion he'd buried beneath his stories.

Emotion he'd thought he'd carved out of his being by giving them to his characters to suffer through and overcome.

Somehow, this remarkable woman had seen straight through to his core, had tapped into the essence of who he was, and had *seen* him in a way he could not recall ever being seen. Since the publication and success of his first book, *The Blackbird*, he'd never experienced such a thing—someone who knew of his success as a writer and still viewed him as someone who'd lived both before and after a book's publication. Someone who'd experienced a childhood and adolescence, someone more than a figure who scribbled words and strung sentences together for the entertainment of the masses. Someone who'd first begun writing as a way to let the pain out.

She *saw* him.

The welling emotion grew stronger in his chest, and he waited for it to ebb slightly before he dared speak, or he would have wept in front of a lady, and he couldn't have borne that. "I have experienced them," he said simply. "All of them."

Grace reached across the table and placed a hand over his. The unexpected weight and warmth melted him inside; he never wanted her to let go. He yearned to turn his hand over, palm up, so he could clasp hers.

"I don't know the details of what you've endured," she said, "but I suspect there is much that only you know. If I'm guessing correctly, and I think I am, your life is far less glamorous than people assume, and perhaps far lonelier."

How did she know? He nodded, not trusting himself to speak until a second wave of emotion retreated slightly. Hearing such words from someone else, even from Grace while she wore her mask, he might have been offended. But Grace Thompson was no ordinary woman, and her question came from a place of not just compassion, but empathy.

When he could speak, he looked into her eyes, which now glinted with unshed tears of her own. "How did you know? Are you a writer, too?"

She shook her head and laughed lightly, sending a couple of tears down her cheeks. "Definitely not." She removed her hand from his and tugged a handkerchief from the cuff of her sleeve, then dabbed her eyes with the corner. "My work requires similar skills, is all."

"Such as?"

"Attention to detail. Deductive reasoning."

"Then you'll have deduced that I don't talk of myself or my background easily or often."

"Indeed." Grace tucked the kerchief at her wrist.

"I see that any attempt at keeping secrets from you is futile." He held out his arms in surrender. "You know all of my secrets."

"Now *that* I doubt very much."

In a moment of what was likely unrestrained but foolish impulse, he leaned in and asked, "Would you care to spend more of the trip with me? If, after an afternoon together, you determine that you cannot bear the sight of me, I'll never show you my face again." He worried that he sounded too pleading or weak, and nearly withdrew the invitation with a self-deprecating joke.

And she did laugh. Not in a mocking way, but in a beautiful, joyful way. Once more, she rested her hand upon his. This time he did rotate his hand palm up and close his fingers about hers.

"I can't believe I'm saying this," Grace said with a wondering shake of her head, "but I'd be delighted to."

Relief and anticipation came over Marshall, but before he could imagine what the next two days would bring, a waiter appeared, ready to take their orders. Marshall reached for the menus, which were upright against the wall, and opened his to peruse the options.

"Sir. Miss," the waiter said with a nod to each of them. "Good afternoon. How is your day so far?"

Marshall looked up at Grace, amazed at his great fortune of finding such a traveling companion, someone so intriguing and fascinating. How was his day so far? "It's grand altogether."

The waiter acknowledged the response with a nod and turned to Grace. As if a physical wall had dropped between them, she went silent. Marshall lowered his menu and found a familiar, discouraging sight: anger. Her gaze bored into him, and he felt certain that if she'd had her way, he would have become a victim of spontaneous combustion.

When she finally spoke, it was to the waiter. "I won't be having anything, thank you."

Befuddled, Marshall attempted to save the moment. "Grace, I—"

"You continue to lie to me, Eldrick. Or Marshall, or whoever you are."

His brow furrowed. "You know who I am. I haven't lied to you."

"You say you're from London?"

"Yes. I live in Kensington."

"And before that?"

An uneasiness appeared in his middle. "Manchester," he said slowly.

She stood abruptly, leaned against the table with both arms, and said, "Then please explain why you speak like an Irishman."

Before he could answer, before he could gather his wits at all, she marched out of the train car. Marshall dropped his head to his hands and groaned. He hadn't lied; he currently did have a flat in London in Kensington, and prior to that, in Manchester. But he hadn't mentioned that he'd come to Manchester from Dublin, nor that he was born in a tiny flat to poor factory workers of no name or consequence.

He'd built a life and a career on being English, but in a moment of excitement and perhaps a little joy, which he wasn't used to, he'd let his defenses slip. The Irish heart inside the English exterior he'd constructed had become visible, if only for a moment.

It's grand altogether. No Englishman would say that, you dolt.

Why did having her walk away, no matter how angry, make him feel as if he'd lost something dear that had been within his grasp? He'd sworn off women long ago, and he could not think of a single time when losing a woman's favor for any reason had chafed.

But this . . . this felt entirely different.

For a moment, I wasn't lonely. The realization made him even sadder. To an outsider, his melancholy wouldn't make sense: he often spoke to crowds or spoke with one person after another in a long queue as he signed books. He spent his life mostly either alone, writing, or with throngs of people. But no matter how many individuals gathered to see him, he was never truly *with* anyone.

He'd learned from painful experience that one could be entirely alone even while surrounded by readers who adored his work. He wanted to have someone in his life who truly knew him. Someone who would buy strawberry preserves for no reason other than that she knew they were his favorite. Someone who knew that he loved gazing at the moon at night.

Someone he could learn similar things about.

He'd lost the opportunity to learn about Grace's favorite foods and activities. He might never know what her life had been like as a child. He'd felt a connection with another person—with a woman, no less—for but a moment.

He'd forgotten how pleasant conversations deeper than surface greetings and shallow exchanges could be. *Happy.* That's what they could be. Instead of savoring the feeling, instead of nurturing the moment so it might last, he'd allowed it to evaporate as quickly as a splash of water dried on sunbaked Jerusalem limestone.

The waiter appeared at his side, holding an uncorked bottle of wine. "You look as if you could use a glass."

"Indeed I could," Marshall said, and watched the wineglass before him get filled. He'd drink it, but the truth was, for how miserable he felt, he'd need several pints of authentic Guinness to numb the pain.

Eight

G race walked back to her cabin quickly, angry at herself as much as she was at Marshall Bailey, or Eldrick Stiles, or whatever his name really was. She didn't trust him as far as she could throw the train.

He'd confided pieces of a childhood and adolescence filled with hardship, and she'd listened, believing every word, her attention so fully on his words that the dining car could have gone up in flames and she might not have noticed until the smoke obscured his face.

How, after nearly a decade working with a detective agency, had she let her guard down?

She'd been hired by hundreds of women to uncover the misdeeds of their unfaithful husbands. Grace knew all too well what men were really like in their private lives, the secrets they hid from the world because they could. The secrets other men knew and, cigar tucked between their teeth, chuckled over, viewing such behavior as manly and acceptable, even as those very things proved to be the greatest betrayal of their wives.

When the truth came out, the women were at best humiliated. Too often their lives were destroyed, especially when the affair involved an unmarried woman, who might never find a suitable match or employment after being ruined, no matter how high her birth had been.

I listened to him, she thought, fuming, as she withdrew her key and shoved it rather roughly into her door. *I believed him.* How could she have fallen victim to the very charms and shallow claims that so many of her clients became victim to? Had she learned *nothing?*

She marched into her room and slammed the door behind her. When she flipped the lock, she wished she could have done so with a loud noise, perhaps by throwing something at the door, rather than merely sliding the lock into place. Such a small act seemed unfitting for the moment.

A few steps in—about all she could do in the sleeper room—she dropped to her bed with a huff. What bothered her most wasn't the fact that Marshall had been born in Ireland. Unlike many of the English, including a good portion of those who hired her, she didn't view the Irish as lower-class citizens. Rather, they were victims of fate, having had the misfortune to be born in a land where a monarchy treated them like chattel, or like a factory to produce products to sell abroad, not as people with minds and hearts and loved ones.

She'd read "A Modest Proposal." She knew about the Great Famine. Had she known that Marshall Bailey was Irish, the detail might have elevated him in her estimation, not the opposite. Granted, he had no way of knowing that, but he needn't have lied about his origins. Not to her, to whom he'd confided some of his deepest feelings, things he didn't easily share with others. Or so he'd said.

I suppose confidences mean nothing nowadays. If he lied about something so inconsequential, what else would he lie over? What else *had* he lied over already? About being Eldrick Stiles?

No, something told her in her middle that he truly was

the famed author. But he could easily have lied about a dozen other things since boarding the train. He also had too good of an eye for noticing things, something she found disconcerting after so many years of being the observant one in any room or situation.

What has he noticed and deduced—rightly or wrongly— about me? She shuddered, not wanting to know.

Her eyes landed on James Miller's copy of *Of Flame and Ash*, which she'd tossed into the room to avoid Marshall seeing it. The green volume had landed on her pillow at a jaunty angle, front cover on top, as if she'd intentionally placed it so.

To her horror, she watched her arm reach out for the book. Clearly, she had absolutely no self-control at all. *He probably lied about the kinds of things he's experienced. This novel is probably full of inane observations—and extensive descriptions of boring smokestacks and cobblestones. Read it as a way to study another type of mind.*

The last thought was all she needed by way of permission to read the book. She fanned the pages—once, twice, three times—all in an effort to get up the gumption to actually begin. Finally she opened the front cover and turned to the dedication.

To Mother, who is no longer with us. Her example and teachings formed the man I am today. I would be nothing without her. Pretty, but was it sincere? Anyone could pen such a dedication, truth be damned, knowing that such words would appeal to readers and make them all the more senti-mental about the author.

She licked the tip of an index finger and turned to the first page of the first chapter. Not quite prepared to read his words, she looked up at the ceiling, then closed her eyes. When her trembling hands calmed, she tilted her chin down to the book and began to read.

The story told of a young boy forced to work long hours, often walking to and from work in the dark for an hour each way. How the boy worked for wages so meager they barely provided a couple of meager meals for the family each week. Yet without his work, the family would starve. The little boy was only eight years old at the beginning of the tale. He quickly matured, and those passing him on the streets often commented that he had the wisdom of an old man in his eyes because he'd had to learn the ways of the world. Being the man of the house after his father's death a year prior changed him forever.

Tragedy after tragedy befell the boy, continuing until his twentieth year. By then, he'd lost his mother to cholera and three younger siblings in succession to dysentery, measles, and consumption. He'd become bookkeeper at a bank, where he'd started working lowly jobs, such as cleaning the floors.

Grace read and read so long that soon she'd tucked herself into the corner of her bed where the wall that separated her compartment from the next met the outside wall of the train. When the sun disappeared and darkness claimed her space, Grace turned on the electric lamp to read by.

By the last chapter, the boy, named David, had at last found some happiness in work that allowed him to eat, replace his threadbare clothing and hole-riddled boots, pay rent, and even buy coal so as to not be too cold in the winter months.

A woman named Violet entered his life, bringing a new type of joy and purpose to his life . . . and then the book ended.

Tears streaming down her cheeks, Grace flipped through the last few—blank—pages, hoping to find a little more of the moving story, but found not a single additional word. She occasionally found herself wanting more from a book, but not at this level. David had become as real to her as Grandpapa had been. She yearned to know more about Violet and to find adecía

out whether she and David married and had a happy life together.

Yet the ending was fitting. She knew that David and Violet belonged together and would live as one for the rest of their lives, no matter what befell them. She simply wanted to know how their entire love story unfolded, to experience it vicariously.

Perhaps another book continues with their story, she thought hopefully. *I'll ask James in the morning.*

Reluctantly, she closed the book and looked out her window, noting that dawn had crested the horizon. Somehow, she'd read all the night through but didn't feel tired. Grace glanced at her travel clock to check the time—six o'clock. Much too early to find the Millers out and about. She'd have to find James later to both return the book and ask if it had a sequel.

Had Marshall written one? Now that she was no longer in the throes of the story, now that she'd come up for meta-phorical air and returned to the reality of the train chugging along, eating track as it crossed the Alps, her mind kept returning to him. She'd connected with David and his struggles so much that he felt real, his problems visceral. She felt whatever he endured—the freezing cold, the gnawing hunger, the yearning for a home, the worry for the future. Not only the future that was years away, but worry over how he'd eat tomorrow or pay rent in a fortnight.

While she'd personally never experienced privation to such a degree, David most certainly had, and vividly. How did Marshall know what such a life was like? He could have spoken with the poor, the destitute, the homeless. He could have visited debtors' prisons. He certainly never worried about his next meal or whether he could pay rent, not if he lived in Kensington.

159

Could he have endured such a childhood himself? The question hung in the air, barely out of sight in the corner of her eye. She didn't want to look at the question, for that would require inspecting it and answering it. And *that* might result in feeling more for Marshall Bailey than she was prepared for. And that would not do at all. Yet the question refused to be ignored. Did he know such privation?

He is Irish, born in a land not known for its riches, likely of parents who suffered through the Great Famine. He probably did grow up very poor.

How much of this book had been taken from his own life? Quite a lot, if her guess was correct. Even if his past had been easier than David's, even if Marshall had lived through but a tenth of such a life, he was . . . well, she wasn't sure what.

He is someone to admire. The thought appeared unprompted and unexpected. In her experience, *no* man, save Grandpapa, lived a life worthy of admiration. For all she knew, Marshall Bailey had taken advantage of women, embezzled money, and benefitted from the misfortune of others. But the person who'd written the story about David could not have done those things. The man she'd spoken to last night was not a devilish knave.

She debated whether to change into her nightclothes and attempt to sleep for a couple of hours, but David weighed on her mind so much that she knew that sleeping would be impossible. She felt as wide awake as ever, but a few hours from now would likely be another story. A nap later in the day would be in order.

Where should she go now, seeing as she couldn't bear to stay in her quarters? She didn't care how luxurious the Orient Express happened to be; it was still a train, and trains were only so large, with so many possibilities of places to go and things to do.

Perhaps one of the dining cars served breakfast at this early hour. She retrieved her key from the bedside table, and only as she slipped it into her pocket did she realize that her dress was wrinkled after wearing it curled up with a book all night. The chances of anyone but a waiter or porter seeing her in this state seemed remote, so she didn't concern herself with her appearance beyond tucking in a few stray wisps of hair.

What if I see Marshall? Her heart hiccuped at the thought, but she shook her head at herself. Since when did a confident woman with a career and no need for a man—a highly unusual creature to be found anywhere in the world in the nineteenth century—care one whit whether any man, talented and famed writer or not, made an appearance in her day? *Since today, apparently.*

The undeniable refused to be ignored: she had a hankering to learn more about Marshall Bailey. She wanted to uncover what parts of David's story had come from personal experiences and which were from his remarkable imagination. He had a way of empathizing with all kinds of people, of showing the human, frail side of even those one might label a villain in a story context. How did he spin words and sentences into images and emotions that made her care for and feel for so many kinds of people, especially when most of them were nothing like her? So many questions she wanted the answers to.

Could she bear to eat the hearty serving of humble pie that asking Marshall himself would require of her?

Perhaps I could instead ask James Miller. He might have some idea as to what parts of the story were inspired by the author's own life. Yes, that is what she would do. She wouldn't seek out Mr. Bailey.

Grace patted the key in her pocket, then exited her room, heading straight for the dining car she'd twice met Marshall in. Minutes later, she paused just outside the car door. Perhaps her breakfast needs would be better served in another dining area. This one held so many confusing emotions, many of which rushed back as she merely looked through the small window. Foggy condensation blurred the interior, so all she could make out—barely, at that—were general shapes of tables and windows. Her fingers felt cold, and they trembled slightly, though not enough for someone else to notice unless they had a particularly keen eye.

Like Marshall Bailey.

She turned to leave, but suddenly felt cowardly, as if *not* going into the place she'd spoken with—fought with—Mr. Bailey was more than she could bear. But Grandpapa had never shrunk from a challenge or from a fear, and his grand-daughter never would either. Grace Thompson of Harward and Sons was anything but a coward.

She gathered up every drop of fortitude she could and turned on her heel. She walked into the dining car, head held high so she'd appear confident even if she didn't feel it. *Act as you wish you felt*, Grandpapa had often said. *No one will know the difference, and the feeling will often follow.*

So Grace pretended to be confident and nonplussed, even after spotting Marshall Bailey at the far end of the car, reading a newspaper. Fortunately, his back was to her. A ripple of emotions went through her, not all of them unpleasant. She clutched his book to her chest, only then realizing she'd brought it along. A sliver of her wished to remain alone for her early breakfast, but another significantly larger part of her wanted to see him. To speak with him. To sit before Marshall and ask him, not James, how much of David's poignant life had come from his own.

How he'd been so perfectly able to create people and places that had to be from his imagination yet felt so real. And, truth be told, she desperately wanted to know the author's opinion of what David and Violet's future would be.

The door had closed behind her, but she didn't move, only watched Marshall with a very different set of eyes from before. He might be rich. He might be famous all across the globe. He might be traveling under an assumed name—or, rather, traveling under his real name, which in his case amounted to the same thing. He might have not been entirely forthcoming about his past and heritage.

Except in his writing. Within the pages of his book, he'd been utterly, almost nakedly, honest. His creation, David, was Irish and struggling to survive, hoping for his own drop of happiness one day. Not riches or wealth, but common, simple happiness.

Is Marshall happy? Has he found his Violet?

A waiter appeared before her, from where she did not know, but he was the same man who'd recognized Marshall as Eldrick Stiles. "Good morning, miss."

The sound of his voice made Marshall glance over his shoulder, but instead of turning back to perusing the newspaper, he did a double take and stared at Grace. He looked surprised, but she couldn't tell if her arrival was a pleasant or an unwelcome one. His eyes left her face and landed briefly on the book clutched to her chest in one arm. He had to have recognized it at once, because his cheeks pinked, and he turned back around to his paper.

In that moment, he'd looked downright insecure, which she rather liked. That put her back into a position of control. But why did he feel insecure? Did he care what she thought of his book? She dearly hoped so, because she was starting to like him—as the creator of David, but also recognizing that to a great extent, David had to contain parts of Marshall himself. The two were not interchangeable, of course, but they shared enough similarities to merit admiration and compassion.

Who would have thought a man *would elicit compassion from me?* She had so many questions about Marshall, and she was drawn to him in a way she could not explain any more than she could explain why her resistance to the feeling was slowly but surely slipping away.

Instead of fighting the pull she felt toward Marshall, she let it build, warming her and sending a thrill of excitement through her like nothing she'd ever experienced. Reminding herself that he was *a man* only intensified the sensations, in a good way. Not only was he a man, but he was a handsome, intelligent, compassionate man.

The waiter leaned closer to her and whispered conspiratorially, "Few people know this, but I'm somewhat obsessed with following Eldrick Stiles's movements, so I've learned a few things you may find interesting."

Grace turned her back so Marshall couldn't see her face or attempt to read her lips. "Oh, definitely," she said, matching his whisper.

The waiter glanced briefly over her shoulder at Marshall and then focused on her. "He has spent most of his fortune helping the poor and needy. He's been known to use book tours as excuses to secretly do charity work in the cities he visits."

She resisted the urge to turn about to look at Marshall. He'd know they were talking about him if he caught her gaze. "But doesn't he usually tour in large cities, like Paris?"

"And where do you suppose the greatest number of poor live, but in a grand metropolis? He's fed and clothed people not only in Paris, but also in Madrid, Berlin, Rome . . ."

"Really," she said, as admiration and respect for Marshall grew in her chest.

"Sometimes he does more, such as on the trip he's returning from. I got him to speak of it last night."

One side of her mouth curled into a smile. "He told you on the condition of keeping his confidence."

When the waiter tilted his head back and forth as if he were helpless, she chuckled. "What did he say?"

"He's returning from a month-long visit to the Holy Land."

Her eyes widened at that, but the waiter went on.

"He built homes and wells and delivered food and medical supplies for the poorest of the poor. All of which he paid for."

"Truly?" she whispered, though she knew the answer.

"Eldrick Stiles is known for spending his considerable wealth on helping others because he knows what it is like to be poor." The waiter shrugged. "Or so they say, though he's never revealed anything significant about his past."

"My goodness. That is amazing."

The waiter politely cleared his throat and spoke at a regular tone. "May I find you a table and get you something to eat, Miss—"

"Thompson," she said. "Miss Thompson." Saying her true surname felt good. "I would like both a table and a menu, thank you."

Now to get up the gumption to say the rest. Marshall might not want to speak with her, and after learning even more about the remarkable man that he was, she'd likely find herself tongue-tied and nervous—utterly out of control. She could not explain why that possibility didn't change the fact that she wanted to speak with him, share breakfast with him. What were these confusing emotions spinning about inside her?

"And . . . if he doesn't object, I'd like to sit by Mr. Bailey." The moment the words left her mouth, she worried they'd been the wrong thing to say.

She and the waiter both looked at the sole passenger in the dining car, waiting for his reaction. Marshall had turned about in his seat and rested one arm on the back of his chair as he eyed Grace from head to foot. Her hair was still rather mussed, and her dress so rumpled that it looked as if she'd slept in it, which wasn't far from the truth. No doubt he noticed every detail of her unkempt appearance, from her wrinkled skirts to her mussed hair.

What would he say to the suggestion of sharing a table?

In response, he nodded, stood, and gestured toward the chair across from him.

Nine

Grace said not a word as she took her seat across from Marshall. She was allowing herself to think of him as that again, rather than solely as Mr. Bailey. How could she use such a formal term when, after reading *Of Ash and Flame*, she felt as if she knew him intimately?

But she didn't, not really. And she'd judged him, harshly. Grandpapa would be at least as ashamed of her as she was of herself.

The waiter had followed her. Avoiding Marshall's gaze entirely, she looked over and ordered toast and eggs. He nodded with a slight bow and left, which meant that she and Marshall were now the car's only occupants. He had yet to move his eyes from her, and his gaze felt like a heavy blanket weighing her down that she needed to shake off just to breathe.

She hoped he'd be the first one to break the silence, but when he didn't say a word, her eyes remained on the floor beside the table. Her heart thumped uncomfortably, so hard that a vein in her wrist visibly pulsed. Grace tried to breathe deeply in and out, as Grandpapa had taught her when she was little and frightened over a nightmare after hearing about a particularly grisly case he was working on. A case that, of course, she wasn't supposed to know anything about.

That night after bedtime, she'd scampered up their stairs, away from her mother's watchful eye—or had it been Grandmama's? Grace couldn't remember for sure, as her parents had both died when she herself was very young. Perhaps Mama had already been taken so ill that she was in bed and quite simply *couldn't* have prevented mischievous Grace from having her run of the place.

However it had happened, Grace had found herself in the stairwell, hearing a man with a deep, gravelly voice discuss blood spatters and other things that made her freeze in place, unable to move from fear. She slipped back to bed, and when the words she'd heard turned into nightmares, Grandpapa was the one who had responded to her cries. He taught her how to breathe deeply to calm a racing heart, ease frayed nerves, and restore peace of mind.

The technique had never failed her, no matter what she'd felt. But she hadn't ever quite felt this way before, and Grandpapa's breathing trick didn't work on it.

When the weight of Marshall's gaze became too much, she lifted her face to his, slightly biting her lower lip—a habit from childhood that cropped up when she was anxious. She stopped and licked her lips, determined not to do it again.

"Marshall," she began, then corrected herself. "Mr. Bailey, I—"

"Please," he interjected. "Call me Marshall."

At that, she looked directly at him for the first time that morning. His face was ashen and haggard, his hair not slicked back but sticking out every which way, as if he'd combed it with both hands multiple times. Faint blue circles beneath his eyes bore testament to his weariness. And the look in his eyes—in his entire being—seemed to plead with her.

"Very well . . . Marshall . . ."

Now that she was looking right at him, she noted the rumpled state of his shirt and coat and that his cravat was untied and hanging about his neck. He looked positively awful. Perhaps he was drunk . . .

For the tiniest fleck of time, she almost wished he were. Having the author of David's tale be inebriated by night and hungover by day would set the world as she knew it to rights. The Marshall she knew, and the Eldrick she'd read, had done a fine job of tilting her understanding of the world off its foundation. Reading his book had sent her adrift, floundering as she tried to make sense of a man with such compassion and deep emotion, a man who saw the good in humanity and, according to their waiter, actively worked for the good of humanity as well.

How many people did she know—male *or* female—who spoke pretty words about helping the poor and homeless but did nothing more than contribute a few pennies to charitable causes every year? Yet here was a man who secretly spent his money in a way that attempted to make the world a better place. He tried to ease the suffering of at least a few people through his quiet deeds.

"*Of Ash and Flame* made me want to be a better person," Grace said, finally breaking the silence. She set the book on the table before her, then clasped her trembling hands in her lap. She'd faced jealous and jilted lovers threatening her with swords and lead balls, but those situations hadn't made her frame quake like this.

"Thank you," was all he said. Even his voice sounded tired.

Drunk? No. He did not have the bloodshot, red-rimmed eyes of a drunk, and he spoke and moved with perfect ease and intention. Nothing like someone who'd spent a night drinking one cocktail after another.

You've judged him long enough, she told herself. *Unjustly.*

Guilt tugged at her conscience—another feeling she didn't typically experience. In her line of work, she'd often told half-truths and occasionally outright lies to uncover the information she needed, and she'd never felt a twinge of conscience over any of it. The ends, as they said, justified the means.

Yet this morning, she seemed to be drowning in guilt over her own actions. And the amazing man before her, the mind who had written the story of young David, had borne the brunt of her assumptions.

"I must apologize to you ... Marshall." Saying his Christian name was harder than she'd expected, but she wanted to do as he'd asked.

"I thought apologies were something *I* did."

She looked up to see a sardonic smile, and she smiled in return, then let her gaze drift back to the table—and to the book. "I judged you most harshly without ever giving you an opportunity to defend yourself."

"True," he said.

"You must know that my reaction was not due to your birth in Ireland."

"It wasn't?" he sounded genuinely shocked. Considering the difficult and painful relationship between England and Ireland, she could understand why. Many of her own country-men looked down upon the Irish, viewing them as barely human.

"Not at all. My grandpapa was Irish, you know, though he came to England when he was but ten, so he acquired an English accent."

Marshall, who'd been leaning back on his chair, now came forward. "Are you saying that your grandpapa—whom

I can tell you deeply love and respect—hides his true place of birth, as I do?"

"Yes. Rather, he *did*. He passed away five years ago."

"Oh, I am so sorry." And he sounded sorry. Grace could not understand a world in which a man this *good* existed.

"What bothered me is that after confiding part of your past, you'd hid that part from me." Grace lifted both hands, palm upward, in a sign of surrender. "I don't know why that mattered so much. Of all people, I should understand."

"And yet." Marshall said the two words as a statement, a way to encourage her to continue, not as a question.

"And yet," she repeated with a nod of acknowledgment. "My line of work has, shall we say, jaded me."

"What *is* your line of work?"

Should she tell him? She quickly weighed the possible risks and settled with, "I work for Harward and Sons." If he didn't know the company name, let him think what he would of the nature of the business.

"The renowned detective agency. That's where you took your false name from. Fascinating." He leaned against an arm of his chair as if settling in for an enjoyable tale.

"You've heard of it," she said, and when he nodded, she figured that there was no use in pretending she merely did the books. "I've been a detective for several years now, and in that time, I've seen so many tragic and heart-wrenching situations, so many disloyal, cruel, and downright evil men, that I've learned to approach them all with caution—"

"Suspicion, accusation . . ."

Grace lifted one eyebrow at him. "Yes, I suppose those, too." How could she make him understand? She settled with, "Alas, men continually prove their mettle as being precisely what I predicted."

"Do you suppose you're seeing what you expect to see?"

Marshall's tone was unexpectedly curious rather than accusatory. He genuinely wanted to know, which made her mull it over before answering.

"Perhaps in part, yes." Another difficult admission. "Most often, I have found plenty of evidence to prove men to be rogue, scoundrels, and worse. I've come across precious few men who did not fall under that category. The one exception was my grandfather, who founded the company."

She expected Marshall to be offended by her blunt statements, but instead he nodded thoughtfully, then leaned his arms against the table and steepled his fingers. "Could that be because the people most likely to reach out for your help are the victims of such scoundrels, and not that half the human species is doomed to be vile?"

"I suppose that is a possibility," Grace said reluctantly. She hadn't thought of her experiences in those terms before, but his theory made sense. Why would a happily married woman hire a detective to prove that her husband was, indeed, a stand-up fellow? She'd known Marshall Bailey hardly any time at all, yet she could not imagine him filled with evil, or mischief, or any other vice. Her shoulders softened in her seat. Indeed, her entire bearing softened under his continued attention.

Had he leaned even closer? She couldn't be sure, but suddenly she could smell him—something that reminded her of leather and wood and something else, maybe the hint of paper, which reminded her of vanilla. Perhaps the scent of his leather-bound notebooks contributed.

At last, to distract herself from the heady smells, she shook her head. "I cannot make heads or tails of any of this."

"Of what, precisely?" He looked both amused and confused at once.

"Of you." She took a steadying breath and looked straight

at him. "I thought I understood men completely. For years, I've known how to—"

"Get what you wish from them." It wasn't a question, but he hadn't understood her intentions.

"Not quite."

"Are you saying you don't intentionally flirt with men?"

"Oh, I do." She'd never put her reasons into words, and trying to made her eyes mist up. "I want to prevent more women from being hurt. If I can get a man's attention, knowing how to avoid getting hurt, perhaps I can help save another woman who might fall for a rake, unaware of the dangers."

"You believed I was a danger to other women?"

Heat rushed Grace's cheeks. "I know now that you wouldn't—couldn't—be." She lowered her gaze to the book, and with one finger, traced the gold embossed lettering. "Anyone who could write this story must be a good person."

"Th-thank you." Marshall seemed taken aback by her sincerity.

She lifted her face to his. "I am quite in earnest. This book is . . . remarkable." She could think of no other way to put it. "It changed me. I'll never be the same."

He wet his lips, then ventured, "Should I apologize for that?"

Grace laughed aloud and shook her head. "Not at all. It's a good change. I'm the one who needs to apologize to you, not the other way around."

Goodness, he was handsome. Her cheeks felt hotter. "I am so sorry for how I misjudged you and treated you."

His voice lowered and took on a hushed tone. "Apology accepted." He seemed to mean something more than those two words. His gaze traveled about her face and returned to her eyes. He reached across the table for her hand, and she didn't pull away as the Grace of the day before would have. He gently brushed his thumb across her knuckles, still looking intently at her. She felt so giddy, unsure of herself—and grateful to be sitting. Otherwise she might well have dropped to the floor in a heap.

"Grace?" he said, still with that soft, tender voice.

"Mm?" She could hardly think straight as he stroked her hand; her skin felt afire in the most delicious way.

"Would you spend your days with me for the remainder of the train journey to Paris?"

Once more, her heart hiccuped, and when she regained control of her voice, she said, "No." His face paled, and his brows drew together at the rejection, so she hurried on. "What I mean is that I'd prefer to continue as traveling companions all the way to London."

His face lit up again, his dejection gone as if rain had washed it away. "Across the Channel and everything?"

"Unless you decide I'm too much to bear, in which case, *I* promise to leave *you* be."

"Hmm," he said, clearly pretending to concentrate. "Very well. But on one condition."

"Oh, and what might that be?"

He reached for her other hand, now holding both, each one of hers wrapped inside one of his. The heat warmed her fingers, and she could have sworn that a thread of warmth shot up her arms and filled her body. "Let me see your life—experience your life—after we reach London. If *you* can bear getting to know me better, all the better. And if not, well, perhaps I'll have learned a few things I can use in my next book."

She was enjoying the banter now. Grace squeezed his hands. "What of my life might you put into a book?"

"Perhaps my next heroine will be a detective."

She tilted her head in challenge. "Writing such a character would require intense research."

He smiled just enough to make dimples appear, which made her middle flip and soar. He leaned even closer now, until she could feel his breath on her face. "Perhaps years?"

She could not have remembered her own name in that moment, so overwhelmed was she with his presence and attentions. "Years," she said. "Definitely years."

"Then there's only one way to settle such an agreement."

"Years?" she said again, her voice scarcely more than a breath. "Promise?" As scared as she suddenly was, she was equally drawn to him and could not bear to pull away. Any thoughts of future investigations automatically included Marshall in some way. She could not imagine her life without him. How could they have met so recently?

Nearer and nearer he drew, until their lips nearly touched. "I promise. I'll need years and years to do my research."

Unable to wait a moment more, she closed the remaining distance by pressing her lips to his. Something in her middle twirled and exploded and settled only when she pulled her lips a hair's breadth away from him.

"Yes," she said. "Years and years."

Annette Lyon is a *USA Today* bestselling author, a four-time recipient of Utah's Best of State medal for fiction, a Whitney Award winner, and a five-time publication award winner from the League of Utah Writers. She's the author of more than a dozen novels, even more novellas, and several nonfiction books. When she's not writing, knitting, or eating chocolate, she can be found mothering and avoiding housework. Annette is a member of the Women's Fiction Writers Association and is represented by Heather Karpas at ICM Partners.

Find Annette online:
Blog: http://blog.AnnetteLyon.com
Twitter: @AnnetteLyon
Facebook: http://Facebook.com/AnnetteLyon
Instagram: https://www.instagram.com/annette.lyon/
Pinterest: http://Pinterest.com/AnnetteLyon
Newsletter: http://bit.ly/1n3I87y

Married on the
Orient Express

NANCY CAMPBELL ALLEN

One

Detective Vincent Brady stood in the shadows of a cluttered warehouse, straining against the noise outside and attempting to overhear the muted conversation taking place behind several large crates of whiskey.

"... got a telegram today from Bernard in Constantinople."

"Jon, I can explain . . ."

"Says when his captain realized what you were trying to get from the American, he took the bloke hostage to collect the thing for himself." The voice was low, controlled, the calm before the storm, and Jimmy Mattingly clearly realized it.

He cleared his throat and answered, "I didn't know Bernard would tell his captain why we needed the American."

"And why do we need the American, Jimmy?"

The pause was pained, and Vincent almost pitied the younger man. "He has the statue, the one missing from the crates."

"*Why* does he have it?"

Jimmy's answer was slow and reluctant. "I lost it over a bad hand, thought it was one of them fakes you sometimes pass off to rich toffs what don't know better."

A thud sounded, the unmistakable hallmark of fist hitting flesh. "Who is this American?" Jon ground out.

Jimmy coughed and spit. "Trevor brought 'im along." More coughing. "I didn't know, Jon, I swear. I didn't know it were real gold."

Vincent winced on behalf of the young man, who was the recipient of another loud smack—one that sent him stumbling, as evidenced by the crashing of crates. Jon Mattingly was not a criminal most trifled with, and his younger brother, Jimmy, ought to have known better. For Jimmy to have lifted an artifact from Jon's stolen stash and lost it in a card game—the fool must have had a death wish.

"Why in blazes did you contact Bernard with this?"

Vincent chanced a peek around the crate. A stocky man stood over a slighter figure sprawled on the floor amidst a broken crate and several whiskey bottles that spilled onto the dirty wooden planks. Jimmy groaned and rolled to his side. He slowly regained his feet and wobbled before his brother, cradling his jaw.

"I wanted to handle it on my own—it was my mess, I wanted to clean it up—but before I could get it back from the American, he left town," Jimmy mumbled, and held out a hand when his brother growled. "Went with Trevor on the Express."

Jon pulled the cap from his head in clear frustration. "Multiple stops on that line!"

Jimmy nodded miserably. "Sent a telegram to our contacts in each city."

Jon looked at his brother, jaw slackening. In all the months Vincent had followed, spied on, and investigated the kingpin, he'd never seen him at a loss for words. Clearly the criminal was regretting promoting his younger brother to second-in-command.

"You're telling me every contact between here and the Bosporus knows we're missing a gold Egyptian statue worth a fortune?" Jon paused. "Do you realize what you've done?"

Silence stretched, and Vincent wondered if Jon would hit Jimmy again. He didn't envy the younger man—Jon Mattingly had fists the size of wine barrels. He took several deep breaths, turned and paced two steps, and slowly returned to his brother.

"Our contacts' loyalties are not blind. Every one of 'em will be looking for this American, and not all will feel obliged to return the statue to us." He sighed and rubbed his face. "Stupid bloke oughta consider himself lucky he's already been caught—half of Europe will be looking for him."

Jimmy nodded and ran a hand over his matted hair. "I'll fix it."

Jon shot a dark look at his brother. "How are you gonna do that?"

"Don't know, but I'll do it." He coughed, winced, and put a hand around his ribs.

"I need to think," Jon muttered, and turned when a door leading to the alley opened a crack.

Vincent leaned quietly back into the shadows as a sliver of light spilled in from the waning daylight outside.

"What is it?" Jon barked.

"'Gram for ye, sir," a young voice echoed into the cavernous space.

"Bring it."

The light tread of small feet, a clink of two coins into a half-gloved hand, and Vincent heard the child exit, closing the door quietly behind him.

Jon paused for a long heartbeat, then two, and cursed soundly. "The bloke don't have the statue. It's with his sister, heading back to America. They're holding him there until she brings it to 'em! That'll take weeks, and I have a buyer comin' in ten days."

Vincent heard Jimmy's exhalation. "Wait, wait! What's today's date . . . she's still here!"

"How do you know that?" Jon's voice rose in volume.

"He said . . . he said he and Trev were goin' the next day on the Orient Express, and his sister were staying behind another week to visit some dusty museums and then goin' back home. The game were only four days ago."

Vincent snuck another look around the crates. Jon paced like a caged beast, and Jimmy put a thumb to his mouth where blood trickled from a split lip.

"Find her," Jon growled. "Find that woman. Do you know her name?"

"Last name's Grant. That's all I know. But I'll find 'er."

"Get in, get out, make it quick and clean. Bring it to me the minute you have it and maybe I'll let you live."

Vincent waited until the two men left before slipping out behind them into the dank alley that ran along the warehouses near the quay. A blast of wind caught him, and he turned his collar up, shoving his hands deep into his pockets.

He'd been tailing Jon Mattingly for weeks, hoping to track down artifacts recently stolen from an archaeological dig in Egypt that was funded by an influential Italian countess. Jon was clever, though, and had slipped through the Yard's clutches for years. His criminal network was extensive, and he had resources that allowed him to evade the law repeatedly. If he had a weakness, though, it was his younger brother. Had the other man in the warehouse been anyone but Jimmy, Vincent would have been witness to a murder rather than a tame thrashing.

Vincent pulled his hat down against another cold blast of wind and rain as he hailed a cab and gave the man instructions to take him to the Yard. He wasn't far on foot from MPS offices but felt a sense of urgency in the light of his newly acquired information. The woman, Miss Grant, was in danger and completely unaware.

But for the grace of God, Vincent might be where Jon Mattingly was. A stern ultimatum in his youth from a judge who had known Vincent's grandfather had put him on a path leading to the right side of the law, but Vincent often wondered if his past would eventually chase him to ground. His life now put him in direct opposition to the people he'd run with in his youth. His knowledge of the streets made him invaluable as a Scotland Yard detective but had him constantly watching his back. His former friends didn't find his position humorous in the least, and he couldn't blame them. He supposed he'd have felt the same way if one of his cronies had turned himself into a bobby and then a detective and had worked to shed the grime and coarse manners of his youth.

Vincent looked out of the carriage window to the darkening streets, gaslights shining against the backdrop of a steady misting rain. Before long, New Scotland Yard appeared to his view, and he quickly paid the driver and jogged to the front door. In recent days he'd resisted the impulse born by long habit to turn his steps toward 4 Whitehall Place. The Yard had outgrown its former home, whose back door had opened onto Great Scotland Yard and given the Metropolitan Police Service its nickname, and now made its home on Victoria Embankment overlooking the Thames. The former buildings held a sense of nostalgia for Vincent, but he had to admit the move had long been necessary. A decade shy of a new century had nearly thirteen thousand police constables and detectives working the force, and the administrative staff required to support it made the move inevitable.

Vincent removed his hat and ran the steps to his chief detective's offices in the Metropolitan Crime Division.

"Brady, come in and close the door," Chief Inspector Lampley said, glancing up from his desk. "What do you have?"

Vincent sank into the chair opposite the desk and exhaled. He recounted the conversation he'd heard between the Mattingly brothers and ran his hand along the base of his neck. Tension had been building for weeks, and the resulting headache had become so familiar he was learning to be comfortable with it.

"So close," he muttered to Lampley. "What I wouldn't give to be able to haul them all into the cells right now."

Lampley nodded and tossed his pen on his desk. He sat back in his chair with a deep breath and exhaled; Vincent knew the chief inspector's exhaustion matched his own. "Can't chance it until we have evidence enough to convict. Now, however, we must locate the woman. This Miss Grant. I'll task Hansen and Ashman immediately with checking local hotels."

"Yes, sir. And I'll do the same. Jimmy's desperate to atone for his mistake—he'll bring the woman to harm if she resists or stands in his way."

"Offer police protection and bring her in with the artifact. We'll lock it up until the home office can send someone for it, and we'll put Miss Grant under guard in a safe house until we can retrieve her brother." Lampley yawned and rubbed his eyes. "I best get on the telephone and have Andrew send some telegrams. A stolen artifact from Egypt, from a dig funded by an Italian countess, and an American citizen abducted by criminals in Constantinople who have links to an English crime ring. This may well become an international embarrassment to the Crown, at the very least."

And the lives of a hapless American who won in a card game what he likely believed was a quirky trinket, and his innocent sister, were now Vincent's responsibility. He quietly exhaled and stood, stretching his tired limbs. He was cold and uncomfortable and wanted nothing more than to return to his rooms at his quiet boarding house and settle in with a fire, a good book, and a nice glass of brandy. It would have to wait; resigned, he greeted Hansen and Ashman as the constables entered to receive instructions.

Two

Emily Grant stood at the ferry window as the ship crossed the English Channel, but saw only her reflection in the glass, as the world outside was dark. Mercifully, a purser dimmed the interior lights and she finally saw, without obstruction, the twinkling lights of the French shoreline. She was fortunate to have caught the last ferry heading across— sprinting to board had wreaked havoc with her coiffure and forced her to crush her hat in her gloved fingers lest the wind snatch it away—but relief at her good luck quickly dimmed as she caught her breath for the first time in two hours and considered the reason for her mad dash.

Kenton had gone and gotten himself abducted. In Constantinople. She closed her eyes and leaned her forehead against the cool window glass. Of *course* he had. And why wouldn't he? When Kenton did a thing, he did it with pomp, circumstance, and flair. And a healthy dose of idiocy. He was her elder by five years, and yet from childhood, Emily had been the responsible one.

The holiday to Europe had been a welcome rest from the recent stress of caring for her father; his passing, while sad, was a relief. He'd no longer been himself, had not even recognized her or Kenton toward the end. He hadn't remembered Emily's mother had been dead for ten years, often confused Kenton for his uncle Stanley, who had fought in the War of 1812, and wondered how "Stanley" had managed to regrow the leg he'd lost in battle.

Elias Grant had been a wise businessman in his good years, however, and had left his two children a respectable inheritance. Coupled with savings from the salary Emily earned as a shopgirl, the money from her father would care for her nicely in the future. Even if she never did manage to "snag a husband," as her neighbors expressed it.

The telegram had arrived for Emily at the hotel, and while innocent enough to the casual observer, as she had read it her heart pounded in alarm. *Enjoying the stay in Constantinople. Trevor has gone home, but a fellow here insists I remain until you arrive with the birthday gift I gave you. Board next Orient Express posthaste, as I shall be sad until you are here. You only, nobody else. Yours ever, Kenton Eldon Grant III.*

They had developed a code. If ever one of them were in trouble of any sort, the message to each other would involve the salutation, "Yours ever," followed by the entire name. Their mother had scolded them as children with their full names. "Emily Anne Grant, I am vexed with you!" Admittedly, Emily was on the receiving end much less frequently; Kenton was the one who found himself constantly on their mother's nerves. On the occasions where Kenton sucked Emily into his antics, whether she'd participated or not, they heard each of those names spoken at high volume.

Emily never referred to Kenton as "Kenton Eldon Grant the Third," and when they'd embarked on their holiday, she'd suggested almost as an afterthought that should they find themselves in dire straits but couldn't be plain in raising the alarm, they would explain as much as possible and sign formally. Kenton had called her ridiculous, had said there was nothing about either of them to ever warrant any kind of danger or abduction, and that if such were the case, they should also say "fellow insists I remain here." She'd scowled at him for mocking her, and he'd nudged her and winked and insisted that they would be safe as children in a nursery.

So now, the best Emily could gather, he was being held by someone in Constantinople who wanted the golden pharaoh statue Kenton had given her before he left. The "not truly gold statue I won in a card game, but it is rather pretty and surely worth *some* money, so happy birthday, Em!" Emily had raised a brow, shaken her head, accepted his kiss on her cheek, and then packed away the statue to ship home. The thing was on the small side—perhaps standing twelve inches tall—but was respectably heavy. She'd wondered what sort of metal had been used in constructing it and figured the exterior to be gold leaf or similar overlay. It was extraordinary, she'd realized, and her artist's eye had found no flaw in its construction or design. She couldn't even find a seam to indicate casting.

She drew in a deep breath as the Calais shoreline approached. Clearly, the statue must have been genuine. It gave her pause to realize she'd held a solid gold item in her hands but gave her more pause when she reflected that even as she stood aboard the ferry to France, the statue was on its way back to America. She had packed her and Kenton's numerous souvenirs and sent them ahead the day before, deciding to lighten her load for the remaining week in London.

Upon receipt of the telegram, she had solicited help from the concierge in obtaining immediate passage to France and before departure had dashed to a shop she'd frequented upon her arrival in London. The shop carried items of both Egyptian and Oriental themes, and she'd located a statuette comparable in size to the item Kenton had given her. The one she purchased was of Anubis, a man with the head of a jackal, painted black and girded around the hips with a gold apron.

The statue Kenton had given her, however, had been a gold pharaoh, a man, so she then visited a vendor who sold art supplies. She added a gold tube of paint to her stash of oils, packed up the lot with toiletries and a few changes of clothing into a large portmanteau, and hoped once she boarded the train she would have time to alter the statue enough that a casual glimpse might buy her the time necessary to secure Kenton's freedom.

And if she failed? Her heart sped up again. She didn't know much about Constantinople, but she did understand the tenor of the note Kenton had sent. He knew she'd been set on visiting several small art shows while he traveled to the Orient with his new friend, Trevor. He also knew she'd been angrily insistent about it, as he had balked at every suggestion she'd had their entire trip. He owed her the opportunity to pursue her love of art, because although she'd managed to drag him into a few larger museums, he'd raised a ruckus about "spending all their time in insignificant, dusty places when there was so much more to see." And when he suggested they separate, she'd been the one to insist they remain together. She didn't trust him on his own, and their current mess offered a perfect example. The first time she'd capitulated, he'd come back from a card game with what was apparently an invaluable and probably stolen artifact. And when he'd stubbornly insisted he was going to take an adventure aboard the famous train, she'd known there was no persuading him to see reason.

Emily sighed as the shipmen began preparations to dock the craft and deposit its travelers on French soil. She hadn't

accompanied him on the Orient Express because she needed
to go home if she hoped to retain her employment in a large
New York department store. Now, she wished she'd just gone
with her brother—perhaps she might have been able to keep
him out of trouble.

But perhaps not. She picked up her large portmanteau
and grasped the handle with both hands. Whoever currently
held Kenton probably did so with a fair amount of deter-
mination. For all her sense of responsibility, she wouldn't have
made a difference even if she had been there with him. So
many things could go wrong now that when she thought
about it, she felt light-headed.

Pull yourself together! She heard her mother's voice
inside her head and exhaled, eyes closed. She could do this.
She had no idea what she might encounter, but she could do
hard things. She straightened her spine and tightened her grip
on the luggage. She would find her brother, she would
somehow pass off the substitute long enough to get them both
away to safety, and then she would drag *Kenton Eldon Grant
III* home by his ear.

Three

Vincent scanned the crowd at the terminal, desperation setting in. He had a detailed description of Miss Emily Grant, thanks to the concierge at her hotel, but he'd been searching for well over an hour with no luck. He was torn between relief that the Mattingly brothers hadn't located her in London and frustration that he hadn't either.

"Mais pardon, mademoiselle," a clerk at the ticket counter three windows down was saying. *"Nous n'avons plus de disponible."*

There were several people behind the young woman at the front of the line who groaned in unison. Vincent shoved forward, shouldering aside a man and two squabbling children, and examined the woman at the window. She stood nearly a foot shorter than his own six feet, two inches, slight of frame, glossy black curls neatly arranged in a pretty coiffure beneath a hat of pale blue. When he reached her side, he noted her matching skirt, crisp white shirt, vest, and pale blue necktie, which matched the style description the concierge told him Miss Grant favored. A successful shopgirl from New York City, he'd been informed, who took great care with her appearance and was very much a lady in manner and speech.

Vincent took in her clenched fists, the spots of color on her otherwise pale face, and the sheen of moisture that had gathered in her eyes. "But, sir," she said firmly, and fumbled in her coat pocket for a small French phrase book, "I must depart on this train straightaway!" She flipped through the pages, and a woman behind her with a pinched expression made a snide remark in French. Vincent was fluent in French and noted that Miss Grant's clear ignorance of the language was decidedly in her favor.

Vincent had secured a cabin for himself a few hours earlier and was now grateful he'd taken the time. Making a quick decision, he approached Miss Grant. "Darling! I've been searching everywhere!" He embraced the shocked woman, who stood stiff in his arms. Tucking his mouth near her ear, he whispered, "Trust me. Your brother's life depends upon it."

"*What . . . ,*" she whispered, and when he pulled back with a smile, she stared, bright blue eyes wide, brows drawn.

"Surprise! I know I said we would meet in Vienna, but I was able to finish my business in London early. Now, I've already purchased my ticket and am so glad to have caught you in time." He put a firm arm around her shoulders and tugged her tightly against his side. To the ticket agent, he explained his wife would be traveling with him in his double and he needed to purchase her ticket.

The agent shrugged and asked for Miss Grant's passport as he readied her ticket. Miss Grant looked up at Vincent, mouth slack. He shook her lightly, and her hat bobbed. "Come along, darling, we must be off! And these good people behind us will need to purchase their tickets for the next train."

The grousing behind him spoke to the truthfulness of that, and Miss Grant licked her lips and swallowed. "Of course, dearest," she mumbled, and produced her passport from an inner pocket.

Hoping to reassure her, as she was now so pale he wondered if she'd fainted while still upright, he opened his coat slightly to reveal his detective badge pinned inside. "I know this is quite a shock, but everything will be fine," he murmured, and for the benefit of the nosy, grumbling woman behind them, he tapped the end of Miss Grant's nose and winked.

Miss Grant exhaled quietly and shoved her passport toward the ticket agent, who examined it and named the cost of her ticket.

"I have money right here," Vincent said, and reached into his pocket with his free hand, as the other still clamped firmly around his new bride, who had regained some color in her face but still looked as though she'd rather flee than continue the charade.

She subtly straightened her shoulders and deposited several bills on the counter. "Nonsense, *darling*," she said. "I'm quite independent, you know. A woman of the new era with money of my own."

"Scandaleux!" the woman behind them muttered.

Miss Grant's eyes narrowed. That word she clearly understood. "I suppose new modes of thinking are frightening to some in the *old* world, but in America—"

"Merci!" Vincent reached for the ticket and Miss Grant's passport and pulled the irate young woman away from the counter. He shoved the items into her hand and took her portmanteau, which was surprisingly heavy. "What on earth do you have in here?"

"And what on earth are you *doing*? Who are you?" Miss Grant stopped, breathing unsteadily. She glanced at the ticket before shoving it and her passport into her jacket pocket.

"Do you want to stand here arguing, or do you want to save your brother from a Turkish prison?" A whistle sounded as if punctuating his words, and her attention shot to the train at the other end of the station.

He grabbed her hand and moved quickly, forcing her to jog alongside. "If you knew you needed to board this train, why did you wait so long? I assume you lodged in a hotel nearby."

"I did not wait long! The hotels nearby were full when I arrived late last night from Calais, and I was forced to rest some distance away. And then," she continued, breathing rapidly as she ran, "I took a circuitous route here because I was being followed."

Vincent glanced sharply at her. "Do you know who it was?"

"No, I do not. I can only assume he's an enemy of my brother." She stopped suddenly and pulled her hand free of his. "Which you may well be, so thank you for helping me with the ticket, but I'll be on my way now." She stomped on his instep, catching him by surprise, and a sharp pain shot up his leg. She grabbed the portmanteau handle and tugged, causing a scene he feared would have good Samaritans coming to her aid.

"He took my luggage!" she yelled, achieving her objective as several heads swiveled toward them.

He gritted his teeth. "I did not; she's my wife!"

She began beating at the top of his wrist with the side of her hand. He was thrown off guard enough to loosen his hold on her portmanteau, which she grabbed and ran down the length of the train.

"Why, you . . . ," he ground out, and with a wince, took up the chase. He stopped himself just short of calling out, "Miss Grant!" and instead yelled, "Emily, dearest! I am so very sorry! I will never again discuss our honeymoon escapades over dinner with your family!"

She faltered midstride and stumbled, looking back over her shoulder at him with a squeak of outrage, eyes wide and murderous. Her slowing gave him enough time to overtake her, and he again wrapped his arm around her. He propelled her toward the train, winded and angry. "Here we are, sweetest. This is our car." He snatched the portmanteau back from her and met her glare with one of his own.

" . . . said he stole her luggage!"

Vincent turned at the pronouncement, spoken in French to a man in uniform. He ground his teeth and said under his breath, "I can help you find your brother, or you can do it on your own. Without my help, though, they'll probably kill him. I'm a detective with Scotland Yard and your last hope."

She breathed heavily and looked at him, cobalt-blue eyes open wide. Finally, he read fear there, rather than frustration or anger.

"You'll also be helping me. We've been after the group ultimately responsible for a very long time." He loosened the grip he held on her shoulder and rubbed her back. "When we reach the next stop, you can wire the Yard for verification, but for the love of Heaven, we have got to get on this train now."

She bit her lip and nodded.

The *gendarme* reached them, billy club at the ready. *"Êtes-vous bien, mademoiselle?"*

Miss Grant nodded. "Yes, I . . . *Oui.*" She fumbled again for the French dictionary, saying, "*Mon mari,* uh . . ."

Vincent smiled. "A lovers' quarrel. *Une querelle d'amoureux.*" He winked at the policeman, and the crowd around them murmured in chuckles and appreciation.

He turned his attention back to his blushing bride, whose eyes regarded him with what he could only define as bafflement. He couldn't blame her—their whirlwind courtship had caught him by surprise as well, and he had instigated it. "Come along, my sweet," he said, and on impulse, planted a quick kiss on her lips. Their crowd of admirers laughed and whistled, and some applauded.

She glanced at the crowd with a tight smile, but he noticed a subtle flare to her nostrils. "Indeed," she said, and grasped the railing as she began climbing the steps into the train car. "Although I do hope, dearest, that our compartment is a true double. I'll be sleeping in my own berth, as I am quite vexed with you." He didn't know her well, but the strain in her voice was unmistakable.

"Ah, such is the plight of the husband in his wife's poor graces." He followed her up the steps and put a hand to her back, half-afraid she would bolt down the stairs. "I may revoke my approval of your employment," he said as he ushered her inside. "You're entirely too independent for my peace of mind."

Four

Emily stood just inside the train car, her "husband" at her back, and took in the splendor before her. The train itself was the most beautiful she'd ever seen. A long corridor stretched to the right of the car, the interior paneled in warm, richly toned wood. Doors to individual compartments stood to the left and bore intricately carved designs and brass handles that shone in the light of evenly spaced lamps anchored to the wall.

"Oh," she breathed. "It's beautiful."

The detective nudged her and whispered close to her ear, "There are people behind us, my love. Move forward; I believe we are in the second door to your left."

She flushed. Of all the inconveniences Kenton had imposed upon her throughout her life, this was the worst. She found herself in the company of a strange man she didn't entirely trust, who claimed to be a lawman but had just lied and schemed his way onto the train at her side. The only bright spot was that she *was* on the train. When the ticket agent had said there were no berths available, no seats, nothing, she'd felt a moment of panic that had left her weak.

She moved forward when the detective nudged her again

and scowled at him over her shoulder. He raised a brow, the handsome lout, and indicated forward with his head. *Oh yes, very handsome,* she fumed and walked to the doorway he'd indicated. A conductor appeared at the far end of the corridor—a young man with a bright smile—and told them in accented English that he was there to ensure a comfortable journey.

"Ring for Henri, and I shall come straightaway." Henri placed a hand to his chest and tipped his head. He moved aside as people continued to file in, a mix of happily chattering passengers and a high-pitched bark from a tiny dog with bows atop its head.

Emily entered the small compartment and eyed, with a rush of relief, the couch that would serve as a double berth when converted. The back of the furniture swung up to create two beds, one above the other. Immediately before her were a chair and a small table with a light fixture attached and fresh roses in a vase, and along the wall to her left was a tiny built-in wardrobe to hold clothing and luggage.

She opened the wardrobe to see a satchel sitting there and a suit of clothing hanging from the rod at the top. "Oh, have we entered the wrong berth?"

The detective closed the door leading to the corridor and locked it with a click. "I purchased my ticket earlier this morning, and the porters delivered my luggage then." He eyed her warily—she couldn't blame him—but brushed past her and placed her portmanteau next to his satchel.

Emily quietly exhaled and removed her hat pin and then her hat.

"Have you a hatbox?" he asked quietly.

Do you see a hatbox? was on the tip of her tongue, but she exhaled quietly and closed her eyes for a moment. "I do not," she said and placed the hat carefully on her portmanteau in the wardrobe. "I was in a rush when I left London and had limited capacity for storage. I have the one hat, and it must suffice for the duration of the journey." She tightened her gloved fingers into fists and forced herself to relax. "I . . . this is all . . ." She gestured helplessly. "I suppose you must find me horribly ungrateful, and I do beg your pardon for that. Provided you are who you claim to be." She muttered the last, wondering again if she'd signed her own death warrant by entering the cabin with the stranger.

He seemed content to watch her, one shoulder against the wardrobe and hands in pockets, a smile at the corner of his mouth. So he found her amusing, did he? Well, he could laugh at her all he wanted. If he made one threatening move, she would fight and claw to her very last. She glanced around the cabin, noting items that would serve as potential weapons—the glass vase that held the flowers, two glass bottles of water, a lamp affixed to the wall that she could probably tear down if she were desperate enough . . .

He must have sensed her line of thought, because he held up a hand. "Please believe I mean you no harm. Suppose we talk?"

"Yes," she said, hating that her voice wavered, and cleared her throat. He gestured to the sofa and when she sat, took the chair across the table. He opened his jacket, slowly pulling out his identification, which he handed to her. Scotland Yard Detective Vincent Brady. She wasn't an officer of the law, wasn't experienced in anything involving police or crime, so the identification could have been fabricated and she would be none the wiser.

"Again, feel free to cable London to verify my identity."

She cleared her throat again and returned his documentation. "I must take you at your word, it seems," she said. "I could be dead by the time we reach a location where I could cable anyone."

He eyed her steadily. "You could indeed. I do not, however, mean you ill will, and I hope you will realize that soon. I apologize for my rather high-handed approach." He paused and ran his hand along the back of his neck. "I simply acted as quickly as I could with the only excuse I could conjure."

She studied him for a moment, allowing herself to relax and notice details beyond the obvious. His eyes were a warm chocolate brown, his hair short but probably had a tendency to curl; his features were strong, pleasing, and there was a breadth to him that seemed solid. She certainly hoped his intentions were as he'd stated—as a protector his size would be comforting. As an enemy, it would be frightening.

He had lines at the corners of his eyes that indicated a probable lifetime of smiles, but shadows just beneath implied fatigue. As he massaged his neck, his lips tightened almost imperceptibly, and she wondered if he were in pain.

"I appreciate your quick thinking very much," she said. She lifted her shoulder, and fear for Kenton washed over her again. "This morning I was certain I would miss this train, and the message I received from my brother made it quite clear that time is of the essence. And that no police were to be involved, or I would have asked for help."

He nodded and leaned forward, resting elbows on knees. "I shall tell you what I know." Mr. Brady then recounted a story about a pair of brothers who led a ring of criminals. She again found herself clenching her hands into tight fists. She was terrified for Kenton, and so frustrated with him she wanted to scream.

She stretched out her fingers and began to remove her gloves. "When Kenton returned home after the card game that night, he was giddy. He'd won a pile of cash and this statuette he claimed was not solid gold but still valuable. Suggested we have it appraised when we return to New York and very grandly presented it to me as a birthday gift." She sighed and placed her gloves on her lap. "I ought to have known—I examined the thing quite carefully myself."

"Are you familiar with antiquities?"

"No, but I am fairly well versed in art. I've studied painting and some sculpture, but I'm certainly no expert."

"Tell me about your brother. Kenton, yes?"

"He is an absolute fool." She bit her lip as tears threatened. She would not be a ninny; she would remain strong—at least until she could find two minutes alone.

"He is the younger of the two of you?"

Emily laughed miserably. "Ah, one might suppose." She shook her head. "He is my elder by five years. And in behavior, my junior by at least ten. I have always been the responsible sibling, the one to insist he stop when he's had one drink too many, to bully him into helping me care for our father. I've been the one to gain and keep steady employment." Emily sighed, feeling disloyal. "He has a very good heart. He is generous to a fault but sometimes lacking in sound judgment. Kenton assumes the world is as generous as he and cannot fathom anyone playing him false. He's often a target for cheats, so when he returned from that card game the victor, I was actually happy for him."

"And you work at Gilbert's Department Store in New York City?"

"My, you have done some sleuthing."

His mouth turned up in a half smile. "The concierge was only too happy to sing your praises. I do believe him to be most smitten."

"But hardly loyal, to provide strangers with my personal information."

"He is familiar with me," the detective admitted. "I've investigated in that neighborhood before."

Emily frowned. "It is a respectable neighborhood—very quiet, I found."

He smiled and sat back in his chair. "Crime knows no social boundaries."

She flushed. "Of course. I am not so naïve."

"I did not mean to suggest otherwise. Now, will you show me this thing that has caused all the trouble?"

She blinked. "The thing?"

"The Egyptian antiquity our Turkish friends seem so anxious to obtain from your brother."

Emily looked out the window, momentarily avoiding his gaze. She was uncertain of how well her admission would be received. "It is crossing the Atlantic as we speak. I do not have it here."

Five

Vincent blinked at Miss Grant. "I'm sorry?"

"I do not have it here." She closed her eyes and rubbed her forehead. "The day before I received Kenton's telegram, I packed our belongings and sent them ahead; my aunt will retrieve them from the ship and take them home. I wanted to enjoy my last week in London free from worry over details about all the extra baggage we've acquired on this trip." She sighed and looked at him. "I was being efficient."

He blinked again. "That you were. Most efficient of you." He studied the young woman as thoughts tumbled through his head. How on earth were they to negotiate without the main item at hand? More troubling still, *How on earth had she planned to do it alone?* "Efficient as you are, am I correct in assuming you'd devised a plan to secure your brother's release?"

She nodded and brushed away a wispy curl that teased her forehead. "I do hate being unprepared; however, I wasn't afforded much time." She drew in a deep breath. "I have a substitute."

"A substitute?"

"But it isn't ready yet. It looks nothing like the original, but I plan to alter its appearance enough that his captors will accept it and let Kenton go. I am hoping to get away with him so that by the time they realize it is not the original, we will be headed back to England." She paused. "It isn't a flawless plan, but it was the best I could manage."

"Actually, Miss Grant, it is a good plan." He was reluctantly impressed, despite all the variables that could go awry. The odds that she and her brother would have escaped before the deceit was realized were long indeed. "Perhaps we can use your decoy to our advantage. We shall be joined in Vienna by an associate, a police detective who has contacts in Constantinople. The men who are holding your brother are, regrettably, a small branch of local law enforcement. They avoid questions because they keep the peace and provide bribes."

Miss Grant swallowed and leaned against the wall at her side. "And your associate from Vienna also has sway over the local officials?"

"No, contacts with law enforcement whose influence and reach supercedes those in smaller communities. We will get your brother free, Miss Grant. It will require diplomacy, skill, and probably no small amount of luck, but we will not leave without him."

Her eyes filmed, but she kept the tears at bay. "Thank you. How did you know where to find me?"

He hesitated. "The younger of the two Mattingly brothers is also looking for you. When I learned you'd left for France, I obtained a copy of the telegram you received, figured you were on your way alone with the artifact. Hoped to find you before he did."

She blanched.

He clapped his hands together. "But, here we are, married! We will arrive at Constantinople in four days and then once we find your brother, we leave safely, and you need never lay eyes on me again." He smiled, hoping to reassure her when he was extremely uneasy himself. "I must admit I am glad for this turn of events—with the train as full as it is, I would have been forced to share this compartment with a stranger—probably a man who snores in his sleep."

She blushed, but her lips lifted in a wry smile. "I am a stranger, and perhaps I snore in my sleep."

"But you are charming and easy on the eyes." He winked.

"Detective, Mr. Brady—"

"Vincent. We are married, after all."

"Vincent . . ." She twisted her fingers together and then as if realizing what she was doing, folded them together in her lap. "I do not do . . . this." She waved a hand between them. "I am not this sort . . . or rather, shopgirls sometimes gain a reputation that suggests . . . but I am not, I do not—"

He rose and took her hands in his. "I did not suppose it for a moment."

"But you kissed me."

He frowned. "I did?"

She huffed. "Outside the train! When the *gendarme* thought to rescue me."

He felt heat rise in his face and figured he hadn't blushed in years. "I . . . yes. I hoped to convince him that we were truly a couple. My sincerest apologies for making you uncomfortable, Miss Grant."

She gave his hands a squeeze. "All is forgiven—I wanted to be certain you understand . . ."

"I do understand." As if he would ever have mistaken her for anything but a proper young woman. The kind that would never have given him the time of day in his youth and that would set her sights on a respectable man of business when she married.

"Then I suppose you should call me 'Emily.' We are married, after all."

She gave him the benefit of a full smile, and he caught his breath. She was truly lovely. Lovely and resourceful and incredibly brave. At some point he might need to tell her that they stood in danger of meeting new thieves and ne'er-do-wells at every stop along the line. Jimmy Mattingly had spread the word far and wide that an artifact worth a barrell of money was on its way to Constantinople, and Vincent could only hope Chief Inspector Lampley's subsequent telegrams to law enforcement in each of those cities would have the desired results. He felt some comfort at the thought that his Austrian associate, Berrin Hirsch, would join them when they stopped in Vienna. For all that Vincent was confident in his own abilities, he knew he wasn't up to the task of taking on all of Europe's criminal class single-handedly.

Six

The whistle blew, and the train lurched forward and was on its way. Emily had traveled by train many times but never on one as opulent as the Orient Express. It was everything its reputation claimed, and more.

Vincent took Emily on a tour of the famous train; he had ridden to Constantinople and back twice. It was exquisite, from top to rails. The wood trim and décor remained a theme throughout the cars, with luxury apparent in the finest of details. Their cabin was in a second- class car—the first-class suites were all full, of course, so she was unable to see them—but even in second class, the attention to the littlest of comforts was apparent. Their compartment contained even a small wash area Emily hadn't seen—it was to the right of the sofa and hidden behind a glossy mahogany door—which boasted a sink, tiny soaps, perfumes, and lotions. Fluffy hand towels and washcloths were engraved with the famed *WL*, which stood for *wagon-lit*, and Emily couldn't remember a time when she'd looked forward to washing her face just to experience the towels. There was even a small shave kit for the busy traveler who might have forgotten his soap, brush, and razor.

The restaurant car rivaled Paris's finest establishments and was manned by a chef of great renown who worked magic in a galley kitchen just a few feet wide. Tables were adorned with fine linen and fresh flowers, and a lamp offering soft light attached to the wall at each table. Mugs and glassware also proudly wore the *WL* logo, and chairs were plush and upholstered in rich brocades. The gentle sway of the train lent the whole experience a magical feel.

Vincent and Emily ate breakfast with others who shared their sleeping carriage. There were eighteen, in total, which included two young children, Todd and Maria, ages seven and five, respectively. Emily was not naturally at ease in the company of children, so when the two settled just across the aisle with their parents, Mr. and Mrs. Clawson, she paid them no extra mind. Todd, however, was determined to show Vincent and Emily the space where his first lost tooth had been, and Maria, suffering from motion sickness apparently, vomited all over her plate.

Emily had turned her face to the window, taking shallow breaths and trying to banish the image from her mind amid the horrified apologies from Mr. and Mrs. Clawson. The mess was tidied in record time—the staff took their duties most seriously—and before long, there was no evidence of a mishap.

The rest of the passengers were good natured, with the exception of the British pair seated behind Emily.

"Utterly disgusting," Mrs. Berry complained to her daughter. "Can't imagine why one would even bring children along. It is inconsiderate to the rest of the passengers."

"I suppose if they all must reach a destination, there would be no other way to get the children there," the daughter, Nanette, replied.

"Where could they possibly be going that would require the presence of children?"

"I am with you, Mother."

Vincent's lips twitched, and he spooned a bite of fluffy eggs into his mouth. Emily bit her cheeks and ducked her head. She liked Nanette—the young woman wasn't fussy in her dress or demeanor, had brought a novel to the breakfast table (much to Mrs. Berry's disgruntlement), and in the thirty minutes Emily had been an unwitting eavesdropper to their conversation, she had stifled laughter at Nanette's dry humor no less than three times.

A pleasant conversational hum filled the restaurant car; the languages that circulated included Italian, Spanish, and another Emily couldn't identify. It sounded quite exotic, though, and for a moment Emily resented the fact that she wasn't on the beautiful train to travel and enjoy the rest of her holiday.

"You are far away, my darling," Vincent said with a smile, and she blinked him into focus.

He was very handsome, and Emily wished for just a moment that the ruse was reality. That she traveled to exotic and lovely places with a lovely man at her side. "Lovely" was perhaps the wrong word, and she tipped her head, studying him. He was more rugged than lovely; one would never mistake him for a soulful poet. She found she liked his brand of handsome better, a slightly untamed side that had been wrestled into submission for polite society.

"And now you're here, but you're considering something quite intently." He braced his forearms against the table, fork and knife poised over his plate, and raised a brow.

"Wool gathering." She shrugged.

"What were you thinking just now?"

"There is something about you, sir, that is not quite

polished. You have impeccable manners, your speech is refined, and yet . . . and yet for me to remark on such a thing is as far from polished as one can travel." She flushed.

His eyes narrowed just slightly, flickered, and his expression tightened. Or she had imagined it, because she blinked, and he was as he'd been before. Inquisitive, pleasantly curious.

"I am not a man of business, it is true," he said and resumed his meal, "nor do I claim so much as a drop of blue blood. The only reason I find myself on this train with you and not carousing with the likes of the Mattingly brothers is because an old man interfered in my life at a point when I might have swung either way. I shall be certain to pass along your compliments about my speech to my elocution coach, who labored long hours to mold the articulate man I am today."

His tone was as pleasant as it had been all morning, he winked at her, even, but she'd offended him, and she knew it.

"I, that is . . ." She slid a slice of melon around her plate with her fork. "You asked what I was thinking."

"And you told me."

He was quiet throughout the remainder of the meal, and Emily wished she could shove her observations back into her mouth and lock it up tight. Her life had not been one of opulence, but she had enjoyed comfort, financial stability, respectable schooling, and even now had enough with her inheritance to lose her job (which was now a definite possibility) but still live well enough for a time until she could find another one.

She had also known the sting of inferiority, however, in the company of young ladies whose fathers could have bought and sold hers a million times over. That she had probably caused those same kinds of negative feelings in the detective made her uncomfortably sad.

As their meal ended, however, Vincent smiled at her and offered his arm. "We have yet to visit the lounge car. Shall we?"

She nodded, relieved he had broken the tension, and determined to apologize at some future point. Or perhaps she wouldn't. She would pretend the whole exchange had never occurred and she had never been so gauche.

She threaded her fingers through his arm and noted the solidity. She curled her fingertips against his sleeve and wondered what he would do if she gave an experimental squeeze. Her own muscles had hardened some in her early days as a shopgirl—lifting, bending, toting, carrying inventory from one end of the store to the other—but what was it about men that made them so much more . . . more? Even Kenton, who lived a life of relative leisure, was physically stronger than she was.

Well, she admitted, her brother was also bigger. As was the detective. She glanced up at his strong profile. She *had* managed to catch him off guard for just a moment before boarding the train, and that thought made her smile. What she lacked in physical strength she often made up for with ingenuity. The brain was almost always a woman's strongest asset. Now if she could just be certain to never again be so blunt with a man, she might avoid hurting his feelings.

She was distracted again by the detective's impressive arm as he reached for the door and his bicep shifted in her hand. She gave into the impulse and pressed her fingertips against it, registering the fact that there was absolutely no give. He glanced down at her as he opened the door by reaching over her head and then allowing her to precede him through.

He must have thought she'd been trying to get his attention, because he quirked a brow in question.

She smiled and ducked her head, hoping he wouldn't see the blush she knew was spreading across her cheeks. He'd kissed her of his own accord, so she was certainly justified in testing the solidity of his arm. He may be called upon to protect her in the immediate future with that arm, after all.

As they entered the lounge car, she tried to decide why it bothered her now that he hadn't remembered kissing her when she'd mentioned it earlier.

Seven

Vincent had been correct in his earliest of impressions that Emily Grant would set her cap for a man with "polish." She'd been embarrassed after admitting her thoughts—he saw her dismay in her face—but that didn't mean she hadn't been astute. He had learned to be respectable—he certainly hadn't been born into it. Why her opinion mattered, he had no idea. He'd known her a handful of hours and would be with her for only a handful of days. Then he and his chief inspector would muster all their resources and locate Jon Mattingly's stash of stolen artifacts. One way or another, though, the Mattinglys would move on either Emily or Kenton Grant, and in addition to gaining concrete evidence of the criminals' involvement, he had to keep the siblings safe.

Perhaps her observation wouldn't have stung if he'd not begun to find her interesting and charming, even while worried sick over her selfish brother. From the concierge's glowing report of Emily's finer assets, Vincent had expected her to be pretty. He hadn't expected to find her more attractive as the day wore on, however. She was a perplexing mix of sarcasm and innocence, and there were times as they sat in the lounge car, the restaurant car again for tea and then dinner,

213

and then later that evening in the café car for after-dinner drinks, that he found himself staring.

She'd had the wherewithal to pack a dinner gown, and he'd left her in their compartment with Nanette Berry to help her dress. If Miss Berry wondered why Emily's husband wasn't up to the task of helping her button and tie her way into the ensemble, according to Emily, she didn't mention it. In fact, the young woman seemed elated at the opportunity to spend time with someone other than her mother, and he certainly couldn't blame her.

Emily sat with Nanette and her mother while Vincent went to the bar to get drinks for the ladies—for Emily and Nanette, dry ginger ale, a novelty from a Canadian inventor who had just established a soda bottling plant. Mrs. Berry requested a gin and tonic, as she was "nursing a headache." Miss Berry had rolled her eyes, and Emily had opened her mouth and closed it again, clearly deciding against arguing.

Wise girl, Vincent mused as he returned with the drinks. If Mrs. Berry believed the concoction would relieve a headache rather than cause it, he was not the one to bring attention to the flawed conclusion. Besides, he reflected as he handed her the glass, judging by the daughter's reaction, the matron was clearly fabricating an excuse to imbibe.

Vincent sat on the arm of Emily's chair and rested his hand on the back of her neck as she sipped her drink. She glanced up at him, uncertain, and he wondered if she'd had a beau, had ever been courted in earnest. Of course, she may well have been—that didn't mean she wouldn't find herself uncomfortable now, playing a role with a stranger while en route to a daring rescue that had the potential to end in disaster.

He winked at her and smiled, and she relaxed against the side of the chair, into his hand. Strain was evident around her eyes, however, and she seemed pale despite the warmth of the car. "Are you tired, darling?" he asked. "Perhaps we ought to retire."

Her eyes widened fractionally, but she caught herself and nodded. "Yes, dearest, I am feeling a bit fatigued. What a day it has been."

"I should say so!" A French gentleman, Mr. Beauchand, laughed quite merrily. "After ze excitement at the terminal zis morning I would think you'd have retired long before now!"

Vincent noted the slight flare to Emily's nostrils and pulled her to her feet. "Ah now, gentlemen," he said and propelled her toward the door, "we needn't speak of it with the ladies."

"Ze lady was the most enthusiastic of all!" General laughter followed the comment.

Emily turned in outrage. "I was not 'enthusiastic,'" she sputtered as Vincent put his arms around her, walking her backward. She continued to protest her innocence as he maneuvered left and then right, blocking her line of sight with his shoulders.

"Come along, sweetness, let's not cause an uproar."

She clutched his shoulders for balance as she tried one last time to chastise the group, who had indulged enough for the evening to be well beyond remorse for embarrassing her. "I behaved with decorum," she yelled, and her heel caught on the back of her dress.

She stumbled, and Vincent hefted her up against him with one arm as he shoved open the door. He'd inadvertently lifted her high enough that she had a clear view of the men over his shoulder.

"And it is most impolite to laugh at a lady!"

The door closed behind them, and Vincent carried her into the lounge car, which connected to their sleeping carriage. He paused to allow his docile bride a moment to catch her breath. By this time her arms were around his shoulders, and she breathed heavily, eyes still snapping.

There were a few people in the lounge car, but the lights were low, so they didn't attract much attention. "Are you calm, madam?" he murmured in her ear.

She relaxed, and he slowly lowered her to stand on her own but didn't immediately release her. She remained pliant against him, her hands holding his arms.

"Why do you become so irate?" he whispered, fighting a smile.

She narrowed her eyes but maintained her hold on him. "They are accusing me of something, something provocative! As if I behaved angrily this morning as a precursor to, to . . ."

He laughed quietly. "My darling, that is what we *want* them to think."

"But even if we truly were married," she whispered, "I would not want their commentary on my personal business!"

"You're right, and men can be blasted oafs," he whispered back. "In this case, though, it works to our advantage. You must realize that as we are posing as husband and wife, your good name would be in shambles should the truth be discovered. I would not want that for you."

She fumed for a moment in silence. "Hardly fair that my good name should suffer while yours merely gains notoriety."

He smiled wryly. "You're right, of course. Now that women's suffrage movements are becoming all the rage, perhaps when women gain the right to vote, they will also gain notoriety rather than censure for promiscuous behavior. Equality for one and all."

She scowled. "It would be only fair." She exhaled slowly and finally looked up at him, sheepish. "Perhaps I am an activist and didn't realize it."

"Are you still angry?"

"No, I am calm."

"You're gripping my arms like a fiddler crab."

She blinked. "I . . . uh . . ." She softened her hold on him and stepped back. "Apologies."

He grinned. "None required, but accepted all the same." He clasped her hand, and they walked the length of the lounge car, then made their way through to their small room. It was only after they'd entered and he'd locked the door that he spied the sofa that had been made into two beds and realized Nanette Berry was still sipping ginger ale in the café car with her gin-loving mother. Emily was two feet away from him, dressed in an evening gown that buttoned securely up the back.

He couldn't summon Miss Berry. He couldn't summon anyone without raising questions.

Emily met his eyes, the same realization clearly having settled upon her. She pursed her lips, brows pinched in a frown. "Blast."

Eight

A conundrum. The word played through Emily's mind as she looked around at the tiny room and the man whose presence filled it completely. She couldn't ask anyone for help undressing, and she couldn't reach all those ridiculous buttons by herself. When readying for the evening, she hadn't given two thoughts to the task of un-readying.

There were no options aside from the obvious, so Emily straightened her spine metaphorically and physically. "Very well. You must help me. But close your eyes."

"Close my . . . close my eyes?"

"Yes. I, sir, am an innocent, and while I require your help, you needn't see . . . anything."

"Emily—"

She swallowed. "Perhaps you should call me Miss Grant."

He sighed. "Emily. Look at me."

She did, and then wished she hadn't. He was incredibly handsome, growing more so by the hour, and he was so very *right there*. He even smelled good, and the room was so small, and he was so *not* small, and she suddenly felt very warm.

"Allow me to speak plainly for a moment and pretend I am your brother."

She wrinkled her nose.

"You wear undergarments, I presume? A corset and under corset blouse?"

Her face flamed, but she nodded. Pretending he was her brother was not working.

"I shall close my eyes, if you prefer, but you may rest assured that even unbuttoned, your modesty is still preserved. I am not a mindless, rutting beast with no power over his instincts. I'm fairly certain that even were you to stand there wearing substantially *less* than a corset, I could and would control myself."

Her mouth lifted in a half smile. She appreciated his frankness and his consideration. She also realized she was fortunate in the extreme that she found herself in the company of a true gentleman. The situation could have been so very different.

"You're a very good man, Detective Brady." She met his eyes. "I trust you implicitly."

He scratched the back of his neck. "Well . . . good." He twirled his finger. "Turn around. I'll unbutton the dress and then leave so you can change."

She nodded and turned around, tapping her fingers together and then clutching them to be still. She felt the detective behind her, and then the soft brush of his fingers at the top of her spine.

"Close your eyes," she blurted. "Just . . . just close them."

She heard his quiet chuckle and glanced over her shoulder. He had closed his eyes, but his smile was contagious. She couldn't help but return it, and he opened his eyes.

"Turn your head around," he said with an exaggerated nod, and closed his eyes again. "Remember—I'm just like your brother."

"Psh." She faced forward and swept up the curls that had escaped her coiffure. "My brother does not help me undress."

"Praise all the saints," he muttered.

She laughed and braced her hand against the wardrobe as his fingers slipped deftly through the buttons at her back. "You wanted me to think of you as my brother!"

"Yes, but I had no wish to hear that this is your customary sibling routine. When I marry a woman, I prefer she come to me unencumbered by problematic family relationships."

She laughed again and realized he'd reached the end of the buttons and turned toward the door. He'd distracted her, made her laugh, and true to his word, behaved like a perfect gentleman. She held the dress to her chest and turned around. "Vincent," she said, and he paused at the door handle. "I offended you earlier today with a thoughtless comment, a badly expressed comment, and I apologize sincerely."

He turned his head slightly, and she caught the little smile in his profile. "Already forgotten," he murmured and stepped out into the hall, closing the door behind him with a soft click.

She quickly shrugged out of the dress, fussed with the strings at the back of the corset—Nanette Berry tied a very tight knot!—and pulled it open, taking a deep breath. Life held few pleasures as wonderful, as elemental, as removing a corset at the end of the day. She quickly changed into her nightgown and robe and made good use of the scented soaps and wonderfully fluffy towels in the vanity cupboard.

When finished washing her face, she opened the door and peeked out into the hallway, which was empty save Henri, who sat in his chair at the end of the corridor. He popped up, and she waved him back with a smile. Vincent was nowhere to be seen, so she ventured into the corridor and closed the door behind her. She entered the room next to their compartment, which was one of the two lavatories in the carriage.

Even the necessary was beautifully appointed. She would

be spoiled for further train travel after riding the rails in such luxury. The door handle suddenly twisted downward, and her heart skipped a beat. Grateful beyond words that she'd locked the door, she called out, "A moment, please." Nobody responded, but she heard quickly receding footsteps.

She finished and stepped back into the corridor, looking right and left but finding the narrow space empty. Her reflection in the window looked back at her as the dark night outside raced by. She looked ghostly in her nightdress; feeling ridiculous but frightening herself nonetheless, she reached for her compartment door handle, surprised when it swung open on its own.

Vincent must have returned, she supposed, and she entered the cabin. It was empty, and she felt a chill chase up her spine. She'd closed the door firmly behind her, had pulled it until she heard the handle click, and then had been in the water closet for only a few moments.

She hugged her middle and looked around the small compartment, examining it for further signs of disturbance. Nothing seemed amiss until her eye stopped on the wardrobe. The door was ajar an inch, and heart pounding, she quickly opened it. Her portmanteau was still there, beside Vincent's satchel. The extra suit of clothing was still in its place, along with the dress Emily had hung next to it.

She slowly closed the wardrobe door and stood with her back against it, folding her arms tightly as if to ward off a chill. A quiet knock sounded at the door, and she jumped.

"Emily," Vincent whispered.

She opened the door, grasped his lapels in one hand, and pulled him into the room.

"What is it?" His eyes roamed over her face, and he touched her shoulder. "What happened?"

"Someone was in here," she whispered. "Please tell me you came back for something in the wardrobe."

He shook his head slowly. "I've been in the lounge car." He paused. "You left the room?" He glanced down at her nighttime attire.

She flushed and waved her hand at the door. "Just to the water closet. I was gone for perhaps two minutes at the most."

"And the door was open when you returned? Are you certain you closed it?"

She nodded and swallowed past the lump in her throat. "Yes, and someone tried the handle when I was in the water closet. I ought to have locked this door behind me."

"Is anything missing?" He crossed to the wardrobe and opened the door.

"No, I don't believe so."

"Have you checked inside your bag?"

She bit her lip and moved to his side, reaching for her portmanteau and holding her breath. A quick rifling of the contents showed her nothing had been disturbed, and the statue decoy was still wrapped at the bottom. She frowned and looked at Vincent. "Everything is here. But the main door was open, and so was this one. I swear on my life it was not how I left it."

"I believe you." He looked inside the wardrobe for a moment, hands on his hips and lips pursed in thought. He shrugged out of his jacket and she tugged on his sleeve when it got stuck. "You get in bed—you're asleep on your feet," he said as he removed his cuff links and set them on the polished tabletop. "I'll check with Henri."

Emily climbed into the lower berth and switched on the light that was recessed into the wall by her head. She pulled the covers close to her chest and shut her eyes tightly, wondering how her life had devolved into such chaos. Kenton, of course, and as she lay still, unbidden images of her brother tied up, possibly tortured, flooded her thoughts. She'd not allowed herself to imagine the worst and since receiving the telegram had been finding ways to keep herself so busy that she had no time to think.

She tensed as the door opened a crack but relaxed when Vincent spoke.

"Henri saw nothing," he said.

Emily stared. "How is that possible—he was there in his seat as plain as day."

"He claims to have used the other water closet after you entered this one." He gestured next door with his thumb. "Did you happen to note whether he was back in his chair when you returned here?"

She squinted and shook her head. "I did look to see who might have tried the door handle, but there was nobody there. Not even Henri, come to think of it."

He nodded and offered a tight smile probably meant to reassure. "Nobody here now, at least." He opened the wardrobe door, rummaged in his satchel, and withdrew a revolver.

Her eyes widened. She'd been terrified of guns since she was a small child and her father had taken the family to his mother's farm to slaughter a pig and shoot hay bale targets for sport. The sheer power of the weapons had alarmed her, and she was forced to admit she'd have made a terrible frontierswoman. She would always link weapons with the slaughter of the poor pig, solidifying her distaste for guns. The detective meant to keep them safe, however, and she would be quite a ninny if she balked at his methods.

He met her eyes as he checked the barrel and then secured it in its holster. He placed it atop his satchel and said, "This remains right here in the event I need quick access to it."

She nodded, tried to speak, but nothing came out. She tried again. "Is that a Webley Mark One revolver?"

He looked at her in surprise. "You know your weapons?"

She grimaced. "Not voluntarily. My father was a collector. I quite detest guns, but I certainly support your use of one."

His mouth turned up at one corner as he placed the gun inside and locked the drawer. "Glad to hear it." He straightened and pulled one end of his black bow tie. "You may want to close your eyes."

"Mercy," she muttered and turned over in the narrow bed, facing the wall and squeezing her eyes shut. "This day has gone from confusing to mad."

She heard him leave the room, locking the door, and then heard the closing lavatory door. She remained still, trying to pretend she'd fallen asleep when he returned and cleaned himself up in the vanity, splashing water—she assumed on his face—cleaning his teeth, and changing his clothing.

He climbed up into his bed and chuckled. "I am appropriately attired for bed. You may open your eyes if you wish."

"No, no. I am very tired." She snapped off her personal light.

"Do you mind if I read for a time? Will the light bother you?"

"Not at all—feel free."

"Are your eyes still shut tight?"

"Well yes, detective, it is nighttime."

"Sleep well, Miss Grant." She heard the smile in his voice. She clicked off the table lamp, leaving only the personal one by his head still illuminated.

Emily relaxed by slow degrees, allowing herself to be lulled by the smooth motion of the train, the pleasant sound of wheels on track. The soft light at the detective's head provided comfort she hadn't known she needed. She felt safe, and for the first time since her father's sanity had begun to slip, she did not feel alone.

Nine

Vincent arose early the next morning and left his bunkmate peacefully sleeping. She looked carefree for the moment, without the lines of tension he'd noted yesterday at her eyes and around her mouth. He'd made a point to step onto the platform when they'd stopped in Strasbourg in the early morning hours, when a good portion of the passengers from Paris had disembarked. Many new faces had boarded, though, and although nothing obvious had caught his eye, a foreboding feeling churned in the pit of his stomach.

Checking his and Emily's compartment door for the second time, he told himself to stop fussing. She was a grown woman; she'd been on her own and ready to confront unknown dangers in Constantinople single-handedly. After her scare the night before, if she left the berth for any reason, she would remember to lock the door.

He began walking the length of the train to reassure himself he had a general impression of the passengers and train personnel. He greeted conductors at each car, spoke briefly with porters, lounge attendants, and servers. He smiled at new passengers, made note of men (and a few women) who might present a fair challenge in a physical altercation.

As time passed, he considered taking a light breakfast to Emily but realized he didn't know what she would want. The morning before, she'd eaten fruit, so he procured a small tray with fruit and tea and carried it back to their coach. He knocked lightly on the door and when he heard Emily respond, opened it with his key.

She was seated at the table by the window with a small palette of paints and three brushes. She was dressed in an ensemble similar to the day before, looking every inch the modern woman with her button-down shirt and necktie tucked neatly beneath a tan waistcoat and skirt. She'd donned a pinafore smock splattered here and there with bright colors of paint.

Her hair was neatly coiffed, with a few dark curls framing her face. She'd had the berths reconverted to a sofa, which spoke of her habits. She paid attention to detail and preferred order to chaos. He'd gleaned that much of her personality the day before in observing the preparation she'd made to embark on her impromptu journey. Between her penchant for control and the temper that sparked when she felt unjustly accused or harassed, the situation in which she currently found herself must have been disconcerting in the extreme. Most women of his acquaintance, and more than a few men, would not remain so poised, and he was impressed.

She smiled at him, and he caught his breath. She was lovely. "You've been gone for some time," she said. "And you didn't wake me when you left—you're very stealthy for such a large man."

He smiled. "Practice."

Her smile grew. "You've made a habit of posing as a husband and sneaking away in the early morning hours unnoticed?"

He laughed. "As it happens, you are my first faux wife. I

had to hone my stealth skills when I became a bobby." He gestured with the breakfast tray. "I brought you some fruit and tea, but if you prefer something different, I'll ring the porter."

"How kind of you. Fruit sounds delightful." She indicated the sofa, which provided a seat across from her, and moved aside her paint palette and brushes. "I am certainly glad to be your first faux wife. If you truly made a habit of this, I'd be concerned for my welfare."

He raised a brow and handed her the folded napkin. "You still must take my word for it—I confess, knowing more of your personality, I'm surprised you acquiesced."

She snapped open the napkin and spread it on her lap. "I had no choice. And if you'll recall, I did try to shake you loose. I do apologize for that. I was prepared to take advantage of your offer and steal this cabin. One whistle had sounded, and I knew departure was imminent."

He chuckled. "What would you have done if you'd made it aboard but the train still hadn't left? I would have followed you, of course."

She chewed on her lip and selected a large grape. "I didn't have much time to consider alternatives. I suppose I would have locked the door and prayed."

He tipped his head. "Why did you believe me?"

"You knew details about Kenton's situation."

"I might have been an accomplice to his abduction."

She shrugged. "But why the ruse, then? I followed instructions specifically and was already bound for Turkey to hand over the ransom demand. And had you suspected the statue was in the portmanteau, which it was, you could have taken it and run. You didn't run; you dragged me with you." She popped the grape in her mouth and smiled as she chewed. "You have an air about you."

He leaned his elbows on the table. "What sort of air is that?"

"A trustworthy air that says, 'Fear not, I am here to help!'"

He laughed. "You are the first person to describe me that way."

"Well then, I am your first for many things, it seems."

His smile lingered, and he must have made her feel self-conscious with the attention, because she blushed.

"You know"—she waved her hand airily—"first sister of an abductee underfoot, first woman to assault you at a train station, that sort of thing."

"My first female partner during an investigation." He smiled and realized it was true. Had someone told him a week earlier that he'd be in this situation, he'd have been horrified. But Emily Grant was smart and talented and didn't easily panic. Something about her prompted chivalry, but he also viewed her as his intellectual and behavioral equal. What an oddity his associates would find it.

"Well! That is something. Pinkerton has hired women for years to investigate, but not everybody is convinced women are up to the task." She placed her hand on her chest and inclined her head. "I am honored." Her smile slipped. "I wish I could claim objectivity, but I am assuredly too close to the subject of your investigation to be truly impartial."

"We will find your brother," he said quietly. And he did most definitely mean it—but he hoped they would be bringing Kenton Grant home under his own power and not in a pine box. Vincent knew that those who held Kenton were not inclined toward fair play. He was an American citizen, though, and they had to know by now the Yard was involved. Their instructions had dictated that Emily refrain from contacting the police, but they weren't naïve enough to believe their network wasn't monitored by law enforcement in every country.

She nodded. "I do believe we will find him. I hope he is alive when we do."

Well, good. At least the lady didn't harbor delusions. For a moment he wished she would. It would be easier for her if she lived in blissful ignorance for a time.

"At any rate," she said, and slid the fruit plate aside, "I have a pharaoh to make." She reached down and produced the Anubis statue. "It will not fool anyone who has seen the original, but it will buy time from any who don't know better."

Vincent had his doubts. He couldn't imagine how she'd transform the thing.

"I wish we knew exactly what Kenton's captors think they are getting. How many details do they have, for example? Do they know it's a pharaoh? Will they release Kenton right away, or will they demand authentication of the statue before allowing him to leave?"

"Regrettably, I do not know exactly what Mattingly told them. Told everyone between here and there, as a matter of fact."

Her gaze jumped from the statue in her hands to his face. "Told who?"

He inwardly cursed. He hadn't informed her that criminal elements between France and Turkey were aware of her and the ransom prize. He explained the conversation between the Mattingly brothers to her, leaving nothing out. He should have told her yesterday—he now knew she'd rather be worried but aware than deluded into a false sense of security.

She slowly nodded. "Then it is very good news that your fellow officer will be joining us soon, isn't it? We could do with more help." She closed her eyes for a moment. "And I thought I could manage this on my own."

"Your instructions were to avoid police, and you did that in concern for your brother. You've no reason for regret." He paused. "How did you know it was not a hoax? Your brother sounds like the sort that would enjoy a good prank."

She looked at him flatly. "He may be carefree, but he is not entirely stupid. He complained about every art show and museum I wanted to visit on our holiday. His going away on this train adventure was a gift to me, so I could go anywhere on my own without listening to his whining."

"You couldn't have done that anyway?"

She sighed. "Yes. I could have, but I didn't trust him." She laughed, but it smacked of sadness. "Kenton was a sweet child, but to escape punishment for misdeeds, he told white lies and usually involved me in the process. My parents didn't know who to believe, so I often was chastised for things I didn't do. I suppose that is why I get so frustrated now if I feel unjustly accused or misunderstood."

She shook her head. "He's my brother, and I love him, but he's my senior by five years—most men are married or settled into a career by his age. But therein lies the answer itself. He's *not* married or settled into a career. The employment he has attempted through the years has never lasted more than a handful of months. He grows bored, he feels he should be making more money, nobody appreciates his talents." She shrugged. "He's charming, though, so my parents, while irritated, indulged him. And then my father was ill and not himself the last three years, so it didn't matter."

Vincent eyed Emily and bit his tongue when he would have made disparaging remarks about her wastrel brother. "You cared for your father and worked at the department store?"

She nodded. "I wanted to do something for myself—I suppose it was selfish, but I was so tired of spending every moment with a father who didn't even recognize me anymore. I hired a nurse to watch him while I worked."

He kept his mouth from falling open, but only just. "Your brother helped . . . not at all?"

"Every now and again, I lost my patience and gave him a piece of my mind. He would sit with Father or find employment for a time."

"Emily, perhaps you should consider leaving him in the Turkish prison."

She pretended outrage, but a laugh crept in. "I will admit, I was tempted." She turned her attention to the statue, testing her fingertip against the point of Anubis's sharp ears. Vincent didn't know if she was avoiding his eyes because she was trying to defend her brother's defenseless behavior or if she was distracted by the task at hand with the statue.

She sighed and reached for a sketchbook she'd propped against the window. "I keep a visual journal; I drew the statue that night." She flipped through the pages.

Vincent stared—couldn't help himself. When she reached the page where she'd documented the day Kenton had won the statue in that ill-fated card game, Vincent wasn't taken so much with the statue itself as in the journal Emily kept. "You drew this? All of these things?" Alongside the pharaoh picture was a sketch of Big Ben, a scene in Hyde Park, a rough water-colored picture of London Bridge and its surroundings.

"I was rather in a hurry for some of these," she said. "Not my best work, of course."

"Not your best . . . Emily, you are an amazing artist. These could be photographs!"

"Psh." She blushed. "At any rate, you'll notice the statue of the pharaoh differs significantly from this." She held up Anubis against the sketch.

"Have you had art lessons?"

"Detective, focus on the matter at hand, if you please!"

"Small wonder you have a fondness for art museums. Truly, this is amazing. I know this exact spot in Hyde Park," he said, tapping his finger on the sketch. "Lessons, surely." He searched her face, which regarded his in exasperation.

"Yes, I had lessons when I was younger! My mother noticed my penchant for drawing on anything and everything." She held the Anubis statue up, clutched in a tight grip. "What are we going to do about this? I have some ideas but would welcome your thoughts. Do you have any way of discovering what Kenton's captors know about the statue?"

Vincent sighed. "I'll wire my chief inspector when we arrive in Munich, ask if he's learned anything new. He can wire ahead his answer for me in Vienna. What was your initial plan for this?"

She plunked down her elbows on the table and pursed her lips in thought. Cupping her chin in her free hand, she looked at the statue while drumming her fingertips against her cheek. "We must remove the ears. I have a sanding block to scratch off most of this black paint . . . also should remove this staff—the original statue was not holding one." She tipped the statue this way and that. "I'll sand the whole of it to create a slightly textured surface. The paint will adhere better, less likely to scratch or flake at the drop of a hat."

He nodded. "What composes it, do you know? Wood? Metal?"

"Metal, I believe. I do not know how to break the ears off."

Vincent held out his hand, and she gave him the statue. "Something metal with a chisel tip . . ." He smiled at Emily. "I'll get rid of the ears for you. You will manage the paint. It is a sound plan and will buy us time, should we need it."

Ten

The familiar scent of oil paints filled the small compartment. Emily washed her hands at the sink near the door and looked at the table where the altered statue dried. From her vantage point some feet away, if she squinted a bit, the replica quite resembled the original. She sighed, uncertain and worried, and leaned her head against the polished wood wall as she dried her hands on a fluffy towel. Her head moved slightly with the sway of the train, and she wondered if, in spite of the worry about her brother, she would be a horrible person if she allowed herself to enjoy the adventure.

She stood straight and checked her timepiece. Vincent would probably be in the restaurant car for tea, and she decided to join him. She smiled as she secured the statue and tidied her supplies. Vincent had disappeared for a short time earlier and returned with a chisel and hammer procured from the conductor in the Munich-Vienna coach, who was good pals with the train maintenance man. He'd been glad he hadn't been forced to use the butt of his revolver as a hammer, although he assured her he'd been prepared to do just that.

With a couple of quick whacks, Anubis was earless; she'd then filed down the rough edges for a clean finish. She wasn't usually the superstitious sort, but she hoped there were no curses associated with defacing the ancient god's likeness. Between the barbaric ear surgery and her abrasive scrubbing of the statue's finish before painting over the whole of it, she and Vincent would both be headed for a gruesome end.

She locked the compartment door and pocketed the key, making her way to the restaurant car, smiling. She could certainly think of less desirable people with whom to meet a gruesome end. If she weren't the careful sort of female, and she was nothing if not careful, she might find herself falling quite in love with the man. He listened to her opinions, and when she spoke, his attention was focused entirely on her. He was funny and kind. She found him very handsome, and each time he touched her hand or guided her down the corridor with a hand at her back or on her elbow, her heart jumped. Just a little jump, really, hardly worth mentioning. When the business with Kenton was finished, she would return home and would be happy.

A pucker formed between her brows when she considered the fact that she hadn't seen nearly as much of England as she'd wanted to. And now she regretted being close to many other countries and sites she'd dreamed about all her life but had been unable to stop and explore. She would save her money and make another trip. And next time she would also see France, Germany, and Italy. Perhaps she could find a traveling companion with similar interests, or at least one who wouldn't make such a fuss about being bored.

Laughter and animated chatter sounded the moment she opened the restaurant car door. The happy sounds lifted her spirits, and she looked around until she located Vincent, who was seated at a table with three women. One was perhaps an elder relative of the other two, and all three were beautiful. Curiously, Emily then felt her lifted spirits plummet. They lifted again, however, rapidly and with an angry rush. Who were these women dining with her husband?

She approached the table and fixed a pleasant smile to her face. "Darling! Perhaps you'll introduce me to your guests." She placed her hand on Vincent's shoulder and beamed down at him.

His brows lifted in surprise, and a smile crossed his face. He stood and kissed her cheek affectionately. "Emily, dearest! So glad to see you're feeling better. The rest did you a world of good, I trust?"

She blinked. "A world of good. I'm quite rested, yes."

"These ladies are new arrivals—we've all been learning about one another." He indicated the elder of the three, who probably wasn't more than a decade or so older than Vincent himself. "Mrs. Deveux, and her daughters, Collette and Carina. They are natives of London but reside in Strasbourg."

Emily smiled at the three. "Charmed."

Mrs. Deveux's lips curved in a pretty smile, and her daughters dimpled adoringly. Emily guessed Collette and Carina to be perhaps a few years younger than she was, but there was an air about them that spoke of money and social experience. Emily felt gauche in comparison.

"Your husband has been regaling us with tales about your whirlwind courtship! It all sounds very romantic," Mrs. Deveux said.

"Oh, yes," Emily said and looked up at Vincent, who raised a brow at her as if in challenge.

"What did you think when he proposed?" Collette asked.

"I was stunned, of course, but when he read the poem he'd written for me, I cried." She placed her palm on Vincent's cheek, her heart beating a little faster. "He may be embarrassed to admit it, but I saw a tear or two in his eyes as well."

Vincent's eyes widened slightly, and the effort required

to *not* laugh was work indeed.

"Mr. Brady, you most certainly did *not* mention poems or tears," Mrs. Deveux chastised.

"Yes, he mentioned only the hot air balloon." Carina eyed Vincent as one would a frosted cake.

"I do not like to boast," Vincent said, his lips twitching. "Poetry writing is a talent I do not often share."

"Oh, but think, you could be the next Shelley or Keats!" Collette eyed Vincent like a cat with a bowl of cream.

Vincent looked at the young woman and took a subtle step closer to Emily. "Why don't we sit over there, Emily? I am finished eating, but you must be famished."

From my strenuous bout of "resting"? She bit her tongue to keep the thought from spilling out. That was the best excuse he could muster?

"Ladies, my apologies for abandoning your table." He offered a light bow. "Perhaps we shall all see each other at dinner." Vincent guided Emily down the aisle to a smaller table with two place settings. He lifted a hand for the server and ordered tea, seating her solicitously with a strained smile. He took the seat across from her, his eyes flicking down the aisle to the ladies' table and then back to her face.

"What on earth took you so long? I thought you were painting the thing one solid color—'Easy as pie,' you said." He maintained a smile for any observing audience, which was at odds with his tense question.

"Resting? That was the best excuse you could think of? 'My new wife is tired'? Makes me sound like an invalid, Vincent!"

He leaned closer. "You retaliated nicely with your poetry talk! Besides, I was hoping to suggest you were tired because we've been having such a wonderful time as husband and wife!"

"Why would you want to leave that impression?" She felt herself blushing.

"Because those women had designs on me and I wanted to discourage it!"

Emily's mouth dropped open. "You're afraid of three small women?"

"Dearest, you apparently have no idea what women of that ilk are capable of wreaking." He shook his head. "Give me your hand—they're looking."

Emily couldn't see without turning around, but she extended her hand. He brought it to his lips and kissed her fingers, looking at her intently. Her breath caught in her throat, and for a moment she wished it were real. His lips curved in a smile meant for her alone, and her heart tripped over itself.

The server appeared with her food, and Emily withdrew her hand. She maintained eye contact with the detective, though, and his gaze never wavered from her face. He swallowed, then a subtle movement of his throat, and finally he looked out the window at the passing scenery.

"We'll arrive shortly in Munich," he said. "The stop is a short one, however. Just long enough to unload and take on new passengers."

The server nodded his agreement. "We'll fill up again to capacity," he said. "There are a few empty berths after Strasbourg, but not much longer."

Vincent smiled as the server finished and left. "Blast. The compartment next to ours is empty now—I had hoped it would remain so."

"Safer?"

He nodded.

Emily pursed her lips in thought. "I believe I saw Henri finishing that compartment when I left ours just now. It's already occupied."

Two small figures blurred down the aisle. "Todd and Maria," Emily murmured, and watched their progress to the other door. Their mortified mother walked quickly after them and hissed when Todd put his little hand on the door handle. Emily was glad the family's compartment was at the other end of their coach. Although the children weren't necessarily loud, they were mischievous.

She turned back to Vincent, who watched the family thoughtfully.

"What is it?"

"I believe I know who opened our cabin door last night. I've watched those two try door handles and touch everything in here and the lounge car."

"That would be a relief." Emily took a sip of her tea. "I've not spent much time in the company of children; I wouldn't know the first thing about caring for one."

Vincent smiled wryly. "Nor I. And remembering my own behavior makes me uneasy about turning free a small version of myself into the world."

Emily pictured Vincent as a child. Small, probably adorably funny, rich brown hair with its tendency to curl, and those warm eyes. Her heart gave a funny little thump. Wretched thing anyway, her heart. In the past two days it had been jumping all over the place for reasons that had nothing to do with worry about her brother, and that made no sense.

Mrs. Berry and Nanette entered the restaurant car, followed by two young men Emily judged to be in their mid to late twenties. Nanette paused at the table with the two gentlemen. "Mr. and Mrs. Brady, allow me to introduce my cousin and his friend." She indicated the man standing next to her. "This is Peter Berry, and his friend, Thomas Williams. I understand they are occupying the compartment adjacent yours."

Both men sketched a light bow and professed their joy at making their acquaintance. Emily and Vincent both responded in kind, and Vincent kept his eyes on the newcomers as they continued down the aisle to a table Mrs. Berry had procured.

"Our new neighbors, it would seem. Something amiss?" Emily asked.

"Shifty."

She smiled. "Could it be that everyone must come under suspicion? I would not question your instincts, but given the circumstances it would be reasonable to suspect everyone aboard to have nefarious intentions. Even the children."

He grinned, turning his attention back to Emily. "Those children most definitely have nefarious intentions."

Emily finished her tea and sandwiches. "Would you like to see the results of my 'resting'?" she whispered. "I left it drying in our compartment."

"Absolutely." He smiled, and they made their way past the Deveux women (who smiled at Vincent and pointedly ignored her) and the Berry family. Nanette was observing her cousin and his friend with an expression that fell substantially short of genial, and Emily wondered about the conversation at the table. She liked Nanette instinctively and hoped Peter Berry and Thomas Williams were kind. They had an air about them that Kenton often did with his friends at home. Confident bordering on arrogant, a healthy sense of their own grandeur, and a tendency to make light of others for their own amusement.

On impulse, Emily stopped and retraced a few steps to the Berrys' table. "Nanette, I do hope you'll be available for a chat later? Perhaps after dinner in the lounge car for a ginger ale?"

"I would enjoy it very much," Nanette said, and her

glance flicked to her cousin when that one made a remark only his companion could hear.

Emily looked at the men, who exchanged a glance but smiled at her.

"I hope that invitation is extended to all, Mrs. Brady?" Peter Berry asked. "Imagine our delight to find so many beautiful people on this excursion."

Vincent's arm brushed around Emily and rested on her waist. "Many passengers enjoy after-dinner drinks and coffee in the lounge car after dinner. You needn't wait for a personal invitation."

"That is good news indeed." Peter lifted his glass in mock salute. "To the adventure of a lifetime."

Eleven

Vincent stood with Emily in the corridor outside their compartment when the train stopped in Munich. He looked out the windows onto the platform for Berrin Hirsch. He'd known him for several years; they had collaborated on a case involving weapons smuggling from England to Germany and had become fast friends.

Emily stood beside him and also watched the crowd. "You have much in common, then?"

"With Berrin?"

She nodded.

"We do have many things in common, and I trust him as much as one of my colleagues at home." Vincent put his hand on her back and leaned close. "I'm hopeful he has heard rumblings along the grapevine, as it were."

She bit her lip. "I suppose we should be grateful to have had an uneventful trip thus far—for the most part."

"Are you going to knock on wood, or shall I?" She grinned up at him, and he knew he would remember the moment forever. He'd never believed in such fanciful notions as "love at first sight," but if there was truly such a thing, he imagined he would find it with Emily Grant. He'd very nearly confessed his growing affection for her right there over tea in the restaurant car—he thanked his lucky stars for the server who had arrived with her food and saved Vincent from his own folly. She would think him mad, and it would further complicate an already-complicated situation.

"Knock on wood, detective? I would not have imagined such a practical man to indulge in superstition."

"What is the new American phrase? One must 'cover one's bases.' Including superstition."

She laughed. "Fair enough. And how wonderful it is to know you are a fan of American baseball."

"I think 'fan' is an overstatement. The sport is really little more than rounders or cricket made over."

"Oh!" She elbowed him in the ribs. "It is very much an American sport, I'll have you know."

He rubbed his side and chuckled. "A soft spot. I shall use it later for exploitation purposes."

She turned her attention back to the platform, her wry smile reflected in the window glass. "I handed it to you on a silver platter."

"Much appreciated."

She laughed, and he gave her shoulders a squeeze. It was so easy, so comfortable—so incredibly natural. And he wanted to kiss her very much. Instead, he looked out the window again, telling himself to maintain focus on their goal, the reason they had been thrown together in the first place.

He spied a familiar face in the crowd; Berrin stood a few inches taller than the average man, with skin tanned from outdoor activity—skiing, from the looks of it. He had thick, sandy-colored hair and blue eyes that had captured the hearts of many a fair maid. Vincent had always smiled, with a shake of the head, at his friend's continual good fortune, but as he now glanced down at Emily, he wondered what she would think of Berrin, and it gave him pause.

He waved, and Berrin tipped his head in acknowledgment with a broad grin.

"Is that Mr. Hirsch?" Emily asked, her eyes riveted on his friend.

Vincent scowled. "Yes."

"He's very ... Nordic."

"Yes."

"Germanic, of course, but also has a rather Viking appearance, wouldn't you say?"

Vincent's jaw tightened. "Yes. I would say."

"I see all manner of people at home, of course, but I don't know that I've ever laid eyes on anyone quite so ... perhaps in Minnesota or Wisconsin ..."

"For heaven's sake," Vincent muttered. "Would you like to sue for divorce right now?"

Emily took her gaze from Berrin and looked at Vincent. "Silly—you needn't play the jealous husband; there's nobody even in earshot."

"Well stop ogling! Someone might notice, and then rumors will spread."

Emily cast him an exasperated glance and turned her attention to the carriage door, where Berrin had bounded up the steps. "Does he know we're not married?" she whispered askance to Vincent.

"I will not be cuckolded, Emily!"

"Vincent!" She looked aghast.

"Ahem." Berrin looked from one to the other, and it was then Vincent realized he and Emily stood in the middle of the corridor, faces mere inches from each other.

"Hirsch." Vincent smiled, sheepish, and embraced the other man.

Berrin slapped Vincent on the back and then held him at arm's length. "It has been a year? You're looking well, old friend."

"As are you. Berrin, allow me to introduce my wife, Emily Grant. Brady."

Emily smiled and extended her hand. "It was very sudden."

Berrin raised a brow. "Indeed. When Vincent wired with the information, I was quite surprised."

"I am certain my husband will share all the details with you once we are underway."

People trickled through the carriage then, although there were no vacant berths in that coach. It became a thoroughfare and forced the trio to the side.

"I am in the Strasbourg-Munich car," Berrin told them as he was jostled by a small, gray-haired lady half his size. "I shall deposit my things and then meet back here in your compartment where we can speak freely, yes?"

Vincent nodded. "We shall chat and decide on a strategy."

"Have you suspects?"

"Possibly. Too early to tell, and we don't have much time."

Berrin nodded. "I shall return straightaway." He touched his fingertips to his forehead in salute to Emily and made his way down the corridor and into the next car.

Emily sucked in a breath and faced him squarely. He knew a moment's uncertainty—he'd seen her irritated before, and they still stood out in the corridor amid a sea of people. "Vincent," she said, "there is a bee in your bonnet, and you had better turn it loose."

He took her arm and unlocked their door, ushering her inside and bracing himself. "I do not have a bee in my bonnet." He closed the door firmly. "I would rather not have to explain to anyone why my wife is enamored of my friend."

"Oh!" Her eyes narrowed. "Firstly, I am not enamored of

anyone, and secondly"—she threw her arms wide—"we are not truly m—"

He clapped his hand over her mouth and indicated the door, through which they heard voices and laughter as people passed by. "Bear in mind," he whispered, "that Berry man and his friend are in that compartment right there, and they will hear loud discussions."

Her eyes sparked in anger, but she nodded fractionally. He slowly lowered his hand but then realized how closely together they stood. "Are you calm?"

"Yes." She gritted the admission out, and he noted the telltale flare to her nostrils that signaled her irritation.

"We must be so careful," he murmured and traced the back of his fingers along her cheek. "And I apologize for being a cad about Hirsch. He is very . . . handsome."

Her expression softened as his hand lingered on her face. "He is," she admitted. "But not as handsome as others."

His lips twitched. "Others?"

She nodded slightly. "Others. Another."

He opened his hand and cradled her face, his thumb tracing along her cheekbone. "How strange that I do find myself genuinely feeling the part of the slighted husband. Not accustomed to being married, I suppose."

Her lips curved. "Nor am I. We are amateurs, it would seem."

"Yet it is critical that we be convincing." He lifted his other hand to her face, slowly, gauging her reaction.

She tilted her head, her eyelids closing in one long blink. "Absolutely," she murmured. "Critical."

He lowered his head, and her hands came up between them. Waiting, wondering if she intended to push him away, he paused. She placed her fingers on his chest, curling them around his lapels, and sighed.

Feeling a surge of relief mixed with urgency, he touched his lips to hers. He kissed her softly, slowly, gently exploring the feel of her mouth beneath his. She sighed again and pulled him closer, just a bit.

"Emily," he murmured against her lips and put his arms around her, pulling her against him.

She twined her fingers around his neck and into his hair, moving fully into his embrace and matching his urgency. She was an incredible woman—bright, witty, and amazingly brave. He was humbled by her trust and painfully aware that their time together was short. He didn't want to let her go—didn't like the thought of never seeing her again when their business together was through.

He lifted his head, giving them time to breathe. He still held her tightly to him, touched his forehead to hers.

"Vincent," she whispered, "I . . . that is, I do not know—I'm not sure . . ."

"Shh, it's all right. I won't ask for more, won't ask for anything. We must find your brother and return your life to rights. Please say you will allow for time spent together in the future, though?"

"How? I live so far away." She blinked, eyes troubled, but kept her arms around his neck.

He decided that was a good sign. "I do not know how. But say we will manage it. When this task is finished, tell me I will see you again."

She nodded, brows drawn in distress. "I want that very much. But I don't know how I shall manage it—"

He shook his head and put his hand again on her cheek, his other arm wrapped around her waist as if it had been made to hold her. "We'll not worry over details right now." He smiled. "You would have a plan in place, and I wish I could alleviate your stress, tell you exactly what the future holds. I know only that this charade has felt more real to me than anything ever has before. I want to be in your life, Miss Emily Grant; only say you will allow me the chance."

Her eyes filmed. "Of course." She smoothed his hair away from his forehead. "I am afraid, though." She drew a shaky breath. "So many things can go wrong."

He kissed her again, softly, gently. "We will endeavor to be certain everything goes right."

A knock sounded on the door, and Emily jumped and pulled back. He sighed, resigned. "That would be Berrin," he whispered. "Now, you behave yourself."

She thumped a fist against his chest, and he chuckled. "I think you kissed me to muddle my thinking," she whispered back.

"A man does what he must."

She put a hand to her hair and smoothed her dress. "What will he think—is my hair still done up?"

Vincent raised a brow and smiled. "He'll think he's interrupted a newly married couple in a passionate embrace." He winked as he reached for the door handle. "What a coincidence."

Twelve

The next day passed uneventfully, and Emily had found a sense of joy in the moment. Berrin Hirsch was charming and friendly, and he elicited the same sense of safety as Vincent had from the very beginning. She didn't know if it was their roles as detectives or their generally protective natures—perhaps both—that encouraged her to feel safe, as though her problems would be solved. Whatever it was, she was grateful and so glad she wasn't attempting the task on her own.

Vincent hadn't kissed her again since that electric moment in their compartment before Berrin had interrupted them, and she willingly admitted her disappointment to herself. She appreciated his sensitivity toward her—nobody knew they weren't truly married except the two of them—and he could easily have taken advantage of the situation. She suspected he was worldlier, more experienced than she was, but he behaved the perfect gentleman. She was hopeful, in fact, for another stolen kiss and began to wonder if she'd have to initiate it.

The train sped along its path, passing Budapest in the late night hours, and as they neared Bucharest, a light snow began to fall. The track remained clear, the mountain scenery breathtaking, and Emily determined to return again soon and enjoy the rail journey without the looming worry for Kenton hanging over her head. She was going to live her life, to be brave and take chances and see the world as she'd always wanted to. When Kenton was safe, she would tell him that he would live his life on his own, that she would not hover anymore. Perhaps it was what they both needed.

The night before the train was to arrive in Bucharest, Emily made plans to sit with Nanette in the lounge car for after-dinner drinks. Vincent and Berrin joined them, as did Peter Berry and Thomas Williams. The young men had been quiet neighbors; Emily heard them rustling around in their compartment only at night before bedtime. They spent the bulk of their time in the lounge car with the Deveux women, laughing and playing cards. They were innocent enough, but there was a sly undercurrent of superiority that ran through the group, and Nanette had tearfully admitted that afternoon that she often felt the edge of their disdain.

Emily sat on one of the lounge's sofas with Nanette, and Vincent and Berrin stood near the bar, chatting with three gentlemen who had embarked in Budapest and were bound for Constantinople and a large trade emporium. Before long, the Deveux women arrived, and the car was soon filled with sounds of their laughter. Gentlemen flocked to them like flies to honey, and Nanette rolled her eyes.

"I do not know why they bother me so much," she muttered to Emily. "I do not want to be them; I do not even want to be *like* them. I always find myself feeling inferior when they enter a room, however."

Emily patted Nanette's hand. "I understand. But we must consider the source." She tipped her head to the side and studied the trio, who had ingratiated their way into the circle surrounding Vincent and Berrin. "And we, dear friend, have intellect in our favor. And understated beauty that lasts. They are mean, and by the time they are old women it will show on their faces."

Nanette laughed. "Perhaps sooner than when they're old," she said. "They seem ugly to me already."

Emily looked at the group, and Vincent caught her eye with a roll of his. Her lips twitched, and she felt smugly satisfied, as though they shared a secret, and even though he was surrounded by beautiful women who flirted as a matter of course, it was Emily who held his interest.

Peter and Thomas approached, each holding a freshly poured ginger ale.

"I curse the day my mother wired them to join us," Nanette grumbled. "She felt we'd be safer on the rails with a male family member along. That one has never cared for anyone but himself, though."

Something felt slightly off to Emily, but she couldn't put a finger on it. The two men in question reached them, all smiles.

"Ginger ale, compliments of our bartender," Peter said and handed Emily and Nanette the glasses.

"To adventure!" Thomas said and lifted his glass in an informal toast.

Nanette eyed him with distrust but shrugged to Emily and lifted her glass. "To adventure," she repeated, and Emily followed suit.

"A moment," Peter said and looked at the crowd near the bar. "Someone is motioning to me."

Thomas took the seat across from Emily and Nanette and smiled. "I shall have the ladies' attention all to myself, then."

"And since when have you ever desired it?" Nanette asked.

She was direct; Emily was impressed. The young Miss Berry did not suffer fools gladly and made no bones about it.

Thomas Williams blinked in surprise but recovered quickly enough. "Why, always!"

Nanette opened her mouth to argue, but Peter reappeared, concerned. "Nanette, your mother is asking for you. She seems to have fallen ill; was she well when you left her last?"

Nanette frowned. "She was fine, a bit tired, perhaps." She sighed and looked at Emily. "I'll return if I can."

"Shall I walk with you to your compartment?" Emily asked.

"No need, I'll accompany Miss Berry." Thomas Williams looked at Nanette, all solicitous concern.

Emily didn't buy it for a moment. "I'll walk her; you remain here where the fun is," Emily stated and stood, pulling Nanette to her feet.

"A pity," Peter said, frowning. "You weren't even able to enjoy your drink without your mother ruining your fun."

Nanette tossed back the contents of her glass, and Emily again found herself impressed. "There," Nanette said. "Fun accomplished." She handed her cousin the empty glass, and Emily set her drink on the side table near the sofa.

The crowd around the bar was thicker than ever, and Emily caught sight of Vincent for one moment before an ostrich plume from Collette Deveux's hairpiece obscured his face. Emily moved toward the exit with Nanette, still straining to see Vincent. She caught Berrin's attention with a wave and mouthed, "I'll return shortly!"

He narrowed his eyes and moved as if to make his way to them but was waylaid by the crush of people trying to get drinks.

"Come," she said to Nanette, feeling dizzy from the heat

in the car. "Entirely too many people in there." They exited the lounge car and crossed through the empty restaurant car.

"Definitely too many people," Nanette said, and stumbled.

Emily clasped her arm, and when the other girl weaved again with the train's movement, wrapped an arm around her shoulders. "Are you ill, Nanette?"

Nanette put a hand to her forehead. "I don't know—I am so dizzy."

Feeling some alarm, Emily looked back down the length of the restaurant car. It made little sense to return to the crowded lounge car if Nanette were ill. "Let's get you to your compartment. Perhaps you and your mother have caught an ailment."

Emily guided the girl into a sleeper car that adjoined theirs. The corridor was empty, thankfully, for Nanette stumbled again and leaned heavily on Emily, nearly taking them both to the floor. The connecting door opened behind them, and Emily saw Peter and Thomas, not sure if she was relieved or alarmed.

Thomas rushed forward. "Nanette! Allow me to help." He pulled Nanette's arm around his shoulders, and lifting her against his side, walked her to the end of the car.

"Wait," Emily called, her heart beginning to pound. Her head felt fuzzy, and she spun around to run back for Vincent. Something wasn't right.

"Quiet, you," Peter snarled in her ear and clamped his arm around her neck, hand over her mouth. "We're going to walk back to your compartment, slow and easy like, and have a talk."

Emily felt a stab of alarm as his hand pressed firmly against her nose and mouth. Her dizzy state was compounded by lack of air, and she began seeing spots as he dragged her from the vacant corridor and into the car containing their compartments. She saw Thomas near the end of the car; he'd thrown Nanette over his shoulder and was at the last compartment, where he turned the handle and disappeared with her friend.

Emily's final hope was dashed when she looked for Henri, their conductor, and saw his seat was empty.

Peter shoved open his compartment door and hauled Emily inside. He kicked it shut and tossed her down onto the lower berth, which had already been made up for the evening. He stood over her, breathing quickly, his hands on his hips. "Where is it?"

Emily put her hand to her head. She must remain conscious. Vincent would realize she'd gone missing, and she had to yell for him when he came looking. "Where is what? I've no idea what you're doing, Mr. Berry, but it is folly . . . in the extreme." She lurched to the side and shoved herself back up. "My husband is a Scotland Yard detective, you do realize that?"

Peter laughed. "We will arrive in Bucharest in an hour. By the time he realizes where you are, I'll have the artifact and be long gone."

"What artifact?"

He shot forward and grabbed her face in his hand. "The one you're taking to Constantinople to free your brother! I have friends in Munich, Mrs. Brady, who received a very interesting message from contacts in London. That Jon Mattingly wants his property returned, and he'll pay a king's ransom for it. Now, I'll ask you again. Where is it? I've searched your compartment already, and it's not there."

Emily frowned. Not there? She didn't want Peter to find it, of course, but how could it not have been there? "I don't know," she said, but her words sounded slurred. "What did you do to us?" She fell hard against the end of the berth, knocking her head on the wall.

Peter cursed. "Fool put too much in the drinks!"

Of course. They'd drugged the ginger ale. She hadn't finished her glass, but Nanette had drained hers. As concerned as she was for herself, Emily now worried her friend might be dead.

"Look at me!" Peter slapped Emily's face.

She cried out, and her head snapped back; she fell heavily on the berth, the compartment spinning and turning her stomach. Peter crouched down next to her face. "Where is the statue, Mrs. Brady?"

She struck out as hard as she could, and although she raked her nails down his face, her movement was clumsy. She was too slow to react when he snarled and backhanded her again, sending her spiraling into darkness.

Thirteen

Vincent shoved his way past the cloying women and the gentlemen who flocked around the bar. "You saw her?" he called to Berrin, who followed him.

Berrin nodded. "Looked as though she said she would return and left with Miss Berry." The Austrian detective frowned. "Miss Berry's cousin and friend also left—I do not trust those two."

Vincent's unease began to climb as he rushed to the door and through the restaurant car. He tore open the door and passed through to the car next to his, running by the time he reached his and Emily's car. He stopped abruptly at his compartment, alarmed when the door opened easily and showed an interior that had been turned upside down.

"*Mein Gott,*" Berrin whispered and clapped a hand on Vincent's shoulder. "You were right to move the thing to my cabin."

"But where is she?" Vincent said, shoving past Berrin to the corridor. He turned to the adjacent compartment belonging to Peter Berry. He banged on the door and tried the handle. "Berry! Open this door!"

He heard movement inside and a muffled groan. He looked at Berrin, who nodded once.

"Kick it in," his friend said. Berrin looked down the corridor. "Where is your conductor?"

Vincent registered the empty seat at the other end of the carriage but turned his attention to the door handle. Sick with fear, he kicked at the door repeatedly, his leg jarring against the sturdy hardware.

Berrin frowned. "Where is the conductor for that car as well?" He nudged Vincent aside and took over, kicking repeatedly until the wood splintered. The door swung open, and a gush of frigid air swept into the corridor. The window was open, Peter Berry was nowhere in the room, and Emily lay across the bottom berth, unconscious.

"I'll find a doctor," Berrin said. "And those two missing conductors," he said as he left the compartment.

"Emily." Vincent rushed to her side and pulled her close, relieved to feel a pulse in her neck. She breathed evenly, might have been merely sleeping if not for the fact that she wouldn't awaken no matter how he shook her. Her cheek was red and beginning to swell.

He moved to the window and peered out. Nobody was hanging on the outside of the swiftly moving train, and snow and wind rushed past in a fury. The odds that a man might survive the fall were slim, but he hoped that if Peter Berry had actually jumped and not died, that he was at least wounded. It was nothing compared to what Vincent wanted to do to the man.

Emily groaned, and Vincent slammed the window shut, rushing back to her side. A commotion sounded in the hallway, and before long, two conductors had entered the room, expressing their dismay rapidly in French.

"Emily, I'm here," Vincent told her and gently brushed

her hair away from her face. "Can you tell me what happened?"

She winced and put her fingers to her temple. "Peter Berry," she mumbled. Her eyes widened then, and she tried and failed to push herself upright. "Nanette," she managed and sucked in a deep breath. "They drugged us. Thomas carried her to their compartment at the end . . ." She clutched Vincent's fingers, her eyes filling with tears. "She wasn't moving."

Vincent barked quick orders in French to the small group of train personnel that had now gathered at the compartment. Two porters immediately turned and ran toward the Berrys' room, and another walked past bracing Henri, who clutched his head in one hand.

"Can we go to our room?" Emily whispered.

"Yes, of course." Vincent acted automatically with little thought. His terror was so complete he relied on habit and instinct to keep moving. He remembered then that their compartment had been ransacked, and he mentioned it to the head conductor, who was jotting notes and firing orders to the other employees.

The conductor insisted they allow him to move them to the first-class carriage—they had a vacancy and would hear no argument about it. Vincent helped Emily up and then lifted her into his arms. She winced as her head jostled and rested it against his shoulder, her arm around his neck. Berrin appeared with a small man who carried a black bag, and the two of them followed Vincent as he carried Emily to their new compartment in the carriage farther ahead.

Once there, he placed Emily on the large bed, whispering to her. "You will be fine, you'll see. There's a doctor here, and we're in a lovely new cabin—once you're feeling better, we'll have a little tour of it. It's bigger than the other one—I think you'll like it." He was babbling and couldn't seem to stem the flow of nonsense.

He stepped aside at the doctor's insistence and cleared the room for privacy. He hovered near the door and spoke tersely with Berrin in the hall. "Search for Peter Berry. Looks like he jumped, but we can't be sure."

Berrin nodded. "We have the other one in custody. We'll turn him over when we stop in Bucharest and check for messages at the telegraph office."

"How are the Berry women?"

"Both drugged, apparently, but alive."

"Has Thomas Williams said anything?"

"I'll go question him right away." Berrin clasped Vincent's arm and then left.

Vincent reentered the suite and stood quietly near the doctor, who listened to Emily's heart, looked carefully at her eyes, and asked her in French specific questions about how she was feeling. Vincent translated for her and was relieved when the doctor wrapped up his examination with some words of comfort and instructions to drink plenty of bottled water and then rest. He told Vincent to expect that she would be groggy for a time but that he would check on her again in the morning. Vincent shook his hand with a murmur of thanks and asked that he next check on Nanette and her mother.

The first-class conductor hovered near the door and asked if there was anything they required. "I want to examine the lounge car, and I need it cleared immediately. Tell the porters and the bartender to leave everything exactly as it is." Vincent felt the anger settle in, heavy in his midsection. He made his way to Emily's side and sat next to her on the bed. "Emily, I must check on some things," he whispered. "I'll return shortly, I promise."

She grasped his hand. "How is Nanette?"

"She's well. The doctor is with her now."

"And you will return quickly?"

He smiled, hoping he looked serene but worried his fury and gut-wrenching fear for her were readily apparent. "I will. Do you remember where you set down your glass in the lounge car? The one Peter gave you?"

"On the side table next to the small sofa." She rubbed her head. "The servers are so efficient, though. I doubt it will be there still."

"I'll look anyway." He paused. "Shall I find someone to help you change? I believe there are two female maids that usually service the Strasbourg-Munich car."

She began to refuse, but he saw the moment when she changed her mind. "Actually, that would be lovely. Thank you."

He kissed her forehead and left her to rest, deciding to put his angry energy to good use. After securing help for Emily from a soft-spoken, young French maid, he found Berrin and got to work examining the lounge car and questioning the few passengers who had moved to the restaurant car to finish mingling and drinks. Emily had the right of it—the glasses had been cleared away already, and there was no way to prove what their drinks had contained. Nobody had noticed anything untoward—their attention had all been occupied with their own affairs.

"What did Williams have to say for himself?" Vincent asked Berrin as they made their way toward the Strasbourg-Munich car.

Berrin shook his head. "Cried like an infant. Peter Berry received a telegram from his aunt that she wanted companionship for herself and her daughter on the trip. Peter had discovered from a friend the rumors about an American with an artifact traveling to Constantinople and jumped at his aunt's invitation. He also invited his friends, the Deveux ladies, to help and promised a portion of the reward he was sure to receive."

Vincent smiled grimly. "And here I was, feeling guilty for awakening those ladies at such a late hour." They reached the Deveux compartment, and Vincent thumped on the door. "I now look forward to explaining why they'll be put off the train at Bucharest."

Fourteen

Emily freshened up for the evening in her first-class suite, feeling a strange combination of pampered and nervous. After the unfortunate episode with Peter Berry, Emily had slept for hours. When she awoke, Vincent had informed her of everything he'd learned while she rested.

The Deveux family and Thomas Williams had been put off the train in Bucharest and placed under arrest. As the crime had occurred while the train was in Romania, they would face whatever judgment awaited them there. Peter Berry was missing, presumably dead. Crews were searching the area he'd last been with Emily.

The telegraph office at the train station in Bucharest had received a message from Vincent's chief inspector. The Mattingly brothers had been caught moving their stolen stash of artifacts from a warehouse to a ship docked at the quay, and because there was finally evidence enough to convict them, had been arrested.

Emily was glad for Vincent that one part of his work had been resolved. There was still the issue of her brother, however, and her heart was heavy. A telegram had awaited her in the morning when they reached Bucharest, with instructions for Orient Express officials to be sure she received it. The contents of her telegram were specific—she was to board a carriage at the train station in Constantinople, alone, where she would then be taken to her brother and the men demanding the ransom.

Berrin had immediately telegraphed his contacts in Constantinople, with whom he'd communicated since receiving word from Vincent. Police officers would be strategically placed at the train station and would follow her carriage without being seen. Vincent would also follow and would be there at a moment's notice as soon as she turned over the statue. The delicate part of the operation would be to secure Kenton's release before allowing the policemen to swarm in and arrest those corrupt lawmen responsible for the entire scheme.

Emily finished readying herself to disembark and sat in one of the chairs at the small table in their cabin. The countryside rushed by, and architecture so unlike anything she'd seen continually caught her eye and pointed to something new. She was nervous to the point of nausea, and she hoped Vincent had believed her when she'd told him she'd not wanted him to return with a dinner tray. He'd been more attentive than a nursemaid in the hours that had passed since the incident, and she'd repeatedly assured him she was fine. She'd seen the panic flare in his eyes, though, an hour earlier when she'd told him she didn't want to eat anything.

Her portmanteau was packed, and the altered statue, which Vincent had had the foresight earlier to hand over to Berrin for safekeeping, was now wrapped and settled at the top of her belongings in the bag. A light knock sounded at the door, and Vincent entered. She did her best to smile at him, but she was afraid it probably wasn't very convincing.

"I will be right behind you," he said, as he had since putting the final plan into effect. He sat in the other chair at the table and clasped her fingers in his.

"I know, Vincent. Truly. I shall be fine." She paused. "Please know that if anything happens to me—"

"Emily—"

"No, allow me to say it. I want you to know that you are dear to me, and I am so grateful to have had your help. I bless the moment when you found me in that ticket line and made me your wife."

He laughed, and she felt a lightness about her heart. She quite adored him, and the thought that something special they might have together could well be over before it was begun was well and truly sad.

"How much longer?" she asked.

He checked his timepiece and looked out the window. "Thirty minutes, at most. See there?" He pointed to a city that grew larger by the mile, full of domed spires, mosques, and densely packed residences and commercial districts. Dusk approached, and the city's lights blinked into life as the sun set.

Saying very little, Emily and Vincent sat at the table as the train moved ever closer to her destination. He held her hand, fingers threaded together, and occasionally pointed out an interesting landmark or something of historical significance. She figured he probably spoke to distract himself as much as her, but it was a comfort.

They drew closer to the train station, and the speed slowed. Emily sucked in her breath and released it slowly. She stood, and Vincent did the same.

"You can stay here until it is absolutely time," he said, his voice gruff.

She shook her head and smiled. "I cannot remain still another minute. Let us be done with this thing."

He nodded and pulled her hand to his mouth. He kissed her fingers with his eyes closed and then exhaled and pulled her to him, kissing her with an urgency she quite understood. She responded with her whole heart, reveling in the feel of his arms around her, his strength ever supporting her, and his lips moving over hers in a gentle assault she wished would never end.

"I will keep you safe," he finally said against her ear, holding her tightly.

"I know," she whispered. "I know you will." She pulled back. "You have your revolver, of course? Because you know how much I love those!" She punctuated her words with a bright, intentionally false smile, and he chuckled.

"I do indeed." He patted his side. "I'd let you carry it if I thought it would bring you comfort."

She shuddered. "I appreciate the sentiment."

A knock sounded at the door as the train continued to slow. Vincent opened it to reveal Berrin, who looked at them in question. "We are ready?"

Emily inhaled and exhaled slowly. "Ready." She gathered her portmanteau and walked ahead of the men to the carriage door. The portmanteau itself was light—Vincent had removed all but a few garments so she could lift it with ease. She gave Vincent's hand a squeeze and stepped forward alone to descend the steps.

The air was cold, and daylight faded fast. Lamps lit the train station platform, and she turned to her left, as instructed, and followed a line of people to several carriages that lined the nearest road. A man in a uniform approached her, saying in a heavy accent, "Miss Grant?" At her nod, he motioned. "Follow."

She kept a firm grip on her bag when he motioned to take it, and he let her keep it. He walked her to a nondescript black carriage, and she climbed inside, wanting to look behind her but not wanting to draw the least attention to Vincent or anyone else aiding her cause. Her escort climbed into the carriage and sat across from her. He rapped quickly on the ceiling, and the driver clucked the horses forward.

The streets were hardly visible through the wavy glass, especially given the waning light. Her companion remained silent but watched her intently as one minute became five, and then ten.

"Do you know where my brother is?" she finally found the nerve to ask. "Are you taking me to him?"

He didn't answer but continued to watch her without a smile or inflection of any kind. The carriage wound through streets, making so many turns she knew she'd never find her way back to the train station on her own. She knew a moment's panic when she wondered if Vincent would be able to keep pace without being noticed.

The carriage finally came to a stop outside a nondescript building at the end of a heavily wooded street. Emily clutched the portmanteau and exited the carriage, an involuntary shudder resulting from the cold and her fear.

"Come," her escort said, and took her by the arm. She was forced to match his stride and was breathless by the time they reached the door. He pushed her in first and followed, closing the door behind them with a solid bang. The room was cavernous and filled with boxes and crates. To her right stood a small group of men in an area that had been cleared of everything except two chairs, a sofa missing its legs, and a battered lamp, which provided the only source of light.

The men wore uniforms that matched her companion's, and one stepped forward. He was of middle age, tall, with clipped hair and a graying mustache. The clear leader of the group, he extended his hand toward one of the chairs. "Please, miss."

Emily swallowed. "Surely this will be a quick transaction? I prefer to stand. And where is my brother?"

The man eyed her for a moment and then smiled. "As you wish. Your brother will be returned to you when I have studied the artifact."

Emily felt faint. Perhaps she should have taken the seat. She tried speaking, cleared her throat, and tried again. "Those were not the terms of the arrangement. I want to see my brother before I hand over the statue. I do not know if he is even still alive." She was absolutely powerless to make demands—they knew she had the ransom with her and could simply kill her and take it.

"Do remember I am an American citizen," she said, grasping at straws but strengthening her spine. "I should think carefully if I were in your position. Family at home know where I am and have instructions to contact officials in New York."

The man pursed his lips. "An American who is now married to an Englishman, it would seem."

"You had spies on the train, of course."

He smiled widely. "A mother of two rowdy children is so easily dismissed, is she not?"

Emily couldn't help but shake her head, and a small laugh escaped. "At any rate, America or England, you will want to avoid an international incident. Give me my brother, I give you the ransom, and my brother and I leave unharmed."

"Where is your husband now, I wonder?"

Emily's heart thudded. She was so far out of her realm of familiar she felt sick with fear. "Waiting for me at Pera Palace," she said steadily. "We are staying for a few days and then returning home."

"You remain in the city where your brother has been held prisoner? You do not want to whisk him immediately away?"

"I am quite angry with my brother. He ruined my honeymoon, and he will be my prisoner now. He'll stay in a room where he can cause no trouble, and I will enjoy my holiday with my husband!" She allowed tears to form, as they threatened anyway, and hoped an irate female might be disconcerting, if nothing else. "He has ruined my wedding, *you* have ruined my holiday, and I wish I'd never laid eyes on this confounded, stupid statue; now where is my brother?" The last came out on a tearful shout that echoed through the huge room.

He extended a hand, palm up. "The statue, if you please. I shall have your brother collected."

She had no more time to stall, nothing with which to bargain. A tear trickled down her cheek, followed quickly by another. She didn't even know if Vincent and the authorities had been able to follow her. She blinked, sniffed, and opened the fastenings on the portmanteau.

Fifteen

Vincent sat, once again, crouched behind a crate in a large warehouse, but this time his heart was in his throat. Emily had given it her best—she'd tried to demand her brother's release before giving them the statue, which they were bound to note as a forgery once in decent light. The only positive thing about the situation was the dim lamp. It had allowed him to sneak into the back door while Berrin waited just outside with several other policemen.

He held his breath as Emily opened her bag and withdrew the cloth-wrapped statue. She'd been meticulous with her paintwork; she'd applied multiple coats to prevent any of the original from showing through.

A pebble bounced on his foot, and he glanced quickly up and to his right. Berrin had entered and approached silently and then cupped a hand around Vincent's ear. "Kenton Grant is at Pera Palace. My contacts located him forty minutes ago at an abandoned police station just outside of the city."

Vincent's mouth slackened. For a moment he could hardly process a single thought. He whipped his attention back to Emily, who was unwrapping the statue. *Think,*

269

think ... He turned to Berrin and whispered, "I'll cause a diversion. Instruct the men outside to be ready."

Berrin nodded and slipped out the back door.

"What statue is this?" the man in charge was asking Emily.

She shrugged a shoulder. "An obscure god from the second dynasty, from what I've been able to discover. It's different—I've never seen it before. Now, where is my brother?"

"I shall have you taken to Pera Palace. I will authenticate this piece, and when my man assures me it is genuine, you will see your brother."

Emily's hands clenched into tight fists, and Vincent bit back a groan. *No, Emily, no no no* ...

"Wait for how long?" she demanded. "Is he even alive?" Her voice trembled, but to his utter amazement, she leaned forward. "I have followed your demands, and I have one of my own! I want my brother now!"

Her voice echoed through the room for a protracted moment before the man backhanded her, sending her flying into the man behind her.

Vincent saw red, fury pounding through him as he shoved over a large stack of boxes. They hit the ground with a smash, and he ran to the cover of another bundle of crates. Chaos erupted, and Vincent knew he hadn't much time. He heard shouts from outside, and Berrin appeared in the doorway. Vincent signaled to him and then ran from stack to stack of boxes until he made his way to Emily's side.

She was dazed, one of the men still holding her around the neck. Officers entered through the rear door, and then the unmistakable sound of gunfire shot through the building. He reached Emily, hit her captor solidly in the jaw, and grabbed her when the man fell. Fire ripped through his shoulder, and he stumbled but dragged Emily away from the clearing. The door behind him was blocked, and he was forced to pull her into the darkness behind the crates.

"Vincent," she murmured. "I'm sorry."

"Nothing to be sorry for, love. Lay low, right here—this will be over soon."

She put her hands on his shoulder. "You're bleeding." She sucked in a breath. "Vincent, you've been shot!"

She ran her hands along his chest and torso. "Oh no," she moaned. "Get down, please get down!" She tugged on him, trying to pull him to the floor. Her eyes widened suddenly, and she gasped. Before he could react, she had unsnapped his revolver from his hip, taken aim, and fired over his shoulder. The roar was deafening, and his ears rang. Everything around him sounded far away, echoing eerily. He strained to see behind him and noted the uniform of the man who had hit Emily. Her aim had been true—the fallen man lay sprawled, his own gun held limply in his hand.

Still clutching the gun, Emily pulled him off balance and heavily down next to her. She wrapped her arms around him and sat with the gun at the ready, protecting him. He knew she was sobbing from her shuddering form, because he couldn't hear to save his life.

"Emily, give me the gun," he tried to say, but he didn't know if he'd shouted or whispered. His head pounded dreadfully.

She pulled the hammer back, her hand shaking, and she braced it with the other hand, encircling his neck. "Be still," he saw her say through her tears.

His heart raced in alarm when a figure ran toward them and Emily steadied her hands. It was Berrin, and Vincent felt the moment when Emily realized it. Her whole frame relaxed, and she leaned heavily on him. She carefully clicked the hammer back into place and limply handed him the weapon. Then she buried her face in his neck, finally releasing him enough for him to wrap an arm around her. Her tears were hot against his skin, and he realized she didn't know her brother was safe.

"It's over, love," Vincent said to her, hoping he wasn't shouting in her ear, as Berrin directed law enforcement to round up the small group of corrupt locals. "Kenton is safe at the hotel. It is over."

Policemen's torches bounced around the room, throwing light and shadows everywhere. She lifted her head, her blue eyes huge. The ringing in his ears was still persistent, but lessening.

"Oh, thank you!" She put her hand to her forehead and released another shuddering sob. "Vincent, thank you!" She lowered her hand and looked at it, her eyes widening again in alarm. "But you've been shot!" She pressed her hand to his shoulder, and he winced. "Oh no, your beautiful muscles!"

He dropped his mouth open in surprise, and he laughed, finding the situation funnier by the moment. He gasped for breath and cupped her face. "I believe it just grazed me, darling, nothing to fear. My beautiful muscles remain intact."

She smiled, sheepish, blood smeared on her forehead and her cheek swelling with a bruise to match the other one still present from Peter Berry. Tears still pooled in her eyes, but he easily read her relief. "What will happen now?"

Shouting and chaos still abounded, his shoulder was on fire, and his head throbbed, but he smiled, feeling cocooned with her in the large storage house somewhere in the bowels of Constantinople.

"It is my opinion, Miss Grant, that we have grown to know each other in this short period of time as much as if we'd been acquainted for years. Would you agree?"

She laughed and nodded, sniffling. "I would agree. And yet I would enjoy getting to know you more."

"As would I. Marry me, Emily Grant. In truth, this time. It makes little sense, it probably wreaks havoc on your sense of responsibility and future planning, but nothing has ever felt more right."

She stared at him, dumbfounded.

"Come back to London with me. Let me be your husband. I do not have much, but what I do have is yours. I will take care of you and love you, and you will be an artist. I promise fidelity, and—"

She wrapped her arms around his neck, cutting him off, and held her cheek against his. For a moment he was terrified she would refuse.

"Yes," she whispered in his ear, and he heard her clearly. "Yes, a million times, yes." She pulled back and kissed him gently. "Undoubtedly the most impulsive thing I've done, but I shall follow my heart. I love you, Detective Brady."

"And I you, Miss Grant." He paused. "Will Kenton be bothered?"

She rolled her eyes. "Kenton can finally become an adult. He can stay in London or go home, but either way, he must choose his own destiny as I'm choosing mine."

"Will you marry me here? In Constantinople? Then we can share a carriage on the return trip without worry."

She lifted her shoulders and smiled. "What else would I do at this point but get married in Turkey?" Her brow creased in a light frown. "But your shoulder—you won't feel well; that is, I worry any activity might be harmful . . ." She blushed, and he grinned at her.

"I'm certain I'll manage. And we'll return first class. We didn't have the time to enjoy our suite, and that was a shame."

She lifted the corner of her lips in a smile. "We'd best rectify that."

"Most definitely." He kissed her again, content.

Author's Notes

This story is set roughly in 1890, so a few discrepancies with timing are an issue; ginger ale actually came into being in 1904, and Pera Palace in Constantinople was built in 1892.

Nancy Campbell Allen is the author of 14 published novels and several novellas, which encompass a variety of genres from contemporary romantic suspense to historical fiction. Her Civil War series, Faith of our Fathers, won the Utah Best of State award in 2005 and two of her historicals featuring Isabelle Webb, Pinkerton spy, were finalists for the Whitney Award. Her steampunk novel, *Beauty and the Clockwork Beast,* was released August, 2016, through Shadow Mountain. She served on the 2015 LDStorymakers Conference Committee and currently serves as the contest coordinator for The Teen Writers Conference. She has presented at numerous conferences and events since her initial publication in 1999.

Her formal schooling includes a B.S. in Elementary Education from Weber State University and she has worked as a ghost writer and freelance editor, contributing to the releases, *We Knew Howard Hughes,* by Jim Whetton, and *My Life Encapsulated,* by Kenneth Brailsford.

Her agent is Pamela Howell of D4EO Literary Agency.

Nancy loves to read, write, travel and research, and enjoys spending time laughing with family and friends. She and her husband have three children, and she lives in Ogden, Utah with her family and one very large Siberian Husky named Thor.

Visit Nancy's blog: http://NCAllen.blogspot.com
Facebook: Nancy C Allen
Twitter: @necallen

Made in United States
Orlando, FL
27 September 2023

37330289R00157